W9-BXV-055

The Heart that Truly Loves

A Novel By
Susan Evans McCloud

BOOKCRAFT
Salt Lake City, Utah

Copyright © 1994 by Bookcraft, Inc.

All rights reserved. No part of this book may be repro-
duced in any form or by any means without permission in
writing from the publisher, Bookcraft, Inc., 1848 West
2300 South, Salt Lake City, Utah 84119.

Bookcraft is a registered trademark of Bookcraft, Inc.

Library of Congress Catalog Card Number: 94-78750
ISBN 0-88494-952-4

First Printing, 1994

Printed in the United States of America

All characters in this book are fictitious,
and any resemblance to actual persons,
living or dead, is purely coincidental.

This book is for
Matthew D. England,
my brother,
who is also soul of my soul,

With love

Chapter One

It was twilight on Beacon Hill. The cool shadows of afternoon that flecked the quiet, tree-lined streets were tinted now by a sky the color of damask roses. The Charles River stretched like a broad gold ribbon beneath the purple silhouettes of tower and steeple that rose like dark veins against a dun-blue sweep of clear, cloudless sky.

Inside the red brick house on Walnut Street, no lamps had been lit yet. In the narrow entry hall two girls stood with their heads close together.

"She would not! Even your mother would not dare," Millie breathed in sympathy.

"Mother would dare anything, I fear. Especially since Father's death." Verity spat out the words. The waning light that slanted through the leaded windows made her red hair glow like a wreath of fire about her head.

"Mormon missionaries right here in the minister's house." Millie's awed voice trembled with the shame of it. "Beggin' your pardon, Verity, but your father would turn over in his grave if he knew."

Verity stamped her small, booted foot in agitation. The color was high in her cheeks. She had the same "touchy Irish blood," as Millie called it, that ran through her mother's veins, and any contest between the two was never pretty. But this, like the rest, would end in triumph for Judith. After all, she was both matron and head of the household now. And Judith had a long and successful history of learning how to get what she wanted from life.

"You'll have to give in at the end, so you may as well do so gracefully," Millie advised.

"I'll not give in this time." Verity's voice held a note Millie had not heard from her before. "She is disgracing everything he ever stood for, Millie. Not to speak of the shame and ridicule she is bringing down on our heads."

"Say your prayers, and don't give up hope. Perhaps we'll think of something to do before tomorrow night comes." Millie gave her friend's hand a gentle squeeze before slipping past her and up the stairs to the little room where she did her sewing. She was completing a frock that the lady of the house had ordered, a difficult piece with a scalloped and embroidered hem and multiple ruffles at the wrists. She wondered suddenly if Judith meant to sport it the following evening when the Mormonites came. She wouldn't be a bit surprised if she did.

The four Mormon men did appear for a meeting in the house of the late and most distinguished Reverend Anthony Thatcher the following evening. And his widow, Judith Boyle Thatcher, did wear a new gown fashioned by her hired seamstress, Millicent Cooper. And the widow's two daughters, Leah and Verity, sat on either side of her and behaved most properly as the guests filed in. If Leah was a little too exuberant to cover her nervousness and Verity a little stiff to conceal her disdain, it was of no matter; they knew none of the guests, and none of the guests there knew them. The group that gathered in their father's parlor to listen to the Mormons preach heresy was a mixed selection of middle-class merchants and lower-class working men—many of them Irish, Verity noticed, and called them "raggle tags" in her mind.

Leah was bored from start to finish. There was not one male member of the company young enough or handsome enough for her to flirt with, except perhaps one of the men who was preaching, and she did not dare to flirt with him. In contrast with her family, Leah had never liked religion much, nor had she cared to make an effort to understand it. She had enjoyed attending the Unitarian meetings because the old church house was such a beautiful place. And her father looked so solemn and powerful, so kindly and knowing, standing at the pulpit. And people were kind, and obviously deferential to the preacher's wife and daughters, and it was all very nice.

The meeting in the parlor began with a prayer, and that was

Verity's undoing. How dare these Mormons speak to God in such common, everyday terms, in such a nonchalant way? She thought of her father's rich, sonorous voice and his grand, ringing phrases and pressed back against her chair, wishing she could dissolve into the very wood of it. Then the sweet chords of the opening hymn began, led by the man with the full auburn beard, who did have a deep, true bass voice:

> A mighty fortress is our God,
> A tower of strength ne'er failing.
> A helper mighty is our God,
> O'er ills of life prevailing . . .

Her father's favorite hymn. Without closing her eyes she could see him standing above the congregation, tall and ramrod straight, but somehow with a vitality, even a gracefulness to the lines of his body. He would sing with a steady, confident voice, and his eyes held the music. The warmth of those eyes reached out to each member of the congregation almost like a caress, with his love drawing each one to him and, at the same time, drawing love and spiritual devotion from their hearts to his, and upward, ever upward . . .

The man was speaking, the man with the beard. Verity forced her mind to listen. If she were to defend herself, her own ways against theirs, she must know what they professed to believe.

"I will begin with some of the first principles which God has revealed, and which it is necessary for mankind to obey before they can constitute a part and portion of Zion. Before the Church of the living God can have any existence on the earth, it is very important and necessary that there should be divine administrators . . . ."

What did he mean, this stranger? Where was he going with such a remark? Verity felt her heart begin to pound rapidly. She put her hand to her chest.

"What I mean by this is, there must be men who have a divine call—being called of the Lord by the spirit of revelation. We must not suppose that God is the author of all these different methods and sects, that he sent all these different ministers. How should true messengers of heaven be sent? In what way . . . ."

Verity stole a glance at her mother. What in the world was she thinking? It was like a slap in the face to her father! This rude, bearded upstart!

". . . Never was a dispensation since God made man on the earth wherein a message was sent to the human family unless there was revelation connected with it, unless the ministers who bore that message were divinely called by revelation. I need not go back . . ."

This was insufferable! Verity pushed her chair back; the legs scraped noisily along the wood of the floor. If her mother thought her unmannerly, what matter? She walked from the room with as stately and dignified a carriage as she could muster. The drone of the powerful bass voice followed her until she put her hands to her ears and escaped into the kitchen, drawing the thick wooden door closed behind her.

"Whatever are you doing here, Miss Verity? You should be out with the guests." The kitchen maid looked up from her stirring with wide, startled eyes.

"I should be precisely where I am, Nancy. Hold your tongue! Where is Millie? I must find Millie." Verity fidgeted where she stood, despite her resolve of control.

"Right here, Verity." Millie's head appeared at the door of the pantry. "Help me carry these plates, and tell me all about it."

Millie was two years younger than Verity, just Leah's age. But she had always seemed older and steadier. That's why she had proved such an invaluable help in their household following the death of her own father. "A bunch of flighty women"—that's what she had called them after her first day in their service. But she had spoken the words with a smile. And who, in all truth, could gainsay her?

Verity set her mouth and strode purposefully toward the pantry. Nancy rolled her eyes, but knew enough to say nothing. Millie thought, *Her Irish blood is up for certain. There's fire in her eyes. What in mercy's sake is going on out in the parlor?*

Every guest had departed, every chair put back in its place, every crumb swept off the table and the worn Turkish carpets before Judith sought out her daughter. The hour was late. She found Verity in the room she shared with her sister. Leah was already a comfortable-looking clump beneath the bedclothes, but Verity sat at the rosewood dressing table, brushing her hair. At a nod from her mother she rose and went out of the room, grabbing a thick paisley shawl to wrap around her shoulders against the night chill of the house.

She followed her mother dutifully until they were safely in Judith's room and the door was shut behind them. This room would always remind Verity more of her father than of her mother. It had a dark, manly air that came from the solid mahogany furniture, the heavy bedhangings, and the deep rusts and burgundies in the patterned wallpaper. And there were books, *his* books lying about on the tables and on the cushioned settee in the corner, as though his hand had just placed them there and would draw them up again at any moment.

"What have you to say for yourself, Verity? I will give you the chance to speak."

Always the democratic one, my mother, Verity thought with some resentment. She drew herself up, unconsciously squaring her shoulders for the encounter.

"What defense need I make, Mother? Yours is the part that offends."

She felt rather than heard the sharp intake of breath as her mother strove to govern her emotions.

"Everything that man said in this house was an insult to Father. His mere presence here was an affront, Mother. And you endured it! You —"

Judith raised up her arm as though warding off the words. Verity paused. Dare she go further?

"You are not entirely accurate in your assessment, Verity. And if you were, even then it is your duty to be gracious and conduct yourself like a lady. Nothing gives you the right to insult your mother and the guests she chooses to bring here." Judith was warming to her subject as she always did, her voice rising a little, her words coming more quickly. "If anything in tonight's proceedings would have offended your father, it would be your behavior. You shame his memory, Verity."

The accusation was too painful to bear. Verity shuddered and hid her face in her hands, wishing with a physical longing that she could flee the room, flee the burden of her mother's presence.

She felt the warm pressure of a slight hand on her arm. How could her mother be so delicate and yet so ferociously strong?

"I am sorry, Verity. But there really is much here you do not understand. Moreover, it is obvious that you do not trust me. You cannot imagine the pain that brings to my heart." Judith sighed. The hand on Verity's arm moved lightly back and forth in a gentle, caressing motion. "Do you believe I would do anything to betray your father?"

Mother always wins, one way or another, Verity thought. *Why do I even attempt the impossible?* She felt suddenly drained and weary. With a small, trembling sigh of her own, she conceded. "Tomorrow is the Sabbath, Mother. What shall we do?"

"Go to meeting as usual, daughter."

Verity could not suppress a shudder at the thought. "In front of everyone? What if Reverend Seabury will not admit us? What if he rebukes us from the pulpit—"

"Wirra, wirra," Judith crooned, lapsing into the Irish as she always did at such moments. "You fret far too much. You always have, dear." With the faintest hint of a smile at the corners of her full mouth, she added, "I know how to handle John Seabury."

"But why all this, Mother? Why?"

Judith paused. "I'm not certain I can answer that to your satisfaction. Not now, now yet."

Verity was aware of the shadow that crossed her mother's features and made her look suddenly young and vulnerable, less than her thirty-eight years. She was a fine-looking woman; neither herself nor Leah had turned out as pretty. Her father used to say, with unmistakable pride in his eyes, that it was her pure Irish blood that set her above most other women.

". . . There is something about this religion," Judith was saying. She shook her head slightly. "I cannot explain it myself . . ."

Verity yawned, trying to cover the offense with a cold hand.

"It's bedtime and past," Judith said. "Off with you, now. Things will look easier in the morning, I promise."

Verity wasn't so sure. She may have felt somewhat reconciled to her mother; it was impossible for most people to stay angry with Judith, and she was no exception. But as for the rest . . .

She climbed into bed beside Leah and rested her head on the down pillow, which was soft but cold to the touch. It was the cold that stayed with her. She fancied she felt the chill on her heart, too deep and aching for her to dislodge, before her eyes closed in sleep.

Chapter Two

Verity dawdled on purpose the following morning, stalling for time, terrified at the prospect of arriving early to meeting. If they could but slip in unseen—and unquestioned—and then escape in like manner! She pretended a clumsy and befuddled mood, and, in truth, she did have a headache. But Judith gave her no quarter. In fact, she sent Millicent up to assist her and prevent any undue delays. So it was that they approached the corner of Tremont and School Streets only three minutes later than usual by the reckoning of the little gold breast watch Judith wore pinned to the lapel of her coat.

The black stone church looked cold and forbidding beneath the lowering March sky. Verity held tight to Millie's hand and led her straight to their pew, merely nodding to those they happened to meet in their quick passage. Millie didn't mind. Though this was not her church, nor her way of life that was being threatened, her sympathies were all with Verity. She knew how important appearances were to her. And, to be fair to her friend, much more than appearances was at stake here. If Judith were *her* mother, she would have felt every bit as mortified.

Judith greeted her friends as usual. Her direct, friendly approach disarmed them. They might talk of her behind her back, but none dared denounce her here and now, as many had hoped to. Leah stood by her side, her tender innocence as much a defense as Judith's calculated aggressiveness. Together they had their way. But then, Judith had learned early how to combat prejudice and the narrow limitations of what was considered acceptable in Boston society. When she had come here as a bride—too young, too red-haired, too Irish—she had had no other choice. She had learned quickly, and though at first her frankness had been an offense to most, it was the only way she could maintain her identity in their midst. With the gentle support of her husband she was able to win them over, or at least reconcile them to her ways. Judith had long since ceased to worry about it. She was one of those rare individuals who had learned to be herself, not what others expected of her. Well she knew that, as widow of their beloved minister and leader, she was going too far this time. There would be no clemency, no forgiveness extended, but for the time being, before she had made up her mind for certain, it would buy her the interval of time she so badly needed.

The meeting was long. The muscles in Verity's shoulders and neck began to ache. She drew a deep breath and tried to relax, allowing her eyes to wander about the room. King's Chapel was Boston's first Unitarian church. It was said that its pulpit was the oldest in all of America. The English royal governors once worshiped here, and the church was the proud possessor of costly silver and vestments presented by King George II and Queen Anne. Even the organ, which she was so used to hearing week after week, had come from England before the Revolution. It was said that Handel himself had selected the instrument at the request of King George. How things must have changed since those days! William Howe prayed here, and General Thomas Gage, and even Washington himself. She could not picture the great man, who seemed more than a mere human, doing the things that she did, living as ordinary men did. What would he think if he were alive now, sitting in this congregation? The notion warmed her somehow and lightened her mood, rather than depressing it.

The Unitarians preached a divinely inspired religion proved by the miracles of Christ. Mortals had the right to spiritual experiences of their own, inspired by the love of God rather than terrified by the Calvinistic emphasis on the sinfulness of their human natures. The gentleness of the doctrine, the hope and dignity embodied in it, had appealed to Verity's father, she knew. How much beyond that doctrine did Mormonism go?

Her skin grew hot and she bit her lip, glancing involuntarily at the backs and profiles of her neighbors. She almost feared they somehow had power to discover her thoughts. Blasphemy to entertain thoughts of such heresy in this hallowed place. *Hallowed by my father, more than any other*, she thought. There had been times since his death that she had fancied she saw him standing behind the pulpit, as warm with life as he had ever been. She had felt she could reach out and touch him. At other times it was more a sensing of his spirit that overtook her, an inner awareness of his reality, of some influence of his being that lingered near her.

She shook her head visibly to dislodge all thoughts, then tried to pay heed to the sermon. The Reverend John Seabury was a dull speaker compared with her father. He was a dull speaker compared with the bearded Mormon who had preached in her father's parlor. Verity put her hand to her mouth. Heaven help her! She closed her eyes and prayed fervently for forgiveness. When she opened them again she saw that her mother was looking at her. Her face bore a curious expression that Verity could not read. She would have given anything to know what her mother was thinking. She had a vague fear that what existed in her mother's overly active mind would have an effect on them all, and she cringed at her helplessness in the face of that fear.

As the day wore on the ache in Verity's head grew no better. Millie brewed a tisane of lemon balm and made her rest after drinking it, which helped a little. But the dull ache was still there, and with it, a growing sense of restlessness. In the late afternoon she told Millie, "I'm going out for a walk, alone. Please don't let anyone follow me. I must think; I must sort things out in my head." She grabbed her shawl and slipped through the side door unseen.

Twilight had not yet begun to gather. A warm golden haze seemed suspended in the very air she breathed. The houses and trees stood in stark relief against the unnatural light that seemed to rob them of dimension and make them appear to be floating— lovely painted apparitions against a backdrop of smoldering sky. Verity drew the beauty into her like a tonic. Hadn't her father's death been enough? Why must her mother contrive to spoil what was left?

She walked the few remaining yards of Walnut Street to where it ran into Beacon, then veered off to her left to find the place where the Long Path headed from Joy Street all the way through Boston Common to meet with Boylston Street on the other end. How quiet the Common appeared this afternoon. Very few people were out. In the early days it had been forbidden to ride or walk in the Common on the Sabbath. Verity could not imagine such restrictions. Whatever would her mother have done if she had lived in that time? Most likely been burned as a witch or sorceress.

Verity took long strides, drawing the cool air into her lungs as she walked, and reached Quincy Lake, or what the children called the "frog pond," before she expected. The bench beneath the tall elms looked inviting. She sat down, drawn by the antics of two gray squirrels chasing one another through the lacework of branches above her head. She did not know how long she sat watching them before she felt a hand on her arm and heard a man's tentative voice ask, "Miss Thatcher, may I sit here beside you?"

At first Verity failed to recognize the big, quiet man who stood anxiously watching her. She hadn't seen much of him before, really. His older, bearded companion had done most of the talking when they had been at her house. She nodded slightly; curtly, she hoped. She could feel her cheeks growing hot. Why hadn't she the courage to send him away with a stinging retort? She tapped her foot on the pavement unconsciously, out of patience with herself.

"I have forgotten your name," she said as the large gentleman settled himself beside her, unaware of her agitation.

"Edgar Gray at your service, miss." With the large, capable fingers of a working man he touched the edge of his hat. "Isn't that the famous Old Elm?" he asked, inclining his head slightly.

"Yes, it's nigh two hundred years old, they figure. Isn't it beautiful in this soft evening light?"

"It truly is. This whole place is a wonder." Edgar Gray's gently modulated voice did not match his large frame and rather imposing appearance, but it served to temper the rough edges that life and experience had not smoothed yet. "Wasn't there once a gallows near here?"

Verity nodded. "Over a hundred people were hanged right there. Isn't it horrid to think of? And not only murderers and pirates, I fear."

"Those were hard times." Edgar Gray's eyes were thoughtful. "A man could be hanged for stealing bread to feed his hungry family. Doesn't even seem to make sense."

"Rachel Wall was hanged for stealing a bonnet that was worth seventy-five cents." Verity's words brought a reluctant smile to the face of her listener. "But then there was Margaret Jones, one of our very earliest women doctors. She was hanged, too." Her companion was listening intently now. "She created an amazing potion of anise seed and various liquors that produced such wonderful results in her patients that the magistrates suspected her of possessing imps. How else could she have done what she did? They wished to seek no other explanation."

"And so she was hanged?"

"Sentenced as a witch, found guilty, and hanged from one of the limbs of that elm." Verity shivered involuntarily. "Those were preposterous times."

Edgar Gray's face held an expression of mingled disgust and horror. Verity nearly wished she had not told him the awful story. Perhaps he was merely a man after all. Surely he seemed to feel things as only the most sensitive of men do. But then he spoke, and she found herself wishing vehemently that she had not been so foolish as to speak to the young man at all.

"Men were also hanged for religious prejudices back in those preposterous times, weren't they?"

The sudden question startled Verity. "Yes, I suppose they were. Yes, men—and women, as well."

"It isn't so unimaginable as we might think it," he continued. "I've seen things myself—in the name of religious persecution—that would turn your stomach, miss."

Verity fixed her wide, angry gaze on him. Why was he speaking this way?

" 'Tis only a thin veneer at best, what we call civilization or refinement," he continued. "It doesn't take much to turn man against neighbor, brother against brother." Verity sensed a shudder travel along his big frame. "We aren't so much different from them as we think."

Verity smoothed her skirts, then stood with as much determination as she could muster. "I must be getting on home now. I don't wish Mother to worry."

Edgar Gray was on his feet before the words were out of her mouth. "May I accompany you home, then? See you safely there?"

She tried to laugh lightly, but it didn't come out right.

"Heavens, no! I'm perfectly safe in the Common, and home is only a little way from here. You go about your business . . ." She paused, feeling the color rise in her cheeks. A faint smile lifted the corners of the young man's straight, serious mouth.

"My business is saving souls, Miss Thatcher. My business is teaching truth to our Heavenly Father's children."

Verity sniffed slightly and began to turn away from him. She was trembling inside.

"You may find me odious, distasteful to your customs and traditions. You may be unwilling to listen, but that doesn't make the message I bring you any less true."

"If you are a gentleman, you will leave me at once, sir. I wish to hear no more of your words. I hope I never see you again— you, or any of your kind!"

She was trembling visibly now. Edgar Gray had the effrontery to place his hand on her shoulder. "Fear does strange things to people, Miss Thatcher. I know that, and I'm sorry. My best to you and your family."

He turned and walked away from her, through the darkening avenue of elms and across the long green of the Common. "How dare he!" Verity muttered. She stumbled back along the path. The golden light had turned gray. The sky was torn into long crimson tatters and faint pink banners, and all was lovely and still. But Verity felt only the cold and saw only the gathering shadows as she scurried back to the house. When she shut the big front door, safely closing the night behind her, she was breathing heavily.

"Verity, where have you been?"

It was her mother, coming down the stairs, looking at her a little too closely.

"I've been for a walk on the Common."

"And was it pleasant, my dear? You look a bit disturbed. Did anything untoward happen?"

"No, Mother. I'm fine. I believe the fresh air was good for me." She would not tell her what had happened and who she had met there. If heaven was kind they would never see those horrid Mormons, would never be disturbed by their ravings again. Oh, why was change the only aspect of life of which one could be sure?

"Well, come along. Nancy has tea ready, with fresh, warm cakes. And Millie has agreed to read to us."

Verity went gladly, anxious only to forget all that had happened that day. She willed the return of simple happiness and security, just as a child, eyes closed tight, wills the terrors of night's darkness to vanish. Could it be so? Verity hoped with all a child's credulity. And when she prayed that night she prayed with the same selfish simplicity, forgetting entirely the things her father had taught: that one should seek the purpose of God in one's life, and strive to love and serve others. Only then would the spirit be illuminated and the path become clear. The path of life. Verity shrank from placing her foot there. Resting here in the warm sun of her girlhood was pleasant and safe. She wished to stay here, heedless of challenge and danger, for as long as she could.

Chapter Three

For the following three weeks the Mormons came every Thursday night to the home of the minister's widow and held their proselyting meetings there. Meanwhile, March gave way to April. With a light hand spring touched the air, leaving the mark of her passage on tree and roadside, meadow and pond. Green was a smell in the nostrils as well as a color on grass and new leaves. The grime and soot of the city's roadways was washed away by a soft, cleansing rain. Something deep and dormant was awakened in Nature, and in the men and women who, dulled by city life, could yet respond to the pure bliss of living, of drawing life in through the senses and finding it good.

For years afterward Verity would say that it was spring alone which made bearable the ordeal they were called to pass through: the loss, the change, the terrible giving up and letting go.

After the third meeting took place, the Reverend Seabury paid Judith a visit. He was excruciatingly polite, but stern, so stern that the very air around him seemed to shrink. Judith received him in the selfsame room where the Mormons had been praying and exhorting. With a pained air of horrified disdain he glanced round him, as though all he cast his eyes on was in some way diseased and unclean.

"Pray, take a seat, Mr. Seabury."

"No thank you, Madam. I prefer to stand here."

Judith acquiesced, knowing her ground, at least, and the direction in which things promised to go. In her characteristic manner she did not wait for him to attack and herself to be forced to defend.

"Yes, this is a lovely room. And both you and I have spent many pleasant and meaningful hours here in company with my husband. But you may be sure that what has occurred during the Mormon meetings has not in any way dishonored my husband's life or his memory. I give you my word on that."

"Judith, please!" The Reverend Seabury forgot himself and called the lady by her first name. Judith kindly ignored his consternation and continued.

"We believe in honestly seeking after truth. At least, we pay lip service to that concept, don't we?" Judith's voice was silky and gently persuasive. Nothing abrasive or argumentative at which the minister could lash out. "Anthony encouraged an honest seeking, as you well know, John"—guardedly she used the familiar form of his name, taking her lead from him—"and that is what I have been doing these past weeks; no more, no less."

Mr. Seabury drew himself up a bit stiffly, and the tight air tingled. "And just what, Mrs. Thatcher, do you think you have learned?"

Judith relaxed a little. The Reverend Seabury could not fail to notice the warmth in her eyes and the softness about her mouth. "I have learned for myself that Mormonism contains God's truth, as revealed in these last days to a living prophet."

Mr. Seabury could not have replied if he had wanted to. His complexion went pale, and he put a hand up to his mouth to stifle a dry cough that was irritating his throat.

Judith took a step forward and placed her hand, just the slender tips of her fingers, on the sleeve of his coat. "In many ways it grieves me to come to such a decision. By doing so I lose my place in a congregation of neighbors and friends who are dear to me. In some cases—knowing human nature as you and I do"— Judith increased almost imperceptibly the pressure of her fingers—"I fear I shall lose the respect and even the affection of some of those friends."

Mr. Seabury frowned. He recognized the trap she had crafted for him. But how in the world had she managed it so quickly and so smoothly? He coughed several times into his hand.

"It will grieve me to lose your friendship and association." She stressed the word *your* ever so slightly. "You have been a great comforter and counselor to me since Anthony's death. I shall never forget your kind services." Judith meant what she said; there was nothing of the hypocrite or the dissembler about her.

But the bold truth is sometimes harder for the mind to digest than mere lies, or a comfortable mixture of candor and sophistry.

"It grieves me to leave my friends, the city I love, this house, which has been home to me for more than twenty dear, happy years." Saying the words out loud had an effect upon Judith. Her voice trembled. She withdrew her light touch on the minister's arm and clasped both hands tightly in front of her. She was not one to show emotion lightly, to let others see into the heart of her. John Seabury knew that. The slight, disquieting awe he had always felt for her rose up like a tenderness in him.

"In fact, John, I have always known how fond you are of this house. So I shall give you the first opportunity to purchase it, before making public its availability." He drew his breath in sharply; Judith did not fail to note it.

"Judith, my dear—"

"Yes, I know. 'Tis an unhappy affair, and I am sorry it had to happen at all."

"Are you quite resolved?" The question was asked gently, but when Judith paused he persisted. "There is always time! If you were to see too late the error of your decision"—his voice was beginning to rise, to take on the timbre, natural to it, of a lawgiver, a master, a revelator—"the horrible tragedy, Judith, the shame, the—"

"Hush, John, please." Judith again placed her hand on his arm. "I know full well the weight of the decision I am making. I have spent many long, sleepless hours alone on my knees."

"Alone, my dear?"

Judith smiled indulgently at his quick, yet pompous, response.

"Yes, much of it alone with my own soul, struggling to find out the will of heaven. Such may be easy for you, but it has not been easy for me."

The reverend softened at her supposed deference to him and patted the hand on her arm. She had always been such a confoundedly handsome woman.

"I shall depend upon you, John, to defend me, to support me when all else fails me." The weakness in Judith's voice was real; there was a vulnerable note that was rarely revealed there.

"Yes, of course. Yes, my dear."

With an effort Judith collected herself. "You will discuss your interest in the house with Janet, then, I assume, and let me know of your decision? As soon as possible?"

"Yes, yes, you will hear from me shortly."

"Good." Judith began walking very slowly toward the door. "Thank you for your time, John, and for your concern. You have always been very good to me."

What could he say to this woman? In the end, standing awkwardly in the entrance of the home he could not help already envisioning as his, he merely gave the hand she extended a kindly squeeze. What to do, what to do? He walked back to his office wrapped in a vague feeling of fatherly piousness, a feeling that suited him and did much to dispel the terrible awkwardness of the situation. He still had his parishioners to answer to. But was not mercy and forbearance always the better way? Was it not the way that Christ taught? For the sake of the Reverend Thatcher, who had been loved by his congregation, might they not condone mercy for his widow and his fatherless children? The Reverend Seabury fervently hoped so. He hoped nearly as fervently that the hours before dinner would pass quickly so that he might return, without unseemly haste, to his own house and report to his wife the fortunate chance that had come their way.

Judith, left on the porch step looking after him, stood there a very long time. She knew that John Seabury had always coveted the house she lived in, and she knew that his wife, Janet Peabody, had money of her own that would assure their ability to purchase it from her. She meant to set the price high and keep it there. Heaven knew she would have need enough of funds in the days ahead. Sometimes the decision she had made frightened and nearly overwhelmed her. But she refused to look back. She didn't believe in that. She had set her course, and she would hold to it now. So she had always done, and look how far it had gotten her, how much of the richness of life she had purchased with what others called brashness but which she knew for certain to be courage and faith— a strange mingling of dependence upon her own inner resources and, when she felt her own powers slacken, upon the powers of heaven. It was the way she did things; it was the only way she knew. She lacked the refinement, even the discernment, of her husband, but that could not be helped. She must go forward in the best way she knew, and trust to heaven for the rest.

She sighed deeply, knowing there was no one to hear her. So her time had run out. She had gotten through the encounter with Seabury, but that had been easy compared with what faced her now. Now she must tell her daughters that she intended to take their comfortable lifestyle away from them and offer them something far less lovely, less safe, less palatable in return. That was the blunt reality of it. If they could see deeper than that, then they might begin to understand and forgive her. But she doubted that either was ready to see beyond the surface and understand beyond the pain and the shock her decision would impose upon them. With a prayer in her heart she closed the door and climbed the stairs, calling for Verity and Leah with a confidence in her voice which she did not feel.

Verity knew the worst had happened when her mother called them into her own room and ceremoniously closed the door behind them, with orders to Millie, who had trailed along, that they were not to be disturbed. She felt a tightness around her heart and a dull ache at her temples. Judith was not one for introductions; Verity knew she would go straight to the point.

"You may guess why I have called you here," she began. Her fingers toyed with the brooch at her neck, and Verity noticed with a sense of shock that her face was drained of color and her eyes looked large and dark and, if Verity had not known better, afraid.

"I have decided for myself that I believe Mormonism to be true." She paused purposefully, letting her words sink in, giving the girls time.

"You can reconcile that with your past beliefs?" Verity demanded. "What of the life you led as a minister's wife? What of Father?"

Judith's lips parted, and her features relaxed a little. "You are so like me, Verity. Do you think I have not considered those things?"

Verity glared back at her, not trusting her voice to reply.

"Your father was not just a minister, one who made his living as a churchman. He was a true man of God. I believe that if he were still here and had been given the opportunity—"

"Mother, really! How can you say such a thing? You wish to believe it, and so you tell yourself it is so. Do you really think he would betray those very things he spent his life teaching? Do you think—"

Judith held out her hand, and Verity stopped in mid-sentence. "You give me scant credit, daughter. He would have to deny none of the truths he taught and believed in. Mormonism contains those, and so much more! It answers so many of the questions he struggled with, things that dismayed him and tortured his sensitive soul."

Verity turned her face away.

"You do not believe me because you do not yet understand as I do or see as I see."

"Not yet?"

Judith sighed.

"Really, Verity, you're not giving Mother a chance," Leah accused indignantly. "You won't even listen to her."

"Do you believe Mormonism is true, Leah? Do you share Mother's opinion?"

Leah cringed before the heat of her sister's gaze. "I like what they teach. It makes me feel good inside." She glanced at her mother and took courage from the warmth in her eyes. "I even like how they pray, as though they were really talking to God, not just repeating high, lofty words."

That's because you've never understood the high, lofty words! Verity thought angrily. "Oh, Leah, do you know what you say? Do you truly wish to become a Mormon and follow their way of life?"

"Perhaps. I'm not certain yet." The withering gaze continued to scorch Leah. "What is so particularly outstanding about the life we live now?"

Verity shuddered. She turned in her seat so that she faced her mother squarely. "So, Mother, what does this mean? Tell me all— and quickly, if I am to bear it."

"Their people shall be our people, and their God our God," Judith said softly. "I have told the Reverend Seabury he may purchase this house if he wants to. I intend to pack up as much as we can carry, sell the remainder, and go to Missouri where the Mormons are building up cities of their own."

"Missouri is the frontier, Mother! It may as well be the end of the world! Have you gone mad?"

Judith did not attempt to defend her decision; she did not know how. She had not attempted to defend her decision to leave the faith of her Irish fathers and marry a Unitarian minister fourteen years her senior, leaving father and mother and all that was dear to her to follow his ways. No one had understood, no one had supported or helped her, but she had made her own way, and succeeded. Of course, she had had Anthony then. But she could do it now, even without him.

As if she could read her mother's thoughts, Verity blurted, "You've done this before, haven't you? Changed religion, changed one way of life for another. What wild, dissatisfied thing is there inside you, Mother, that drives you to such madness?"

Judith would not have endured such disrespect under ordinary circumstances, but she knew how hard her daughter was pressed. She sat silent and composed before the onslaught.

"You may be bored and restless for heaven knows what reason, but I am a Bostonian, born and bred, and I like it here! I wish no other way of life, Mother." Her voice broke, betraying her. She buried her face in her hands.

Judith leaned forward and placed her hand on her daughter's head, running her fingers lightly through the thick auburn hair. "Wirra, wirra," she soothed. "It will not be so bad. You fear overmuch, my little one."

Verity felt herself relax beneath the touch of her mother's fingers. Judith's strength flowed into her like a warm liquid, warming the chilling sensations of anger and fear.

"You are women nearly grown and in truth should have the right to choose for yourselves." Judith formed the words carefully. Verity lifted her head. "I have no desire to force either one of you, but it is my wish to keep the family together, as your father would have wanted it."

Verity sighed. The thin, bright opening in the clouds drifted shut, and she was enveloped again.

"Only in family is there strength," Judith continued, her voice growing stronger. "And I need you right now. I need you both. If you could see your way to come with me, then later, if you were truly unhappy, you could always return."

She was talking to Verity, and both of them knew it. Leah was young, and she had always been pliable. It was understood without saying so that Leah would go with her mother. But Verity was already older than Judith had been when she left her "ain folk" to go with the preacher man.

Verity could not think, she could not really grasp what was happening. She pressed her fingers against her temples to still the dull roaring inside her head.

"Think on it, Verity. We can speak again of it later."

"When would you leave? I mean, when will you leave?" Verity swallowed the bitter bile of the words.

"In three weeks' time. A group is forming that intends to leave by mid-May. We will travel with them."

Verity stood. She felt suddenly weak and light-headed. "I think I had better go to my room and lie down for a spell, Mother."

"Yes, dear heart, do."

Dear heart. So her mother had called them from Verity's earliest memory. She recalled clearly the time when she was fifteen and had come upon her parents unexpectedly as she was going late into the parlor in search of some misplaced item. The room had been dim, with only one small corner lamp lit. Both of them stood with their arms wrapped around each other, in some warm nest of their own. Her mother's head was cradled on her father's strong shoulder, and he was stroking her hair. Her face was tear-streaked, and she looked no older than fifteen herself. "Dear heart," he had murmured, as his gentle hand soothed her. "Hush, hush, my dear heart."

Verity had never forgotten the scene. Now her mother's heedless endearment brought the full weight of her duty upon her. She had not dreamed of bitterness and pain when she had promised her father, on his deathbed, that she would take care of her mother and stand by her, no matter what. She had not envisioned herself as a frightened, caged animal, powerless to escape, though the trap door stood open and freedom cruelly beckoned to her.

"I don't believe it," Millicent said bluntly. "Even your mother—"

"Hush, Millie. You know as well as anyone what Mother is capable of. It is true. We are leaving Boston, and my life is over."

Though they were overly dramatic, Millie did not smile at the words. She understood. Although it was of no great importance, her own life was also being tossed about and disordered by this thing that Judith had done.

"Three weeks," she mused. "Three weeks. That does not give us much time. And you are determined?"

"I have no choice in the matter. I promised my father, Millie."

He knew her all too well, Millicent thought. But she kept her thoughts to herself.

"'Your mother is strong,' he said." Verity's eyes were wide as she repeated her father's words. "'But she is not as strong as she appears. There is a tenderness in her, deep and hidden, and she suffers greatly. Please help her, Verity, when I am gone.'"

Millie shivered at the words. Verity raised a tear-swollen face to her. "Millicent, won't you come with us, too? It would make such a difference!"

Millie shook her head fiercely. "I would if I could, Verity. Don't break my heart! I have my father to care for once his ship comes to port. And besides, I could not live among people"—how could she put it kindly?—"whose beliefs are so alien to me."

Topsy-turvy. Judith had turned their world topsy-turvy overnight. Millie was not surprised when the lady herself called her into her room and put the same request to her that Verity had earlier made.

"I can't go with you, ma'am, as much as I'd like to," Millie told her staunchly. "I'll help with the sewing and packing; I'll help any way I can until—"

"I know that, Millie. And I cannot thank you enough. You are like one of the family, to all of us, and we shall miss you more than you know."

Millie blinked against the mist clouding her eyes. She had no words to say in return. She could not understand people who lived and died by religion. She had been raised by a seaman and the wife of a seaman, and what power she knew was embodied in the tides and seasons, in the ways and wiles of that mistress who held their lives in her hand. Nor would she have marked Judith for being one of those simple souls bound by religion. She with her touchy Irish blood. It didn't seem right. Yet it was happening. Like the tide when it was full and running, there was no holding it back.

"I have friends," Judith was saying. "I will gladly arrange a position for you here in the city, a place where you could be happy. Anyone would be glad to have a girl such as you, Millie."

"Thanks, but no. I believe I'll go home to Gloucester, ma'am. It won't be long 'til my father's ship comes in, and I'd like to be there. Perhaps for me this is all for the best."

There was no conviction in her voice. Judith smiled such a sad smile that Millie felt her mouth start to tremble. Judith caught both her hands up and held them tightly. "I'm truly sorry," she said, and her words were a murmur, like the sea on a soft night. "The path of true conviction is never an easy one. But it grieves me to bring sorrow to those I love best. I am imposing my desires on others; well I know that. But there is no other way, no other way that presents itself to me, my dear."

Such an intimate revelation from the great lady herself stunned Millie. Her own heart cried out involuntarily, "Oh, Mrs. Thatcher, it is a hard thing. And for Verity more than any of us. What shall she do, torn away from the home that is life to her? As for myself, Verity is the best friend I've ever had. My mother is gone; there is little enough in life left for me."

Judith drew the girl gently forward and encircled her in a motherly embrace. "There is much in life left for the both of you," Judith whispered against her hair. "Verity will grow from this experience. The womanly qualities that lie sleeping within her will ripen and bloom. Wait and see. Have faith, Millie. Good will come of this for you, too." She stroked the girl's hair. Millie did not truthfully know much about faith. She could not say she had faith every time her father sailed away that the sea would return him again. She had seen too many fail to return to be as foolish as that. But she was familiar with patience and a quiet kind of hope that might be something like the faith Judith spoke of.

She relaxed in the great lady's arms, soaking up tenderness as the dry sand soaks up the tide. She had known little enough tenderness in her life, and she could not bear to draw back too soon from the unexpected luxury of it. Judith, feeling the girl's need, responded. She held her for as long as she could, held the sweet breath of the moment warm in her hand. For this brief spell there was no future to intrude, trouble, or make afraid.

Chapter Four

All was ready. Time's hourglass stood drained and hollow-eyed, as blind to the future before her as Verity was. The days of cleaning and sewing, sorting and packing, had consumed every hour, every energy, every thought. But Verity had reserved this last evening to say farewell. She would allow nothing to rob her of it and no one to share in it. The few times she had ventured forth on errands of necessity she had been stung by the coldness of her neighbors. Now that the news was out, now that the Reverend Seabury had purchased the house from her mother and everyone knew of their terrible shame, all the pettiness and meanness that sometimes seems hidden in people had come to the surface with a vengeance that unnerved her.

Verity did her best to avoid confrontations of any kind. Not so Judith, of course. She was unabashed when friends appeared at her door demanding some book or household item they claimed to have loaned to her or her husband. She gave up all such belongings gracefully, even offering precious mementos of the dead minister to parishioners who she knew had particularly loved him and would cherish such things. She did not complain when the local grocer seemed suddenly out of her favorite meats and spices, things he had stocked especially for her before. She was quiescent when the blacksmith charged her more than anyone else for services that he was accustomed to discounting for the minister's household. She went her rounds, serene and unruffled as an angel, and Leah traipsed by her side, indulging in tearful farewells of old school friends and chums.

Verity was outraged when she heard her mother announce her intention to visit one particularly odious old lady.

"Mother, why do you submit yourself to the indignity of it?" she demanded in her frustration.

"I do as my Anthony would have me do, Verity. I represent him, especially among these people. I try never to forget that."

Her answer silenced Verity, who responded by punishing herself in turn with her own duty. She would not flinch. If she were to be martyr to her mother's life, she would be so completely. At the end of each long, exhausting day she took the Book of Mormon her mother had given her down from its shelf and read at least one chapter, no matter how heavy with sleep her eyelids grew. At first she read woodenly, for duty's sake only, and the words were mere one-dimensional letters printed on a white page. Gradually, without realizing it, the content began to penetrate her consciousness. Both her parents had taught her to be strictly honest and fair, so she admitted grudgingly, to herself only, that the book contained much of interest, if only as a history. She did not want to enjoy it; she did not want to find anything of merit therein. The fact that she was doing so disturbed her greatly. This was just one more trap, one more means of alienating her from the sweet life she wished to live.

But this last night she meant to wallow in her misery and pain. She meant to soak up, one last time, each sound, sight, and sensation that was dear to her heart. Such an exercise could be naught but agony, and she both dreaded and, in some perverse way, welcomed it.

She took the Long Path through the Common. The elms were heavy with their new spring foliage. Through the tender grass at their feet, gray squirrels ran in short starts and stops, chattering to no one in particular and glancing over their shoulders nervously to see if danger was near.

The Peanut Man was still shuffling his way across the worn cobbles. Verity bought a bag from him and scattered the contents for the squirrels to enjoy. The air was sweet to her nostrils, and a gentle silence sifted down from the sky to envelop her in its peace. She walked past the spot where it was rumored that a beautiful murderess had once been hanged. She had had the effrontery to appear before her executioner in a lovely white gown, and to bow and smile to the cold men who welcomed her doom. Verity felt a bit like the unknown woman as she walked through the still twilight, condemned to a fate that would wrench every bit of courage from her being and lay bare her heart.

She reached the public gardens and spent long, pleasant moments among the purple iris and yellow buttercups and the patches of pale blue forget-me-nots. A low, gnarled hawthorn tree spread a cloud of white blossoms beside the path, and an evening thrush sang sweetly from its branches. In the whole wide world there could be no city more lovely than Boston! Where else but here did the spirit of America breathe from every brick, every stone, every tree? Verity sighed as the weight of her grief trembled through her, like the breath of the wind over the tender spears of new grass. No more lectures in Faneuil Hall, which John Adams had named "the Cradle of Liberty." No more plays, nights of make-believe and magic, at the Boston Theatre, with its circular staircase nine feet in width and the glitter of lights and richly dressed ladies. No afternoon teas at the Athenaeum, with bouillon, cheese sandwiches, and sweet crackers for only three cents. No picnics under the great elm that rose sixty-five feet above them and spread out to become its own sky. And no summer outings on Long Island, with the lighthouse in view and the rocks of Nix's Mate, where it was said a captain was murdered by his wife and buried in the shallow soil of that lonely island, so close to the harbor that would have meant home and safety to him. Home and safety. The harbor of Boston that would be haven to her no more.

Verity's feet moved slowly as she approached the last stop on her pilgrimage. King's Chapel looked stolid and severe in the gray glow. No signs of life here, no movement, no shadow. She was grateful for that. She slipped through the gate to the little path that ran by the side of the chapel. Governor John Winthrop was buried here, as well as many other great men. But close by the path was the humble stone marker of Elizabeth Pain, who had worn a scarlet *A* on her breast. She had loved her minister, and he had returned her love. She bore him a child outside of wedlock, and all her long life her pious neighbors had forced her to wear the scarlet letter of shame.

Verity touched the cool stone with her fingertips. "Goodbye," she said softly. "Your life is done. You are free of it now, whatever its sorrows, whatever its pains. You bore yours well, I know you did. I only pray that I can." She raised her eyes to seek the grave of Mary Chilton, the first woman to step from the Mayflower onto New England soil.

Oh, Father, she cried in her heart, *I leave you in good company, I know. But it is a sore thing for your daughter to be torn from your side.* She stumbled toward the slight rise of ground where her father was buried. She was crying openly now, and past caring. The silence seemed loud to her, with a terrible, unvoiced lamenting that shivered along her spine and made her feet feel like dead weights as she moved among the tall, unmown grass. At last she dropped clumsily to her knees and pressed her forehead against the unyielding stone.

"Oh, Father," she moaned. "How can I do this thing? How can I do it?"

As she knelt there on the ground, chilled by the damp and the shadows within her heart, it seemed the last vestiges of her girlhood dropped away. She remembered the day she had boasted to Millie that she would not give in this time. But she knew now that nothing in life was as simple as that. She was beginning to see with the clarity of a woman's gaze, whether she wished to or not. She closed her eyes and drew into her the comfort and peace of the place. The conviction came strongly that this all belonged to her; she could take it all with her wherever she went. She need not be bereft as long as memory was her comforter and faith was her guide.

When Verity rose at last her eyes were dry and there was enough peace in her heart to allow her to walk home free from the terrible pain that had gripped her before. *Home.* The word would mean something different to her from this day forward, and for the rest of her life.

They left by sea. It was the sea that would bear them away on her breast. There would be a long overland journey to follow, but Millie thought it fitting that the ocean should part them. It had ever been thus in her life.

A terrible loneliness encased her as the time of departure drew near. It seemed to eat away her insides, leaving a hollow feeling similar to the emptiness she had felt when her mother died. She tried to chide herself, talk herself out of it. What were these people to her? Acquaintances of a few years only. She'd had a life of her own before them; she could have one again. Such friendships as theirs were a fleeting blessing, not a stable feature of life one could count on continuing indefinitely. Actually, as she well knew, most of the best things in life were fleeting and hard to lay hold of. Nothing in life ever continued unchanged.

With such gloomy thoughts crowding her mind she stood on India Wharf, her eyes stinging with unshed tears as well as with the glare of the sun on the water. Leah clung to her hand, and the realization struck her suddenly that the girl was afraid, truly so. She gave the small, damp fingers a squeeze.

"Don't worry, Leah. Your mother will take good care of you, and you have Verity. All will turn out well in the end." The sound of her voice saying the words gave them a weight of reality she had not afforded them before.

"Come, Miss Thatcher. All is ready for you ladies to board. Take my arm, and I'll help you."

Edgar Gray had come up behind them. Millie glowered at him from beneath her bonnet, but he didn't notice. His large, expressive eyes were filled with an obvious tenderness as he took the hand Leah offered him.

"Good-bye, Millie, good-bye!" Leah kissed her hand to her friend, and her eyes filled with tears as she clung to the large-framed Elder Gray and hurried toward the ship.

"You will write, as you promised, Millie?" Verity's voice revealed the tight control she struggled to maintain, but her hand trembled visibly as she placed it on Millie's arm. "Sisters of spirit," Verity whispered.

Millie nodded. "I shall never forget," she said, tears brimming her eyes now. "I shall never care for you less than I do at this moment, no matter how many years pass between us."

"Time and distance cannot alter our affection for one another," Verity echoed. "And in letters we'll share the hopes and longings of our spirits, as we have these past years." Her eyes were wet and shining, but she went on bravely. "And, Millie dear, if you become altogether too lonely in Gloucester, will you come to us? Promise?"

Millie nodded again. Verity gathered her into her arms and

held her fiercely a moment. Then she released her, turned, and walked resolutely toward the ship. Millie did not wait to see her friend board, to watch her become a small shape among many shapes crowding the decks. She had experienced too many such leave-takings. She turned and worked her way through the press of people, carts, and animals until she was free of them all and only the salt air, strong in her nostrils, remained with her. She fled, as from the phantoms of every fear and suffering she had ever felt in her life. All was over. They were gone. Standing and staring after them with burning eyes would not change things one bit. Her own bags were packed and ready. She would catch the train to Gloucester and be home within hours. Time enough then to think and plan. Time enough then to grieve.

On board the vessel, Verity did the same thing. She refused to stand on deck, staring pathetically out at the sea of faces that stared back at her. All was past now. Boston was forever behind them. She could envision no future, and the here and now was so distasteful, so precarious, that she must take it one breath at a time or be overwhelmed by it.

She felt her mother's hand on her shoulder and lifted her eyes reluctantly to meet her warm, steady gaze.

"This is more of a beginning than you know, dear heart. Remember what your father always said? 'God is nothing more to us than we allow him to be.'" She reached out suddenly and clasped Verity's hand with a pressure that ached. "He must be our all now, Verity. God must mean all to us now."

Verity closed her eyes and fashioned her mother's words into a prayer in her heart.

Chapter Five

The road to Gloucester had a cleansing effect on Millicent's mind. The coastline, chiseled and torn by the sea, was nowhere more beautiful. In many places forests of tall pines, so green they looked almost black in the weak afternoon light, marched down their slopes to the coast, crowding the uneven stretch of white, wet sand. Topping the rise of a little hill, her first view of the Cape Ann coast stretched before her. The water was placid and blue, as gentle as the May day itself.

Eager to feel the sandy soil beneath her feet, Millie sent her luggage on ahead and walked along the narrow, meandering streets of the town. It seemed every little road somehow rambled down to the sea. She could hear the gentle mew of the gulls and the startling cry of a curlew mingling his voice with the melodious swell of the surf breaking over the land. She closed her eyes and drew into her lungs the smell of Gloucester, a rare mingling of the flesh and bones of countless codfish, perch, and whiting; the oil and hemp and wet wood of the dark ships that rolled in the bay; and the sea—the tang and bite of air blowing in from islands and continents, shoals and reefs strange and exotic; drawing with it the breath of all places and all creatures it moved upon. Since 1623, when the first Adventurers colony was established here, Cape Ann men had drawn their livelihood from the sea. Three years after the Pilgrims landed, Gloucester's men were exporting dried codfish. Their fleet was now the oldest in all of America, and noted yet as among the most valiant in the world. Over two centuries of seafaring had weathered the town's wharves and narrow streets, and the faded roofs and spires had been blown gray and brittle by the ceaseless wind streaming in from the sea.

Millie stopped at one of the shops to buy bread, cheese, and salted smelt to make up a quick evening meal. She would worry about household staples tomorrow, after opening the house and determining just what was needed. For now she was content to trudge up the last stretch to the gentle grassy knoll where her father's house rested, seeming to rise out of the earth itself, as naturally as rock and tree did. No one had been inside the house these many months, with her father off on a whaler out of Nantucket and herself in service in Boston. Perhaps they both had avoided the house since her mother's death. But that had been nearly three years ago. Time enough, surely, to lay her ghost and get on with their own lives.

Millie fitted the key into the lock, and it turned with a loud, rusty protest. She pushed the door open and entered the dimly lit room. She was greeted by the pleasant, musky smell of dried herbs and the instant awareness of loved, familiar things about her: her mother's rocker in the corner with her Oriental shawl draped over one arm, as though she had just left for a moment to put the kettle on for tea; her father's old black sea chest against the far wall; the corner what-not shelf displaying some of the curiosities her father had brought back from his trips to Lisbon, East India, Amsterdam, and the Western Islands. *Those were the days,* she thought, sinking unconsciously into the rocker. Childhood was long and sweet then, and at the end of her dreams was always the coming of her father's ship, like some grand dream of its own, bringing back the whiskered half-stranger who hugged her against the rough wool of his coat and kissed her mother until her cheeks turned red, and dug from the depths of his sea bag the most incredible treasures: carved ivory boxes and miniature animals, silk scarves, rare cottons and nankeens, sugar, exotic tobaccos and fruits, and, once, a doll dressed in a bright flowered kimono, with wooden shoes on her feet, a shock of black hair, and a curved mouth like a small red bow against the pale porcelain of her face. Oh, the magic, mingled with the quiet joy of being together again!

The memories were suddenly too bright. Like morning sun slanting off the sea, they hurt Millie's gaze and accentuated the dull gray reality around her. She leaned forward and blew a layer of fine dust from one of the shelves. It billowed around her like specks of fairy powder, then settled again. There was no life in these rooms, only memories.

She rubbed her arms, feeling a sudden chill pass over her skin, though the sleeves of her rust-print dress went to her wrists and her fichu was still draped round her shoulders. The truth of it was, Millie was all alone in the world, or might as well have been. Her father was some place or other, at the other end of the world, and with the practical honesty of experience she knew that he may never return. The friends who were dearest to her were halfway across this vast country, meaning to live in a society that was as alien to her as any her father had witnessed, and they would never return. Of that she was certain. How dreary the prospect! A pox on the Mormons and their radical audacity. They had robbed her, and she entertained the most unkindly thoughts about them as she rose and made preparations to sweep out the room before taking her solitary supper, with nothing but the whispers and shadows of memory for company.

Gloucester was a thriving seaport these days. The Sandy Bay Breakwater, which the government had begun to construct the year before, protected the fishing coves on the exposed side of Cape Ann and brought new families and trade to the area. But "the harbor" in the heart of Gloucester itself remained the hub of all activity. In the heart of Gloucester lived the old families who not only minded change, indeed, who tended to shun it. Thus, it took Millie no time at all to realize the subtle alteration in her status among the townsfolk. She was looked upon as part of the change. She had been gone these three years and had come back with city clothes and city tastes. They were wary of her. In what other ways might she have changed? She was no longer comfortably and entirely like them. She understood how they felt—understood why the young women going to market gave her a wide berth when they passed on the streets; why the old women did not include her on their rounds of visits from door to door, exchanging tidbits of news and baked goods and herbal remedies; why the men down by the waterfront mending nets and exchanging yarns shut up like clams when she ventured too close. She understood, but it hurt just the same. She took to wearing the old, plain shawls and dresses she had packed away when she left for the city. She took care to buy in the same shops that had served her mother and father since before she could remember, although as she glanced through the windows of some of the new places she could see enticing wares she had grown accustomed to in Boston. Perhaps in time. Millie knew how to be patient. This was her home, and worth being patient for. But then something happened, something that changed things beyond her wishes or control.

Early on a fair June morning Millie was weeding in the garden. She had been home for nearly five weeks. In that time she had pruned and nourished and planted, and the results were pleasing. Right now the grass at her feet was blue with pretty Gill-go-over-the-ground, and her mother's rich red wallflowers and hollyhocks were as lush as she had ever seen them. She had planted additional tea roses, poppies, pinks, sweet peas, and much more, not to speak of her herbs in the far sunny corner. Here she had gone a bit wild. In addition to basil, bay, and bergamot, and half a dozen various mints, she had angelica, borage—which the bees loved—sage, chamomile for teas, chives, comfrey, coriander, and fennel. The list went on and on. Each herb had half a dozen uses and pleasures that she had seemed to grow up knowing but that she now realized had been taught to her by her mother in wise, natural ways.

Her mother was everywhere about her. She was thinking, as she dug at the clover and mallow and uprooted a tough clump of plantain, of what her mother might have been like when she had made this cottage her home and planted the first fruits and flowers, then later the herbs and spices her husband brought back from all parts of the world. She had been young then, and Millicent had not been her first child. There had been two little sons, but both had died of diphtheria before she was born. Millie knew little more than that they had been born within a year of each other and had died within the same week, and were buried down by the bayberry bushes that skirted her father's property.

Millie's parents never spoke of their lost children, but Millie had felt that her father sorely missed the companionship of sons to raise up to his trade, and that her mother missed the calm, steady help a son would have been when her husband was gone with the ships and she could have used a strong hand. Millie had done all she could to compensate, improving every household skill her mother introduced her to—doing the hard, heavy work of washing, perfecting soap and candle making to such a degree that the fragrance and texture of her bayberry was admired by all the village women, which was high praise indeed. She could do little to break into the world of her father, no matter how hard she begged and pleaded with him. But as she grew older she took over the task of laundering his heavy wools and cottons. Then once he cut his arm badly and was out of commission for over a week, right at the beginning of July when he needed to get ready for the trolling of the great swordfish—that could be done at no other time of the year. So, grudgingly, her father had taught her how to use the various needles—some curved, some straight, some fashioned of bone—to make the different stitches needed to mend his nets and thick canvas sails. Millie had a natural skill with cloth and needle, but it was not her father's way to praise her. Nevertheless, from then on it was she, not her mother, who acted as seamstress for him.

Millie was deep in reverie, tugging away at the past, when the stranger approached her. She resented the interruption and dropped her tools with an ill-concealed reluctance.

"I beg your pardon, miss. That's a fine garden you've got there. But I was wondering if you might assist me for a moment."

Millie raised an eyebrow at his clumsy praising of her work. He spoke with the accent of a stranger; he was from nowhere around these parts.

"Yes?" She made the word a question that invited nothing more than was necessary. Yet the stranger stood back upon his heels and smiled.

"You do have the prettiest yellow hair I've ever seen in my life." He looked for a moment as if he were going to reach out and touch it.

Millie stood frozen in place.

"Soft," he said. "Like the colors on a young fawn when the sun dapples its coat."

She took a good look at him, frank and open, a trait of her kind who must look life squarely in the face to be able to endure it at all. The stranger was young, with good, strongly drawn features: chiseled chin, fine cheekbones, a bit of a beak nose, but Millie didn't like small, pinched noses on men. His skin was smooth, not tanned rough as were the faces of the men who made their living by wind and weather. His hair was thick, as blue-black as a raven's wing where the sun lifted and lit it.

Millie adjusted her bonnet and rubbed absently at a streak of dirt along her apron. "And just what may I do for you?"

"I fear I am lost."

"In Gloucester!" The words came out unbidden. She couldn't help smiling at the expression they brought to his face. "All roads here, sooner or later, lead down to the sea. And from the harbor you can find your way to any place in the world." Her own boldness in bantering him astounded her. She felt heat rise to her face and suppressed an urge to lift her hand to her cheek.

He was a good sport. "'Tis embarrassing enough, miss, without you making it worse. Do you happen to know a Jonathan Hammond?"

She didn't. But when he described where he lived, she said, "That sounds like the old Copley place off Norman Avenue, just below Hesperus Road. But no one's lived there for years."

"That's the place. Mr. Hammond purchased it six months ago. It's getting to be quite livable."

"He's one of the new ones, then." Millie pushed her bonnet back from her forehead. "And is he a landlubber as well?"

The stranger smiled again. "Yes, I suppose you could call him that. He's a businessman, really, and has plans to build an iron-works factory hereabouts. But I don't truly know much about that. I am merely his guest, and an unexpected one, to boot. But I am trying to earn my keep by helping with the building and refurbishing. There is certainly enough to be done. And I'm more handy than some with a saw and a hammer."

He was rambling on as though they were old acquaintances. Millie stiffened and took a step back. The stranger was quick to sense things.

"Forgive me, miss," he said. "I have not even introduced myself. Nicholas Todd, at your service." He touched the rim of the low cap he wore.

She nodded, reluctant still. "Millicent Cooper," she offered at last. "And I can point you safely back to where you came from. It's not really far from here."

It hadn't been by the route Millicent gave him that he had wandered her way, though he had rambled aimlessly, deep in the sights and impressions around him. He had no choice then, really, but to thank her and leave.

Millie watched him start down the road. She liked his long, easy stride, the way his shoulders and hips moved. For some reason he disquieted her. She turned back to the earth, which was still disturbed by her diggings. But it was too warm now to be working outdoors. She picked up her things and walked back into the dim coolness of the cottage. It was so still here, so silent, that she could hear the distant whisperings of the sea. So different from Boston. But she liked it. Or, at least, she always had liked it before. Inexplicably, the silence sat uneasily upon her this morning. Had the stranger done that?

With a sigh of frustration she walked to the sink and began rinsing her hands. The cold water felt good against her skin. There was work in plenty to keep her mind occupied. Thank heaven for that.

Chapter Six

The hills above Gloucester were thick with ripe berries this time of year: blueberry, raspberry, gooseberry, and wild currant. Millie meant to harvest as much as she could over the next few weeks and to put up syrups and preserves against the winter months, as well as to enjoy them fresh with sugar and cream. The fragrance in the woods was a heady mingling of the ever-present sea air with gorse and yarrow, the mulch of leaves underfoot, and mosses, with small woodland flowers scattering a light scent over all.

Millie was busy filling her pails, humming under her breath, when she heard the approach of someone or something. She looked up in alarm. She had been too long in the city. Solitude and its natural interruptions would never have caused her apprehension before.

He saw her before she saw him, and he approached her with caution this time and a sense of reserve. Millie felt it and was not altogether sure she was pleased.

"Miss Cooper, is it not? Millicent Cooper." His smile, too, was slow. "We are well met, I hope."

"There are berries in plenty," Millie replied, shifting her position slightly as if to make room for him. He did come up closer and begin to fill the basket he carried. After a few moments of silence she ventured, "You must serve in a variety of roles at Mr. Hammond's."

Nicholas Todd relaxed a little. "You mean, are there no women or children in residence who could do the berry picking?" He swatted at a fat bee that was circling too close. "I'm afraid we are a bit short of such luxuries right now. Mr. Hammond does not have a wife."

"And yourself?" Millie asked the question casually, though she felt an annoying quickening of her pulse.

"I have a sick companion. That's why I'm out here in the first place, looking for luxuries to tempt his palate." He saw the uncomprehending dismay on her features, and his expression grew kinder. "You see, I am a preacher of sorts," he explained. "A missionary. We travel by twos, and we literally are companions."

Millie felt a chill at her heart. It could not be! No, it could not.

"That sounds odd to me," she said saucily. "Might you by any chance be Mormonites?"

"Mormons. Yes. How did you know?"

"A group of Mormons left these parts not long ago for the ungodly place where your kind have settled. What in the world brought you here?" She had blurted out the words before she could help it. Now she bit her tongue in annoyance at herself. But her dampened mood remained.

"We are on our way to Great Britain."

"Great Britain! There are Mormons there, too?"

"A great deal of us." He was watching her closely, trying not to smile at her vexation, but curious, too. "How do you know anything about Mormons?"

Millie did not wish to tell. She felt instinctively that it would put her at some disadvantage. Nor did she wish to answer his questions or to see his pleasure when he realized that friends of hers had been converted—and might he construe some hope from that fact?

She remained quiet, as though he had never spoken. *What ill luck!* she was thinking. *He appeared such a pleasant young man. Now all that is spoiled.*

"All right," he said, drawing her back. "You don't like Mormons much. I'm used to that." *And I refuse to be offended,* his look implied.

"What's wrong with your friend?" Millie would not use the word *companion.*

"We met with an accident some weeks ago on the Susquehanna. He suffered quite a gash in his leg and caught a bad chill. By the time we reached Boston it had turned into pneumonia."

"He must be very ill, then."

"Yes, yes he is. We knew Jonathan Hammond's brother, who

lives in the city. He sent us here. Elder Howlitt must have complete bed rest until his fever breaks."

"And after," Millie cautioned. "Pneumonia is not a disease to take lightly."

"Well, he may not have the luxury of that. Depends in part when a ship arrives that will take us."

"You care so little for your friend's well-being?"

"We are greatly needed where we are going," he tried to explain. "Besides, there are ways beyond medicine whereby—" He consciously stopped himself. "Never mind now. I shall take good care of him." His eyes gently chided her. They were a deep blue, streaked and multi-shaded, more alive than his ebony hair.

She looked away from his gaze. "I must go now," she murmured.

"Please don't. Your bucket isn't half full. Don't let me chase you away."

Millie hesitated. "I'll keep still, I promise," Nicholas Todd said. "Or better yet, I'll entertain you." He turned his back on her and resumed picking, humming lightly under his breath. Then, suddenly, there were words and a rich, tender melody.

> Oh Shenandoah, I long to see you,
> Away you rollin' river,
> Oh Shenandoah, I long to see you . . .

Millie lowered her eyes, feeling shy in the presence of a young man singing as though he were unaware of all else around him, even herself.

> Away, we're bound away,
> 'Cross the wide Missouri. . . .

When the first song was finished he went on to others.

> Believe me, if all those endearing young charms,
> Which I gaze on so fondly today . . .

Soon Millie relaxed and forgot herself, too, and let the music rush over her like the soft ocean wind.

No, the heart that has truly loved never forgets,
But as truly loves on to the close,
As the sunflower turns on her god, when he sets,
The same look which she turned when he rose.

Singing seemed as natural as talking or breathing to Nicholas Todd. Millie envied him that.

"Here's one for you," he said, glancing at her sideways. He cleared his throat and began:

I have a ship on the ocean,
All lined with silver and gold,
Before I'd see my true love suffer,
That ship should be anchored and sold.

He burst into the chorus, and she couldn't help singing it with him under her breath. Then, before she knew it, she was singing lustily along:

The wind blows cold in Cairo,
The sun refuses to shine,
Before I'd see my true love suffer,
I'd work all the summertime.

Both her buckets were heavy with fruit, and the young man's basket was filled. There was no reason to linger any longer.

"The sun's hot," Nicholas noted.

"Yes, it usually is this time of day." Millie lifted the pails and slung one over each arm. "Well, I guess I'd best get these home now." She turned and took a few steps away from him.

"Thank you for the company," he said.

She did not know what to reply to him. It was not until much later, as she lowered herself, hot and sticky with berry juice, onto the cool wood of the settle, that she realized she had not even thanked him for the songs he had sung. *I'll make up a nice gooseberry pie,* she thought. *His sick friend would enjoy that, and I would feel more comfortable myself.* She disliked the idea of being beholden to a Mormon in any manner at all.

*   *   *

She took a small crock of strong borage tea along with the pie, which had turned out well, baked to a turn with a light, flaky crust. She had done little baking during her years in Boston, and so was all the more pleased with her success.

The walk to the Copley place was pleasant in the cool evening air. She found herself humming the tune of the last song Nicholas Todd had sung; she couldn't get it out of her mind. As she approached the house she hesitated a little, then chided herself for her cowardice and knocked with such energy on the door that it was flung open immediately and a startled face stared out at her.

"What be the trouble, ma'am? What can we do for you?"

"Are you Mr. Hammond?" Millie asked, feeling a bit foolish.

"That I am."

"I am Millicent Cooper, and I have come to see your boarder . . . your . . . your guest," she stammered.

"Young Todd?" His voice was booming. His salt-and-pepper hair hung over his forehead, and curly mutton chops festooned his broad cheeks. "Bring yourself right in, miss, and I'll go fetch him."

She walked timidly inside. Her host had already crossed the long room, bellowing for Nicholas as he went. It was easy to note the lack of a woman's touch here. Glancing round, it appeared to Millie that chairs and tables had just been thrown together in any which way they landed. She felt her fingers itching for a feather duster to attack the layers of gray grime that sat over everything.

"Miss Cooper! How kind!" Nicholas Todd had come up behind her. She started at the sound of his voice. A nice voice; not deep, and yet sonorous, with a pleasant lilt to it, like the lilt in his step. "What have you there?" Like a curious boy he peered over her shoulder, trying to see inside the basket she carried.

"I've brought a fresh gooseberry pie," she said. "I thought your sick friend might enjoy it."

"My sick friend? So there is to be none for me?" His eyes were sparkling, but he did not mean to discomfit her.

"I made it for you as well. Payment for the songs," she said.

He took a step closer. "Those songs were free. How can a song be anything else, Millie?"

A warmth spread through her at his words, and a sense of confusion. She lifted the cover on the basket. "I brought some strong borage tea for your friend as well. It is excellent for chills and fevers. In medieval times it was believed to comfort the heart and purify the blood."

"Is that so?" He was interested.

"Yes." She stumbled on. "It was also said that borage contained properties that would grant a man courage." She shrugged her shoulders and drew her shawl a bit more snugly about her.

"Comfort and courage," Nicholas mused. "Well, bless your heart." He removed the basket from her arm. "These kind gifts will be much appreciated."

"Yes, 'twas right kindly of you." Mr. Hammond entered the room again, blaring out as he came. Millie raised her eyebrows, and he grinned at the gesture. "This young man here," he continued, "isn't like other men. Says he's a minister of the gospel. Does he look like a minister of the gospel to you?" He winked at Millie with a bold, bright eye. He was enjoying himself. "Young man like him should be out courtin'. What do you say to that, miss?"

"Leave her alone, John." Nicholas moved so that he stood between them and the older man could not see the uncomfortable effect of his words. "Pay him no heed, Miss Cooper."

"I'd best be going," she said.

"Come again, my dear," boomed Mr. Hammond. "Often as you like. We old bachelors could use a pretty face around here."

Nicholas opened the door and walked outside with Millie. "The man is hopeless," he said. "But he means well."

Millie swallowed because her throat felt suddenly dry, and her hands were clammy. "Nevertheless, he was right back there, wasn't he?"

"What do you mean?" A shadow, brief but chill, passed over his features.

"You aren't like other men your age. Missionaries don't mingle with young ladies. They don't do anything but—" Millie could not go on. An anger that surprised her rose to choke her words.

"Please . . . please tell me, just what do we do?"

Millie made an impatient gesture with her hand and walked away from him.

He matched his stride to hers. "Tell me, Millicent."

She turned, without knowing she would. "You entice innocent women in other ways. Entice them to leave their homes and beliefs of their fathers, to give up all that they have and go to some wretched place in the middle of nowhere—"

Nicholas put his hand on her arm as if to stop her. She could not control her own trembling. "Miss Cooper, you do not understand." He was grieved. There was a sorrow in his gaze that reached out to her. But she knew what she knew.

"I understand! Far more than you realize." She wrenched away from his touch and began to half run, half stumble away from him. He let her go. He had no right to do anything else. Mr. Hammond had spoken the truth and so had Millicent. He was not like other young men. He had a calling, a mission.

He turned and walked slowly back to the house. Millie fled through the night, listening for the sound of his footsteps behind her. By the time she reached the cottage and let herself into its haven, there were hot tears in her eyes.

Several days passed before Millie saw Nicholas Todd again. While going about daily errands, gardening, or even taking her evening walks along the shore, she had watched for him, half-expecting, half-dreading the sound of his voice or the sight of his tall, well-knit frame approaching her, his raven hair red-streaked beneath the sun. She chided herself for having any thoughts of the young man at all. But life here was quiet, and sometimes her days edged on boredom, accustomed as she was to the social life of the city: luncheons at the Athenaeum, shopping at the new Faneuil Hall Marketplace, afternoon literary teas at the Old Corner Bookstore, and occasionally a play at the elegant theater on Washington Street. She had been in a position of service in the household, true, but her status had been ill-defined and unusual. When Judith had said that Millie had come to be as one of the family to them, she had been speaking the truth. There, for the first time, Millie had experienced what family life truly could mean, knowing nothing before but the kindly, though dour, association of her aging parents. She had loved the giggling and screeching, the girlish confidences and tears, even the emotional squabbling that went on between sisters. She had enjoyed being part of it all. She missed it more than she would allow herself to admit.

It was early evening when she walked out, skirting the busy streets and veering off to a long, lonely stretch of sand where the shoreline curved and the tide rolled in gently. The day had been warm and fair. A mackerel sky danced above her, with row upon row of small, fleecy clouds, reminiscent of the blue-striped back of the silver-bellied mackerel. She hummed as she walked, thinking of nothing at all, giving herself over entirely to the beauty around her, until she almost felt that she herself was part of it, integral to the sand and the air, the sea and the sky. The cries of plovers and killdeer quavering over the water seemed to issue forth from the pulsings of her own heart, and the hushed wash of the sea upon land trembled against her warm, parted lips like a prayer.

She walked the damp, darkened line of sand until her bare feet tingled with the chill of the spray and the hem of her skirt was wet nearly up to her knees. She never could get enough of the ocean; the sound of its desultory voice in her ears, the push of its sweet tide against her legs. She moved up the gentle slope and spread a blanket across the rough sand, then sat there with her knees hugged to her chin and looked out to sea.

He whistled as he approached, so she saw him and was not caught off guard. He slowed uncertainly as he neared her, hesitating visibly, not certain whether to speak. He appeared to make up his mind, and said abruptly, "I have a new song for you. I learned it from the men on the wharves."

Without waiting for her reaction, he placed one foot on a rounded hillock of marsh grass and began:

Some men plow the open plains, some men sail the brine,
But I'm in love with a pretty girl; for work I have no time.
My truly, truly fair, truly, truly fair,
How I love my truly fair,
There are songs to sing her, trinkets to bring her,
Flowers for her golden hair.

Millie was smiling, but she couldn't help herself.
"Golden hair," he said. "This song was written about a girl like yourself. Listen to the second verse":

Once I sailed from Boston Bay bound for Singapore,
One night out I missed her so, I swam right back to shore.

He laughed in the delight of the bright tune and lyrics.

> My truly, truly fair, truly, truly fair,
> How I love my truly fair,
> There are songs to sing her, trinkets to bring her,
> Flowers for her golden hair.

The music of his voice seemed to end on a long, pleasant sigh. He settled down in obvious contentment on the sand, but not too near where she sat.

"Your pie was the best I have ever tasted," he said, "and I do not exaggerate. Elder Howlitt much appreciated it and, fear not, Jonathan ate his fair share."

"And the tea?"

"The tea helped! I should like more of it. And I wanted to return your dishes, but I was not certain I should."

A sudden heaviness filled the air around them. "It would be all right, would it not, for you to return dishes to a neighbor?" she asked. "You need do no more than stand at the gate." He said nothing. She did not look at his face. "I should be happy to brew another infusion of borage for your friend. Really. I am happy to hear that it helped."

"What book have you there?" She could hear the tightness in his voice.

"A volume of Tennyson's poetry."

"Will you read to me? One of your favorites."

She opened the cover very slowly and thumbed through the pages until she found what she was looking for. Could she trust her voice? She drew a deep breath and began:

> What shall sever me from the love of home?
> Shall the weary sea leagues of sounding foam?
> Shall extreme distress, shall unknown disgrace,
> Make my love the less for my sweet birth-place?
> Tho' my brains grow dry, fancy mew her wings,
> And my memory forget all other things—
> Tho' I could not tell my left hand from my right—
> I should know thee well, Home of my delight!

"That's very lovely. I don't know that. Have you others?"

Millie glanced through the pages. "There's one here about sea fairies, but I do not think you should hear it, being what you are." She stressed the last phrase slightly. "Here's one you should like":

O God! my God! have mercy now, I faint, I fall.
Men say that Thou didst die for me, for such as me . . .

Her words glided onto the air, pushing the feeling of oppression away. The sound of her voice, with the murmur of the sea beneath it, had a soothing effect, apart from the fine words themselves.

And what is left to me, but Thou, and faith in Thee?
Men pass me by; Christians with happy countenances—
And children all seem full of Thee!
And women smile with saint-like glances,
Like Thine own mother's when she bowed above Thee,
    on that happy morn,
When angels spoke to men aloud,
And Thou and peace to earth were born.

It was a lengthy poem, but Millicent read it straight through. When she finished she closed the book with a sigh.

"I don't know your Tennyson," Nicholas confessed. "But I should like to. Those seem inspired words."

The air hung sweet between them. "What is your book?" she asked, catching sight for the first time of the volume tucked under his arm.

"One I am quite certain you are not familiar with," he replied. "May I read you a passage or two?"

She nodded lightly. He opened the pages as though he knew right where he was going. "'And it came to pass that he commanded that their little children should be brought. So they brought their little children and set them down upon the ground round about him, and Jesus stood in the midst; and the multitude gave way till they had all been brought unto him. And it came to pass that when they had all been brought, and Jesus stood in the midst, he commanded the multitude that they should kneel down upon the ground. And it came to pass that when they had knelt upon the ground, Jesus groaned within himself, and said: Father, I am troubled because of the wickedness of the people of the house of Israel. And when he had said these words—"

"Stop this minute! What are you reading me?" Millie sat bolt upright, her eyes smoldering. He held the book out. She read the words, printed in gold lettering across the cover: *The Book of Mormon.* She drew her breath in sharply. "I do not wish to hear. You have tricked me, and that is ungracious behavior toward one who has trusted you."

"Trusted me to what, Miss Cooper? Trusted me to deal justly by you? That is what I am trying to do."

She made a low sound in her throat that expressed her annoyance.

"There is naught in this book that can harm you," he said gently. "Why do you fear it so?"

"I do not fear it, I abhor it!"

"Have you read it? Have you read even one page?"

Millicent glared at him.

"Are you brave enough and fair enough to allow me to complete this one small story, Miss Cooper?"

He had trapped her again. Resentful and tight-lipped, she nodded. Unbidden to her mind came the words that Verity had once spoken to her: "I am forcing myself to read the book nightly, Millie, and to be fair, there is much of interest contained in its pages."

Nicholas was reading again. Millie caught the words in her mind unwilling, wishing she could push them away.

"'. . . He himself also knelt upon the earth; and behold he prayed unto the Father, and the things which he prayed cannot be written, and the multitude did bear record who heard him. And after this manner do they bear record: The eye hath never seen, neither hath the ear heard, before, so great and marvelous things as we saw and heard Jesus speak unto the Father; and no tongue can speak, neither can there be written by any man, neither can the hearts of men conceive so great and marvelous things as we both saw and heard Jesus speak; and no one can conceive of the joy which filled our souls at the time we heard him pray for us unto the Father.'"

Millie rose. Her legs felt weak beneath her. "I really must go." There was a ringing in her ears. The words he had spoken had broken through to her heart. She wanted to ask him, "Who were these people, that the Lord Jesus would pray for them? How was it so?" She had never prayed in her own life, not really. When her mother had died some anguish deep inside her had cried out through the darkness, longing for someone to hear, longing for someone to save and succor her. She blinked her eyes and looked out to the pale, restless sea.

"There is more."

"It is late. See how dark it grows." Millie caught up the blanket on which she had been sitting and shook out the sand. "Please, let me go."

He said nothing more and made no move to detain her.

The sky was a darkening plain above Millie as she hastened homeward. The sea was a muffled roaring inside her head.

She went to bed early, but she could not sleep. She tossed and turned in her bed and suffered strange, erratic dreams she could make no sense of at all.

Nicholas Todd sat up late with his companion, administering to his needs. His mind was disturbed. He read in his scriptures longer than was his habit, even though sleep thickened behind his eyelids. It was also his habit to pray on his knees before going to bed. He knelt there, pleading with heaven for a long, long time, needing more than ever before to feel his way through the mists and find the answers he sought.

Chapter Seven

Millie had not hoped for a letter so soon. When Almira Fenn's youngest, Amos, brought it out to her on his rounds, she found it difficult to hold back the intensity of her feelings. He watched her as children do, with a straightforward and impersonal interest that was disarming. Knowing his mother as she did, Millie was certain the boy would be questioned concerning her reaction to so great a thing as mail that had traveled all the way from the Missouri territory to the edge of the east coast.

As soon as the boy was safely away, Millie sat in her mother's rocker and hugged the letter to her, just savoring its reality, for a long, foolish time. She was almost afraid to open it and discover what had happened to her dear friends since they had parted. At last she slit the envelope and lifted out the thin, folded pages. The words Verity had penned were well formed, the lines crowded close against one another. Bless her heart, she had crammed in as much as any two sheets could hold. With trembling fingers Millie smoothed back the creases and started to read.

My dearest Millicent,

I take up my pen but know not where to begin in telling you the strange saga which now is our lives. We arrived safely in Far West, Missouri, which is known as the central gathering place of the Saints. It is a fair city that sits atop the highest swell of ground in this vast prairie country, where fields of corn and meadowlands stretch on all sides, as far as the eye can see. The city boasts above three thousand inhabitants, and more arriving each day—many who were converted in the British Isles and have made that long journey, leaving all behind them, to join with their fellows here. I had thought my own sacrifice so great, so to be admired! How small I feel, Millie dear. No one speaks in terms of "sacrifice" in this place. It is simply part of their way of living from day to day. And they embrace it as I don't think I ever could!

I must say in truth that the people here are very kind to each other. They use the terms *brother* and *sister* most freely, but such still feels awkward to me. Everywhere the eye looks one sees growth and change—so many houses being built, and yet there are not nearly enough. We have found living quarters in one-half of a small home belonging to an elderly widow. She and her daughter (whose husband is dead) and her daughter's four children dwell in the other half. The rooms are quite small, of course, but are adequate for our needs, and clean—thank heaven for that! Mother minds nothing. She loves the excitement in the air. She calls it "freedom of spirit," claiming she has never felt less stifled, never more her true self. People like her, and she thrives. As for myself and Leah, we struggle more than Mother does, each in our separate way.

The strangest thing about these people is their cheerfulness in the face of hardship, and their fearlessness in the face of threat and real danger. I made a promise to myself not to complain, Millie, even to you. But this is not complaining, merely informing you of the facts as they do truly exist. Several years back the Mormons were gathered in Jackson County, in another portion of this same state, and the other settlers there, jealous of their unity and prosperity, formed themselves into an angry mob and drove them from their homes, stole their property, and left them destitute. And yet, these Mormons remain in such a hostile environment. Even now, in Far West, there are rumors of "enemy activity." *Enemy,* Millie! Imagine the reality of living with real enemies at your back. Mother laughs at it. "We were raised in such a manner in Ireland, and we survived," she says. I do fear sometimes that she almost enjoys it. I am frightened more than I let her see, and poor Leah is indeed like a ship without moorings. She has lost weight and appears more white of skin and frail than ever. If it were not for Elder Gray, or Edgar, as we now know him, I believe she would sicken and fade away like a lovely shadow.

Since you and I are at such a distance and communication between us so hazardous and yet so invaluable a thing, I will not demur, but rather speak my whole mind, knowing, as I do, your tender indulgence and quick and generous understanding. Brother Gray, no longer on an official mission, is free to court, and I fear that is what he is doing, with Mother's approval. To tell you the truth, I at first believed he harbored an interest in me. But I think I tend to frighten him just a bit, or at least disconcert him. He is very tender with Leah and enjoys fussing over her. You can picture, I am sure, his big brown paw of a hand closed over hers, white and bird-thin. He brings her sweetmeats and small treats whenever he can manage it. Needless to say, Leah thrives, as she always has, on indulgence and pampering. Yes, I fear if you were here you would raise one of those fair arched brows of yours and remind me that I am not far behind her in that regard. Yet, for the first time, Millie, I thank God—and you—for what usefulness I might have. Little did I know while you sat patiently teaching me in that high, square room in the dear house on Walnut Street how to make patterns, how to cut, how to stitch, and I sat despising the tedium of it—little did I dream what need I would have of such precious skills! I have pieced and mended our few clothes several times already. Sister Shumway (the woman in whose house we are living) gave Mother a small end of cloth, and I contrived to make a new apron for Leah, which cheered her considerably. How little we have here, Millie! But no—I promised myself! How I do miss you! How I do miss Boston, and the clean breath of the sea, and the sounds of—well, you must know how I miss it. What need be said?

Several days after our arrival Mother and Leah were baptized in the shallows of the Grand River. They were part of a large group, and there was much singing and rejoicing. But I could not commit myself to such an immutable step as yet. Leah, unable to perceive my feelings, pronounced me foolish. But Mother did not press me, and I am most grateful for that. I read daily in the Book of Mormon and try to perform faithfully all duties that fall to my lot.

Millie sighed and paused in her reading. Such a dismal picture! Dare she go on to the end? She tried to imagine the scenes her friend was describing, tried to picture the girls in such a setting, but had difficulty doing so. How alien—how pointless such an existence seemed to her. With a tightness at her heart she turned back to the letter again.

I have seen the man who is responsible for all of this: Joseph Smith. They call him Joseph, the Prophet, or simply Brother Joseph. He is without doubt very pleasant to look upon—a tall, fair-haired man. His eyes are blue, and they pierce right through you, seeming to enter your heart, but not as with judgment, more like a light, like a pleasant warmth surging through your whole being. He has a kind manner and a noble bearing, and something beyond that which I cannot pin down, but which draws all people to him—men as well as women and children, enemies as well as tried-and-true friends. I have heard the stories of his marvelous influence. For myself, I cannot deny what I have felt and what I have seen with my own eyes.

I have no more room, and my hand is cramped from writing. Besides, I must put venison on the fire and potatoes to bake in the ashes. No seafood here, but we are beginning to harvest fresh vegetables, despite our lateness in planting. I bid you a fond, fond farewell, dearest Millie, and pray God to take care of you and comfort you in your loneliness.

Your loving friend,
Verity Thatcher

Millie let the letter fall into her lap and sat for long, silent moments contemplating what she had read, struggling with a range of emotions that exhausted her feelings. She realized, with a stab of dismay, that Verity's letter, rather than warming her and drawing her closer to old affections and memories had made her feel even more isolated than before. How could that be? She placed the sheets back in their envelope and tucked it carefully inside her silk-lined handkerchief pocket, which smelled pleasantly of lavender. A letter from Verity. The first letter. The first of many, she prayed.

*　　*　　*

Just the sight of him made her feel anxious, almost angry. He sat on the waterfront, dangling his feet like a boy, listening to the old men tell tales. She was jealous; she knew that in an instant. How had he worked his way into their confidence when they still shunned her, their eyes cautious whenever she approached, their mouths set thin and tight below their weather-lined cheeks. Watching him, she could endure it no longer. She marched up until she stood directly behind him.

"Elder Todd," she said, keeping her voice firm and even, "may I please have a word with you?"

He was on his feet instantly. She could feel his amusement at her use of the Mormon title for him. Could he feel her anger as well?

She turned and walked off from the group of now-silent men, who hid their curiosity as they did all other emotions. Nicholas was forced to follow, and he did so graciously, walking a little behind her and whistling under his breath.

Only when they were quite removed from the men and all other possible listeners did Millie turn on him, her skirts swishing around her ankles. "Did you come here from Missouri?" she demanded. "Tell me about it. I wish to know all you can tell me."

His forehead furrowed into lines of concern, pinching his face in and making his nose seem larger. Millie moved to a cluster of large rocks jutting out of the land a little above the shoreline. She leaned against one that was smooth and green in places with lichen, and waited. He kept his distance and took his time in responding.

"My family was converted not far from here, in upstate Vermont. One of my father's older brothers, as it happened, knew the Prophet's grandfather, Asael Smith, knew him when he was an elderly gentleman."

Millie was impatient, but he did not appear to see that. He plodded solemnly on. "My mother had lost, as it were, an entire family—her first three daughters to cholera. She liked the Mormon belief in the continuation of family units after this life, and of our eternal natures and possibilities."

"So, when you joined the Church you went to Missouri." She was urging him on rather than questioning him.

"Yes, we moved to Jackson County in '33."

"Jackson County!" Millie felt a chill shiver along her backbone. "Then you were driven out of your home by a mob." Wasn't that what Verity had called it?

He was clearly curious now. "How do you know this, and why are you asking?"

"I have my reasons. Will you help me or no?"

Perhaps the word *help* prompted him that there was something at play here which was not apparent to him. Regardless, he continued.

"There isn't much to tell. The settlers in Missouri are a wild lot. They like their own way and resented the sheer numbers of the Mormons, the way they bought up the land and organized into communities, each man helping his brother. They didn't like that at all."

"It can't be that simple. There must be more—more reason than that to cause people to harm, to destroy, to—"

"You may as well say 'murder,' for so they have done."

"With no cause but jealousy?"

Nicholas shook his head. "Who am I to explain human nature or the forces that move upon the spirits of men?"

"So why do the Mormons stay where they are hated, where they are in danger? It makes no sense at all!"

"It is their promised land. It is the will of God that they be there."

"The will of God!" The derision in Millie's voice was as harsh and intent as a blow. "Do you know Joseph Smith?"

"I do not know him personally, but I have been in his presence. He has shaken my hand. I have heard him speak many times to the Saints."

"How does he impress you? Do you really believe he is what he calls himself—a prophet?"

"Would I be here if I did not? Miss Cooper!" A tender light coming from somewhere inside him lit the young man's eyes, and Millie realized they were as deep a blue as she had ever seen in the sea of a morning. "Things of the Spirit must be gained through spiritual means; one must seek and learn for oneself. It is possible to experience enough to *know* of a surety. Tell me, could you describe the ocean, the magnificent range and scope of it, the textures and colors and moods it possesses, to one who is blind, who has never seen water, who has no concept of what a long stretch of anything means? Right now you are unable to judge of such things as Joseph Smith and the work that he does."

"But he is wicked! I think he delights in taking the lives of ordinary, decent people and making havoc of them for his own will!"

Elder Todd's face turned ashen, as if he had just sustained a great shock. "Oh, you are wrong, so terribly wrong, Miss Cooper." He lowered his gaze as though it pained him to look at her. But he said nothing, and the silence between them was palpable.

Millicent was the first to move. "If Mormonism were not so wicked, I might feel sorry for you!" She spoke through gritted teeth, and her words were caught up by the wind blowing in from the water and the pounding of surf on the shore. "I am going. I shall not bother you further." She turned her back on the young man and walked into the wind, its force making a funnel around her, drawing her hair and clothes, even the lines of her skin, tight and strained.

Nicholas watched after her for a long time, until his eyes burned from staring and a dull ache pounded beneath his temples. Millie dashed a trembling fist against her eyes, angry at the sting of the wind that had caused tears to form there, foolish tears that made her head swim and blinded her as she stumbled along.

Chapter Eight

Summer by the sea, with no one for Millie to answer to but herself and the simple demands of living, with the fragrance of blossoms, redolent of sun, in her nostrils: snow pink, sweet william, phlox, and the tangled white and pale yellow honeysuckle that were her special delight. There was more to Millie's life than her disturbing encounters with the young Mormon. True, there was no overt excitement, and little beyond the common to break the pattern of days. But it sufficed, at least for the time being. Then one fine August morning, when the fresh wind spanked the white water and the blue sky shone rain-washed and clear, Luther's boat hove into sight.

The holds were full to overflowing, and the ship rode gaily atop the waves. When the rocks of Cape Ann came into sight they rounded Eastern Point. Now it was in with topsails, down with jibs, lower the anchor, down with foresail, let the mainsail stand. And suddenly there she was, brought to bay, steered into her stall like some graceful, spirited racehorse, spent and panting, neck wet and glistening but held high and gallantly still. A crowd had gathered, but Millie kept to the fringes. She had no real purpose here. It was wives and sweethearts, children and mothers who pressed close, whose faces were too bright, too anxious. This was a triumphant return, safe and profitable, with no flag wilting at half-mast, no heartbreak harbored in the curve of white sails.

Men swaggered off the ship one by one or in small knots. Millie watched the reunions with interest, longing to be part of the terrible intensity of that moment when gaze meets gaze and the very force of life trembles between two loving souls who are united again. She thought of her father's face, stiff with wrinkles, and each one a story, an etching made by danger and challenge, passion and pain. *The men that go down to the sea.* The phrase sang in her head, and the words of the verse she had known from child-hood:

> Gloucester is fair, yes, wondrous fair
> For artist's brush, or poet's pen,
> Yet still its wealth beyond compare
> Is in its race of sturdy men.

After a few moments she turned and walked away slowly. It was time, any time now, for her father's ship to round that fair bend into a safe, well-earned harbor. Pray God it may be so.

It was with surprise that she opened the door to Luther that evening. A black oystercatcher had found its way up the beach and was poking among the rocks on its long legs, as pink in color as the blush in the sunset. "Kervee-kervee-kervee-kervee," it called, the sharp piping sound ending in a beautiful rippling. Millie smiled at the bird, and at Luther who stood looking at her with dark, serious eyes.

"Heard you were back. Looked for you down by the boats, but I didn't see you."

"I was there. Did you have a good voyage, Luther?"

She had nearly forgotten this man: the sound of his voice, deep and almost guttural, the dark brooding of his eyes watching her, ever watching her from the days when she had been only a child, playing with shells and sea creatures along the sand. Luther was seven years older than Millie, so it had been a bit strange when he had set himself up as her protector, fighting anyone who offended or harmed her in any way. It was part of accepted knowl-edge by all the Gloucester folk that Luther had claims on Millicent. That had been part of the reason she left home and went to Boston. He stifled her with his devotion; he always had. She did not see herself belonging to Luther and living his kind of life. He was too stolid, he lacked imagination, and he belonged to the sea. Yet the men in Boston, the few she had become to any de-gree acquainted with—what had they been like? Smoother in manner, yes, more educated. But they had been boorish in their own ways, and just as devoted to business and profit as any seaman was to riding the waves. They had not been the answer she was looking for. And now she was back, and here Luther stood watching her, his tarred canvas hat in his hand.

She let him inside. She listened to his tedious recounting of the journey—Luther was sparse with words, and the few he spoke were painfully utilitarian, commonplace. She served him lemon jelly, blackberry scones, and tea. He was content being near her, as he always had been. He asked very few questions of her, enough merely to ascertain that the threat, as he knew it, was past.

"Your fancy Boston friends are gone, then, for good?" he asked her once more as he stood up to go.

Millie nodded. *Yes,* she thought, *but that does not mean what you think it means. I can be gone from this place anytime I choose to, and well I may!*

He had caught her hand up and now was pressing it against his lips. She was surprised at the warmth of his touch. "Millie, my dear . . ." He murmured the words against her skin. "You don't look a day older than you did the last time I saw you, over two years ago."

His eyes said more. His eyes spoke the sweet, awkward sentiments he had written on countless cards and notes on the countless holidays and special occasions of the past ten years. Why did she feel an impatience with him, rather than the tenderness he looked for?

He walked down the narrow path of stones Millie's father had laid for her mother. She could remember the day the two of them scoured the high, scruffy sands above the tide line in search of them. Some of the rocks had the sand ground right into them, and some were softly streaked with the grays and blues of the sea that had brought them there.

Recalling something, Luther paused and half-turned. "Your father's vessel hove into Honolulu a few days afore we left."

Millie felt a catch at her heart. That meant that they had been successful in hunting the whales and that they had a cargo of oil and whalebone to transfer to commercial ships there.

"Will he come on home, then?" she asked. "Or will he go back with the whalers?"

"I didn't speak to him myself. But Jim Trollop said the half-dozen Gloucestermen who sailed out of New Bedford with the whalers was comin' back on the *Swallow*." He watched pleasure spread over Millie's features. "I thought you'd be glad to hear that."

Millie hugged her arms to her body as she stood watching Luther disappear into the warm evening dusk. A seaman's life was a grueling one, she knew, and at her father's age, service on a whaler must be a punishing thing.

The Gloucester vessels, with very few exceptions, were owned by the well-to-do merchant-shipowners, who also kept most of the general stores. Although these owners stood the cost of all supplies, each fisherman was allowed to keep only half of his catch, and could never hope to own even one-sixteenth of his ship, as the Cape Cod sailors could. The average earnings of a Gloucester fisherman for the working year of nine months were roughly $150. But a fair-sized family needed a hundred dollars more than that to carry it through the winter.

Of course, sometimes there were years—what years!—when a banner season could bring in as much as eight hundred dollars. Millie's father had known a few such years. Thanks to that, the cottage Millie lived in was paid for free and clear, and a modest "nest egg" sat in the Gloucester bank, which dated back to Federalist times and boasted a vault carved out of solid rock. But nothing comes without a price, and Millie thought she understood the price exacted on her father by the winds and the tides and the siren call of the cold mistress who did not reward her lovers in worldly fare. Not to be forgotten was the ever-present gamble between life and death.

The dark curtain of night had lowered while she stood there musing. She walked out into the comfortable obscurity and found her way, more by feel than by sight, to the stretch of shoreline, which was empty save for the voice of the sea and the echoes that moaned ceaselessly beneath the shifting current. Millie heard them only at night. She truly believed they were the murmurs and moans of the countless seamen who had given the sea her toll, and whose spirits wandered restlessly, seeking land, seeking the warm arms of wives and family. Millie gazed out at the expanse of water and thought of the men, seventy-eight of the Cape Cod fleet, who were drowned just last season. She had read of it in the Boston papers, and the tragedy was more than mere statistics to her. She had known some of those men and the families who would see them no more. They were more than names, more than faces, more, even, than flesh and blood. And they were gone, as so many before them, and so many after would be.

Millie shivered. She had no wrap, and the night air seemed to bruise her flesh. But she knew that it was her spirit, not her flesh, that was tender.

She walked back to the house. Her thoughts were in a turmoil that she could not still. The forces of nature could be brutal, but in an unfeeling, impersonal way. For some reason the ugly word *mob* kept penetrating the morass of her thoughts. What about man's brutality against man? Was this some omen, that it beat upon her consciousness and would give her no peace?

Millie moved through the rooms, straightening things, getting herself ready for bed, with the sound of the sea in her head and the lonely moans in her heart—and fear, a fear she could not explain, settling like a damp chill over all.

Nicholas Todd handed Millie the piece of paper with a little flourish. She stared at it blankly for a moment, then recognition and annoyance together flooded over her face. It was a poster announcing a Mormon meeting to be held at Winchester Hall, Boston, on the following evening. Listed below the information concerning time and place was a list of "elders" who would be preaching. Nicholas Todd's name was among them.

"You are an odd one," he said, watching her. "What is it about the advertisement that surprises you? I am here as a missionary. I have been doing more with my time than helping Jonathan Hammond make the Copley place livable."

She handed the sheet back to him icily. "And what affair is this of mine?" she demanded. "Why do you bring this information to me?" He did not answer her, and she added irritably, "You know my feelings!"

"Do I?" he asked. "Do you, Millicent? Do you truly know your own feelings?" There was no effrontery in his voice, only the gentlest concern.

"You know nothing about me, and you've no right to question me. Leave me alone!"

"I was hoping you would come."

Millie could not hide her amazement. "Come! Of my own accord! To a Mormon preaching!" She was incensed. "Have you listened to nothing I have said to you? I have good reasons for hating the Mormons, and I need not explain them to you!"

"I have listened more than you know." He spoke in the same tempered, untroubled voice. "I have heard more than you realize."

"You are full of nonsense." She took a step away from him.

"But I am not wicked, and you know it. Nor were the other Mormons you met. The ones you wish to hate."

He spoke as if he knew—knew all about Boston and Judith and the meetings in the reverend's house. But, of course, he couldn't!

"In three days I leave," he said quietly.

She stared at him stupidly.

"Yes. Elder Howlitt is much improved in health, and we are instructed to take passage on a certain ship. All the arrangements have been made."

Millicent nodded, feeling awkward. "Well, off to England at last. I wonder what you'll find there?"

"Success. Our message is being well received among the British." Again, there was no offense in his voice, though the words themselves held a sting. Millicent chose to ignore that for the time being, in deference to her own dignity, which she was already struggling to maintain.

"Do come, Miss Cooper, for sake of our friendship."

Millie found she could say nothing in reply, and he did not press her.

"You have such poppies as I have never seen," he said, turning his attention to her garden, "and hollyhocks—I do remember hollyhocks from my mother's garden, lining the entire expanse of her fence."

"How lovely that must have been," Millie murmured. "Have you flowers in Missouri?"

"Wild prairie flowers in plenty, though I don't know the names of half of them."

"Is it such a terribly wild and lonely place?" She had not meant to ask that. She felt the color drain from her face as he turned to regard her.

"Someone you care for deeply must be in Missouri. That must be part of the mystery." He said the words as if thinking aloud to himself. And, in truth, Millie caught only a portion of them and refused to ask him what it was he had said.

"It is beautiful country!" he told her. "Good soil, gentle hills, plenty of woodlands."

"But lonely to those who have left homes they love—and hostile to Mormons."

"Love of God is supposed to be first in our hearts," he replied. "But it seldom is. True religion teaches a man to be happy. Mormons are the happiest people I know."

Millicent did not believe him. She thought of the dull suffering in Verity's eyes when they embraced for the last time. She thought of the sad courage in the words she had written, masking her struggles and fears. Nicholas Todd, watching her, sighed.

"You must experience what I speak of for yourself," he said, with a degree of resignation in his voice. "And you have not done that yet."

"No, I have not," Millie replied, and she may as well have added, *I never will!*

"I shall hope to see you tomorrow evening, nevertheless," he responded, with what cheer he could muster.

"You will be disappointed."

For a moment his eyes met hers and held them, and she could not decipher what she saw there. "I've been disappointed before," he said.

What did he mean by that? He walked away down the stone path. "Fare you well, Miss Cooper," he called, waving a hand to her, "until we meet next."

Fare you well. . . . They were ordinary words of parting, but they brought distress to Millie's heart. Those were the last words her mother had spoken to her father when he went out to sea. He was still gone when she died, and by the time he returned she was under the ground, and the perils and hardships of his long journey never really ended for him. It had been her hand that smoothed out the wrinkles and strained muscles, her heart that coaxed the loneliness out of him and set him to rights with the world. Silent, unheralded work for the woman, but every seaman's wife knew how essential it was.

Fare you well . . . the words sat like a stone on her spirit as she walked back into the house.

*　　*　　*

She never meant to go to the meeting, but at the back of her mind was a reluctance to disappoint the young man who had been, after all, a kind and well-meaning friend. *No good will come of it!* a voice inside whispered. *Despite his gentle ways, do you not despise what he stands for? Has Verity, with all her integrity, all her trying, been able in good conscience to be baptized a Mormon herself?* Why did she have this weakness where Nicholas Todd was concerned? she agonized. *You see qualities in him you admire,* she reasoned, forcing herself to honesty, *qualities that would make a good husband. Do not be deceived! Mormonism would spoil that—perhaps it has already. There is no future, no future in thinking about him at all.*

So the weary battle continued within her all day. And then, in the end, the decision about attending the meeting was taken from her.

Luther came himself to invite her to the festivities: a fish bake and dancing in the moonlight to celebrate his ship coming in. He would be there to walk her to Stage Fort Park at seven, and if she had any of her fresh blackberry preserves left, she could bring them along.

"I'll make up some sourdough bread to go with them," she offered. What else could she do? Feeling guilty for the relief that surged through her at having the whole troublesome matter taken out of her hands, she turned with renewed energy to the tasks of the day and promise of laughter and enjoyment when evening came.

Swordfish was one of the specialties of the Cape Ann area, and August was the prime time to find the big fish, by trolling with mackerel, herring, or even squid for a bait. The succulent white steaks, simmering over glowing coals, made one's mouth water.

Millie, with her arm tucked into Luther's, was surprised to see so many people swarming over Fisherman's Field. She wondered what the original Pilgrim settlers would think if they could see the Cape Ann coast today. In old times the fishermen dried their catches here on a stage. Later they built the fortification called Stage Fort, which was never officially used. That had been long before the Revolution, before men had any real notion of what life

63

in this new land would be. She would like to have seen the field then, and the men who worked there—the first white men to cast lines and nets into this vast fertile sea.

"Millie, you're so quiet. I've been among surly seamen for these many months." It was a gentle, well-deserved remonstrance.

"I was just wondering what the men were like who fished here, who raised Stage Fort and built their homes here."

"Not much different from us, I'd guess," said Luther. "Aren't all seamen cut out of the same cloth since time began?"

Millie sighed; he had missed her point altogether. "I'm hungry, Luther," she said. "Let's go fill our plates before all those delicate little pastries are gone."

"There's chowder in plenty, and that's all I care about," Luther chimed as he followed her.

"You mean to tell me your mouth is not watering for some of your mother's lemon cake after all that time at sea? Or the blueberry pie I baked for you at the last minute—"

Luther surprised her by putting his hands around her waist and lifting her clear off her feet. "It's the sight of you I've had a hunger for these many months. This blue dress against your white skin—like a summer's sky against the white of the clouds . . ." He whirled her around before setting her on her feet again, but she was so close to him she could feel the gentle rising of his chest as he breathed and could smell the sweet rum scent of his body. "You do try a man, Millie!" As he spoke, she suddenly felt his warm breath on her cheek. She knew what he was about, but for some reason she did not stop him. When his lips covered hers she was surprised at the tremor of delight that moved through her, seeming to warm her from the inside out.

She laughed and pushed him away. He let it go at that, and they walked together toward the big, steaming pots set in the sand and the long tables laden with food, their bare feet leaving a trail, wet and iridescent, on the soft, sun-warmed beach.

It was late, very late, when Millie walked with Luther back to her cottage. They moved slowly across the sand, now cool to their touch; there was no need to hurry. The waning night was languid and still. The memory of the sunset meeting the sea in a line of fire was still with them, the warmth of bellies filled with good food, skin cooled by the sweet ocean air, then heated again by the touch of flesh against flesh, strange and new in the darkness. Millie had never been kissed before, at least not properly. Luther took no undue liberties with her, yet she found his lips seeking hers several times through the heat of the dancing, when every nerve in her body was tingling, and again later, sitting in the glow of the fires that dotted the beach, while the townsfolk sang the old, old songs of the sea and of the men who had sea eyes and sea ways.

> Farewell to my comrades, for awhile we must part,
> And likewise the dear lass who first won my heart,
> The cold coast of Greenland my love will not chill,
> And the longer my absence, more loving she'll feel . . .

Melancholy thick as sea-mist in every word:

> We're bound out for Greenland and ready to sail,
> In hopes to find riches in following the whale . . .

Death and danger were a part of life, not to be shunned or ignored. Silent as these sea folk were, there was a strength to them that was more ancient than time and memory. Millie felt it course through her veins and knew it was an integral part of her being, something she could never ignore or deny. The question she must ask herself was, how much was Luther a part of that life, that essential essence—or had he nothing to do with it at all?

A voice calling outside her window awakened her. She sat up in bed, rubbing her eyes, wondering why Nicholas was calling her. Then she remembered, and put her hands to her face.

"Miss Cooper, answer me! 'Tis a small thing I'm asking, Miss Cooper."

Millie threw on a long paisley shawl over her nightdress and went to the window, pushing it open just a fraction.

"What do you want so early in the morning?" She did not have to pretend to sound tired; her voice was muffled and still warm with sleep.

"Early in the morning? It's past nine o'clock." His voice was cheerful, and she could hear no anger in it. "So you had a good time on the beach late last night?" She opened her mouth to speak, but he stopped her with a shake of his head, quickly adding, "Never mind about the meeting. It doesn't matter now. But you will come and bid us farewell? We've no one else but yourself and Mr. Hammond, and I've heard it's ill luck to leave on a long journey with no well-wishers at all."

"Of course I'll come. Are you glad to be going? Aren't you frightened at all?"

"Frightened of what?" His voice was calm, and his eyes burned with a confidence that drew her. "If I do what I know to be right, I have nothing to fear. I believe God's power will help me."

The words were too gentle and humble to be offensive. "Good," Millie replied. "I am glad of it." She did not wish to quarrel with him on his last day. Indeed, a vague sense of loss had begun to rise up from within her. "When does your ship sail?"

"One of the afternoon, I've been told."

"I'll be there," she promised.

He nodded slightly. She could read the pleasure in his eyes. "Thank you." There was a little silence between them. She could see in his face that he wished to say more.

"What is it?" She felt no disposition to be harsh with him now.

"Miss Cooper, may I write to you? And if I do, will you answer my letters?"

Millicent stood still, considering the unexpected request. *What harm could it do?* she asked herself. But the voice of warning chanted, *Look what happened to Judith, look what happened to Verity!* "You believe I am still 'convert material,' Mr. Todd, despite all?" She asked the question in a casual, almost teasing manner.

His expression did not waver. "That is not the reason I had in mind when I made my request, Miss Cooper."

Millie dropped her eyes, afraid the telltale color would rise to her cheeks and betray her. He stood unmoving; she knew he wanted an answer, and would wait for one.

"Yes," she said, feeling free and light as she spoke the word. "Yes, you may write, and I shall reply to your letters and tell you what things of interest I can." Good heavens, he was only a young

66

person, much like herself, going halfway around the world and, despite his assertions, probably feeling a bit unsure of himself and his future right now. If she had not enough inner stamina and purpose of her own to combat any subtle Mormon influences he might exert against her, then she was a sorry case indeed. She had never cared much for organized religion of any kind; she was not like Judith, looking for a creed and a cause. Nor was she like Verity, forced to mold her life to another's. No, she had little to fear.

He was watching her still. She attempted a cheerful, friendly smile.

"Thank you," he said, his voice and face solemn. "This means more than you know."

She could say nothing, and she dared not meet his gaze directly. "Off with you," she said, "or I won't be through with my chores in time to come down to the wharf."

It worked. A slow smile spread over his features, and Millie thought again, *He isn't quite handsome, but he has such an interesting face, an air that invites confidence, unstifled and open.* She did not watch him walk away. She closed the window and began to make up her bed, refusing to allow herself to think of what the coming hours would hold.

It was difficult; she had feared it would be difficult. The sun was warm on their heads, the smell of the sea ripe in their nostrils. His friend, still thin and quite without color, stood a short distance away. "Will he be able to stand the journey?" she asked, glancing over at him.

"Elder Howlitt? He's fine. He looks like that all the time— you should have seen him when he was really ill!"

They laughed together, and it helped a little. "This is for you," Millie said, drawing out the hamper of food she had prepared for him. He was moved by her kindness; she realized with dismay that he was fighting back tears. The ship's whistle blew; Elder Howlitt took a few steps toward the gangway and called out, "Make haste, Nicholas."

Millie held out her hand. He lifted it gently and held it as he would a small bird or a rare, precious shell. "There is so much I would say that I cannot," he murmured. His eyes were dark with a suffering that reached out to her. She felt her whole being tremble. "I shall take the beauty of your spirit with me," he said. His voice was firm and sure now. "And I shall pray for you, Millicent, day and night." He bent over and kissed the hand he was stroking. "God keep you," he said.

Her throat felt dry and constricted. She had no words to say to answer the music of his. But for a moment her eyes met his freely, and she did not hold back whatever might be revealed in her gaze. She knew not what he saw there as he turned and left her. She knew not what she thought or what she felt. Something within her was refusing the impressions and feelings that seethed through her like a damp, cloud-driven storm. She stood alone, staring at the ship, staring at the water, staring at nothing at all. She stood until the ache in the small of her back and the strain in her eyes, half-blinded by the glare of sun striking water, bit into her awareness. Then she turned, feeling heavy and tired, and walked slowly home.

Chapter Nine

It has happened, Millicent! And I know you will not believe it any more than I did.

What in the world could Verity be talking about? Millie held the letter to her a moment, fearful of what might lurk within its innocent-appearing pages. But she could bear the agony of not knowing for only a few seconds. Hungrily she started reading again.

I know not how to prepare you, so I shall just bluntly tell. Simon Gardner, with his red beard and his great head of auburn hair, has asked Mother to marry him, and she consented. He has, I fear, been giddy as a schoolboy ever since. When I at last worked up courage to ask Mother what in the world she was thinking of, she laughed sweetly and said, "Dear heart, I could never love Simon as I loved your father—as I love him still. But I am fond of the man, and he loves me. We need him, Verity, and I can make him happy, and that ought to suffice." By the time you receive this letter they will be man and wife, Millicent. And, what is more—to prove how strange life can truly be—big, gentle Edgar Gray has asked Leah to marry him. "How delightful!" she says. "Mother and I can have a double wedding. Think of it, Verity." He, too, seems pleased with his choice, but I wonder about Leah. "Do you love him?" I asked her. "Of course I love him," she replied, her cheeks still pink with the delight of the adventure. "He is so kind to me, and I believe he adores me, Verity." That was her only response. It chilled me a little, so I demanded bluntly, "Do you love him? Do you desire to make him happy?" She looked at me a bit blankly. "You worry too much, Verity," she replied. "I told you I loved him, didn't I?" So I left it at that. I shall give away both my mother and sister to husbands, and be left an old maid myself. And for this I sacrificed all that was dear to me!

Millie choked on the words, as though they had been uttered from the depths of her own heart and the pain was somehow her own. She longed to rush to her friend, to fly as the sea birds, high and strong against the blue, immense sky, and rescue Verity and make everything right. How clumsy and earthbound and powerless she felt! With a sinking heart she read on.

Marriages ought to presage a happy, prosperous future. But I feel none of that under the circumstances, which include an increasing tension between the Mormons and their enemies. On the sixth of this month an election was held at Gallatin, and the old settlers made up their minds that the Mormons should not vote. They started first with threats and bullying which, like wildfire in a wind, soon became an all-out attack. Now the Missourians are arming themselves against the Mormons, gathering support from every county. Does it not seem insane, Millie? Joseph Smith and the other leaders are doing all they can to achieve peace, but it is obvious that some men are simply out for their blood. The small, scattered settlements fear the most. Here in Far West, surely, we will be safe. Such is the feeling we cling to. We go about our activities as usual, but this cloud of fear and injustice, like a black weight lowering closer and closer, shadows all that we do.

By the way, in July, less than a month ago, Joseph Smith said he received a revelation giving him a means to finance the struggling Church. He has asked his people to pay a tithe, one-tenth of all their increase—and, Millie, they do it! In the midst of sacrifice and persecution and pressing needs on every hand, these people accept his word as the word of God. It would astound you to see it. In truth, there is a power when people unite in this way. And, lest you picture this modern prophet as monstrous, inhuman, and conniving in his power, let me in all fairness say that he is none of those things. His power is real, and you feel it whenever you are near him. But such love emanates from his gaze, such kindness, such virtue! Do not laugh at my defense of him; I feel bound to tell what seems true and right. Children flock to him, and that alone is an indicator of something rare and good in a man. I do not know. I live in amazement each hour and try to take one day at a time, in faith, remembering my promise to Father. Sometimes I fancy him near, yearning over me, loving me and helping me. 'Tis a sweet sensation indeed. Do you ever feel thus with your dear lost mother, Millie? I hope that you do. I hope there is some tender power hovering near to comfort and bless you. That is the prayer of your loving friend and sister in spirit,

Verity

Millie could not hold still. With the letter clutched in her hand she paced the room, prey to sensations and feelings that she could not give name to or understand. Then abruptly she stopped, aware of the words Verity had written as though someone had spoken them aloud. "*Do you ever feel thus with your dear lost mother . . . some tender power hovering near to comfort and bless you . . .*"

The sun coming in the small leaded panes of glass spread a rosy glow throughout the room, drawing sparkles like a gleaming gem from the cranberry glass pitcher, a wedding gift to her mother, sitting proud on its shelf. Close beside it was the small oval likeness of her father and mother, a rough, unskilled pen sketch fashioned by one of her father's shipmates. Her parents both looked very young. What expression the man had caught in their eyes revealed an innocence that astounded Millie. The proportion of features was not accurate, but the artist had managed the aquiline line of her mother's nose and the gentle curve of her cheek. The color of her hair, soft and light as new honey, was still fresh in Millie's own memory, as well as the sound of her laughter, resonant and melodic as the murmur of the sea at low tide. For a moment, just the space of a heartbeat, she could feel what Verity had spoken of: a gentle influence, an unheard singing around her, a sense of peace and wholeness, as though someone had uttered a prayer.

"Mother!" She spoke the word aloud. Peace and warmth

flowed through her, so that she sat down on the settle and rested her face in her hands, longing to hold onto what she felt, to hug it fiercely near. The loss and loneliness waited like a chasm to engulf her once the feeling had passed.

"Millie, what's going on? What does this mean?"

Luther had not bothered to knock but had walked into her house unbidden.

Millie looked up from the vegetables she was cleaning, annoyed. "What are you talking about?"

He flung a wrapped parcel onto the hard settle. It slid across the polished surface and came to rest against one of her mother's embroidered pillows. Millicent wiped her wet hands on her apron, walked past him and picked up the parcel. It was wrapped in brown paper, tied with a length of hemp, and only her name was written in the upper corner. "This is addressed to me," she said, her voice tight and controlled.

"Yes, a young man left it with my mother to be delivered to you. Do you know what 'tis, Millie?"

"Do *you*?"

He had not the sensibilities to even pause at her words and the implications behind them. "Mother had her suspicions, and she was right. She knew who the stranger was, and so she took a look for herself."

Millie clutched the book and glared at Luther. "How dare she?"

"How dare you? Do you know what that is, Millie, that you're holding? 'Tis the Mormon book, the devil's book. And what's it doing with your name on it?"

"That is none of your business, Luther." Millie was trembling now.

"'Tis my business, feeling the way I do for you. You've been seen with this Mormonite by the townfolk—talking with him, being right friendly! Have you gone mad, girl?"

Words choked in her throat. She stood silent and frustrated, trying to express with her gaze the horror and loathing she felt. *I will not explain myself to him*, she thought.

"Millie!"

"Luther, do not make demands of me or try to bully me. I will not stand for it!"

Luther's features tightened. He seemed to dig into his position like a tenacious bulldog as he stared back at her. "Millie, you live among these people. They're the only friends you have. You'd better care what they think. Have you no shame? What's happened to you, Millie?"

"Much has happened to me since you last saw me, Luther." Millie drew herself up as she spoke the words. She saw an uncertainty enter his eyes. "I have my own life and my own ways, and I will explain myself to no one."

"It is unwise to talk like that."

"I have done nothing to be ashamed of—nothing even unseemly. Therefore, what right have you, or anyone, to question me?"

"Come now, Millie." Luther ran a hand through his straight brown hair, only causing it to fall limply across his forehead. He was disgusted, and never thought to disguise or soften the emotion. "You know better. You were seen in this man's company— often!—walking the beach alone with him!"

Millie sighed. Luther's eyes had gone dark so as to appear almost black in their distress and intensity. She realized with a jolt what he was probably thinking, and what others might be thinking as well. She had been gone too long from the intimacy of a small, closely woven community. Under Judith's tutelage, she had taken upon herself an attitude of freedom and individual determination that was unknown and certainly unacceptable here.

"I tell you once more, I have done nothing to be ashamed of. That is all to be said on the subject." She stepped to the front door and gave it a tug so that it stood wide open and waiting. "Good day, Luther. And next time will you kindly knock before entering my home?" She stood stiff and silent, waiting for him to pass.

For a moment he made no move. The anger in his gaze had deepened, fed by the frustration and lack of comprehension he was feeling.

"You've no business to offend those who care for you, Millie." There was nothing in his voice but hurt and anger.

"Good day, Luther," she repeated.

With a surly growl under his breath he strode past her. She shut the door so quickly behind him that it grazed the heel of his boot, and then leaned against the closed door, trembling, unable to sort her feelings. Why did this happen on the same day that she had struggled with Verity's letter? It didn't seem fair.

At last she moved to the settle and tore the wrappings from the book she had been clutching. It was a Book of Mormon, all right. What possessed Nicholas to send it when she had so adamantly refused it before? With a sigh she opened the cover. A folded paper fell out. She retrieved it, and with vague misgivings read what Nicholas had written there.

Miss Cooper—Millicent—Please accept this book and do not be angry with me. I could not with any peace of mind leave you without knowing you had it in your possession, for do you or I know what life will bring? You may well need the comfort or strength which this book alone could give you. Even light and knowledge—you may one day stand in need of these. Please do not discard it. And please do not despise me, but believe me to be, as I am, your most sincere and devoted friend,

Nicholas Todd

She folded the note and slipped it back inside the cover. She did not know what to think. Part of her realized that she might very well have spurned the book but for the stubborn pride Luther raised by his pigheaded ignorance and interference. She knew she would keep it, partly for the same perverse pride that would have made her reject it under different circumstances. She wanted to curse Nicholas Todd for bringing this trouble upon her. She wanted to hate him. But she could not. Try as she might, she was able to remember only the kindness in his eyes, his voice singing "My truly, truly fair" with the sigh of the sea like a counter-melody woven into his words. She had not admitted to herself that she missed him, but she knew she could not forget him. Whether that be for ill or good, time alone would tell.

She placed the book on her father's shelf with the few precious volumes the household boasted, rolled up her sleeves, and went back to cleaning the vegetables that now lay muddy and wilting in the sink.

Millie awoke in the morning to the sounds of a squall blowing in from the northeast. A nasty one, she thought, looking out through the streaked glass. Seldom were storms so rough this early in September. She pulled one of her father's gray wool sweaters out of the trunk and boiled up some oatmeal to eat hot. There would be no work in the garden this day; she would have to find something quiet and productive to keep her busy indoors.

The wind carried a high wet whine, and she fancied she could hear the voices of young children weeping. Such a wind always distressed her. She buried her nose in the rough pile of the sweater, drawing in the musky odor of sheep's lanolin and the richer, almost heady fragrance of her father's old calfskin trousers, which were also packed away in the trunk. She thought of the men fishing in the small Chebacco boats. This gale would force them to leave their moorings and head for a safe port. What of her father's ship plying homeward?

As the day wore on the constant battering of wind and rain ate at Millie. She felt cooped up and restless, and a vague apprehension ate at her spirit. The storm was noisy and the sky was dark, and all the earth seemed troubled. She ought to answer Verity's letter, but she could not under this brooding weight. She warmed up some fish balls to eat with what was left of her bread and tried to read a little, but the lethargy borne of fear and solitude stifled nearly every impulse.

By early afternoon she had lit the lamps. When night descended in earnest there seemed to be little difference to her. She shivered, thinking of the countless days and nights such as these that her quiet mother had endured through the years. An old verse came to her mind. With a superstitious reluctance she whispered it under her breath:

> For men must work, and women must weep,
> And there's little to earn and many to keep,
> And the harbor bar is moaning.

She felt she could hear the sifting of the sand under the force of water, pounding at it from the heavens and dragging at it from the cold, foaming tides. She knew the harbor bar could moan beneath the force of a tempest. She trembled at the thought of ships floundering in the shoals of Georges Bank or in the jagged reefs of Norman's Woe, where rain hissed in the brine and the billows frothed up like beaten egg whites.

How bleak the night was, and how weary the watch she kept; now hopeful, now overtaken with nameless, faceless shadows and fears. She sought bed early, hoping to drown out the whine of the wind and the weeping of the rain. But the plaintive sounds followed her into her dreams and she slept fitfully. The night seemed endless, and her dreams were filled with ghosts and nightmares of the lost, the suffering, and the dying, crying out to her in their plight.

In the morning the skies were still gray and wet, but the wind had ceased blowing and the sea had settled. Millie took inventory of the damage done to her garden and, with frustrated resignation, began repairs. There was no sun to dispel the gloom of the previous day and the unrest of the night. Work was her only vent. She was grateful for it but found herself working doggedly, without her usual enthusiasm.

She did not see the *Swallow* slide quietly past Mussel Point and Rocky Neck into the inner harbor, almost limping, it seemed, her flag at half-mast, her men grim-mouthed and sober. But later she did see Norman Pope, captain of the vessel, walking with heavy stride down the center of the road toward her cottage. She put her hand to her mouth and bit hard on her lip to stifle a cry. She could not take her eyes from his solid figure rolling steadily toward her. She stood and brushed the damp soil from her hands. *No! Dear God, this can't be!*

He approached slowly, like a man moving in a dream, his eyes straight ahead. When he reached the stone walk she was there to meet him. He could not meet her eyes, but reached for her hands and cradled them gently in his, which were rough and cold still from the chafings of rope, canvas, and weather.

"Where?" she breathed.

"Grand Banks. You know how wicked the currents are there, the seas steep and short."

Millie drew a ragged breath. She knew.

"A fog settled in. We lost two others besides your dad, Millie. Mark Flynn and Louie Bell—aye, he that had a sweetheart waiting to set a date for the wedding." He shook his head. His eyes, narrow slits below a brown, lined forehead, regarded her with the patience borne of gazing for years on end at a wilderness of sea and sky, gazing and watching, gazing and listening, gazing and waiting. He did not attempt any awkward expressions of sympathy or apology. What had happened was part of life as they knew and accepted it. His being there was enough.

"I'll send some of the womenfolk down to you," he said as he left her. That, too, was the way. Millie did not protest. Right now she was part of them—more part of their ancient, ongoing life than of her own.

The sea has taken him at last, she said to herself as she gathered up her garden tools. *The sea has taken him home.* There was no comfort in the thought, and no horror. Just the weary acceptance that was her ordained and unquestioned part.

Her father's death made all the difference. Luther came to her, all thought of disagreements aside. They were integral to one another again, in the only world he had knowledge of. Her grief was his own. All Gloucester mourned with her. She was no longer a stranger.

The sea, as terrible and mysterious as she had been since the beginning of time, had once more pulled them all together: they were one in submission to her, fear of her, awe of her. They lived under her power. As Millie stood beneath the fine morning drizzle and looked at the pinched, lined faces around her, she wondered how many of these men and women, even for a moment, ever forgot that fact.

As they lowered her father's coffin into the sodden ground she experienced a moment of panic. What madness was this to bury a seaman in the dank hold of the earth? He who could not live without the salt spray sharp on his face, the cold heavens and all the stars of the universe spread out to his gaze. He who was tuned to the wild voices of the wind and the water spirits, lovely or loathsome, that spoke to his ears alone. Here, all would be darkness and silence.

She shivered. Luther put his arm around her shoulders and the warmth of his body, hard and seasoned like her father's, reached out to her. And yet, how fragile he was. He stood beside her with the strength of a thick, straight mast that could withstand any storm, yet he could be broken, hewn down in a moment by a whim of the mistress, the mighty sea, that he served.

They were dropping clods of earth onto the coffin, these men who had ridden the seas with her father, whose eyes were veiled and whose faces revealed none of the vulnerability they felt. Whose turn was next? Who would be missing when they gathered once more in this gloomy place to bid yet another farewell?

Was she growing morbid? She moved away from Luther. But, feeling suddenly weak and giddy, she leaned against him again. The wind had worn itself out. The air about them was heavy with silence. Not even a bird spoke to pierce the thick gloom. She would go home now. The man who had been her father would never return. His shell, useless to him, heedless of the skills with which his mind and will had imbued it, lay here at her feet. She had not been able to see him, talk to him, listen to the sound of his voice. After two years of separation she had been waiting and hoping. But it was not to be. He was gone. Perhaps he was with her mother. She wanted to believe that he was. She wanted to believe that it all made sense somehow. Is that how the others, silent and stoic, felt too? Was courage, then, nothing but terror denied expression?

The people were moving slowly, huddled in small groups together, out of the cemetery and along the sea road that led back to town. Always the sea—beside, around, within you. She hated the sea. But not half as much as she loved it.

Luther got her back to the house. He stayed with her until she could no longer keep her eyes open. Then he tucked her in bed. Why was everyone afraid of leaving her alone? She needed no solace in the daylight; it was the darkness she feared.

"Leave a lamp burning," she told Luther.

"Right here on the table, Millie."

She heard the scrape of the wooden runners along the floor as he moved her mother's rocker into the bedroom.

"I'll be with you," he said. "I won't leave you alone in the murk."

Had he read the fear in her eyes? Had she been that transparent? She was too tired to think about it, exhaustion seeping like a paralyzing fluid through every inch of her body. She could not move her head. She could not raise her hand to pull up the bedclothes. Her eyelids closed, like a heavy barrier shutting out all feeling. Against her will, she slept.

Chapter Ten

She could not say why she did it. For two weeks after they buried her father Millie did little at all, performing by rote the daily tasks required of her, walking the blank line of the shore, or sitting for long hours on the knoll above the cottage, her mind empty and untroubled, if not at peace. Then one morning she got up and, without thinking, sat down to her father's old, scarred desk and wrote a letter—a long, detailed one telling all that had happened and much that she felt, or at least, as much as she was able, for the first time, to identify and put into words. She placed it in an envelope and wrote *Nicholas Todd* with the Liverpool address he had given her. "Anything you send here," he had said, "will eventually find me." Next she wrapped the envelope in a piece of burlap and bound it with string. Over the black dress she was wearing she tied the long gray shawl she had purchased in Boston, pulling the hood over her head, for the weather was still wet and raw.

She carried no shopping basket over her arm, only the small parcel tucked under the folds of her cloak. She was heading for the cottage, bent and narrow, that stood at the point end where Essex Street nearly ran into the sea. But as she passed the post office she suddenly paused. It would do no harm to ask.

She stepped inside. Almira Fenn's face registered surprise when she saw her. Millicent smiled, regarding the older woman who was a thin, wizened, shrunken version of Luther himself: the same dark eyes, like deep pools, with no lights in them; thin, common brown hair; pencil-fine eyebrows that looked as if she had drawn them across the line of her brow; a narrow, beaklike nose; and a mouth that was too small for her face. Somehow with Luther the same features, expanded, lent character to his appearance. But his mother was not flattered by her looks, and her personality did little to make up the difference.

"'Tis good to see you out and about, Millie. But you'll take a chill, all considered, if you're not careful."

Millie proffered no real response but asked simply, "Has any mail come in for me, Almira?"

"Mail?" She spoke the word as if it were foreign to her. With her long, thin fingers she began sifting through a stack of envelopes on the counter before her. Squinting, she looked up at Millie. "You just had a letter from your Boston friend, now, didn't you. But postmarked from some wretched place in the West . . . I don't rightly recall . . ."

Millie stood with her hands inside her cloak, patiently waiting. She would not be put off, even if she had to sort through the pile of letters with her own hands.

Perhaps Almira saw that. She searched again, more carefully. To her own surprise she pulled out a thin brown envelope with Millie's name written across it. She held it out, examining it closely. "There's no postage. Must have been hand-carried on one of the ships—not your father's." She spoke the words matter-of-factly. "Most likely from the week before." She turned it over in her hands. "I'd say the *Hartley* out of Liverpool. Passed through here last week."

Millie held out her hand. Reluctantly Almira gave her the letter.

"You know somebody in Liverpool, do you, Millie?" The older woman could not forbear the question; such was not her habit.

Millie did not reply. "Thank you, Almira. A good morning to you."

She scurried out the door before Almira could stop her, retracing her steps in the way she had come. A strange excitement throbbed within her. A letter from Nicholas! She would read it first, and perhaps add some reply along with what she had already written.

She did not even remove her cloak before opening the letter and reading the words, written in a large bold hand across the page.

Dear Miss Cooper,

I am writing this onboard ship and shall post it at the first opportunity once we arrive safely in port. My companion fares well—better the first few days than I did, for I was made very ill by the motion of the ship, which troubled him far less than I fear it did me. There are few passengers on this voyage, and those poorly organized. Thus Elder Howlitt and I spend much time reading and writing in the journals we carry with us. Your food was a godsend, and we stretched it out to last as long as possible. The common fare consists of navy bread, rice, beans, salted pork, and potatoes, with oatmeal for breakfast. But to me it is quite tasteless and insufficient in quality to truly curb the appetite. How I miss your warm breads and pies, and your kindness to us!

Millie paused in her reading. It was as if he were speaking to her. She could see the earnest cast of his face and the blue shine of his eyes, as though morning's sunlight laughed through them. Here she was, eagerly devouring every word from him! Was she the most foolish of women? What would Verity say? Would she understand, or would she warn her against such error?

The circled date in the margin of the letter indicated a week had passed.

We make good time. The crew is disciplined and efficient and pleasant enough. Now that I am no longer sick, I find sailing full of interest and very pleasurable. I sit for hours on the forecastle and watch the vessel cut through the thick seas, churning them into a white foam about her. How graceful she is, despite the weight and bulk of her. And the moving water, with the play of light upon it, is never for two moments the same. It has made me wish for the power to write songs, like the ones we sang together, in praise of those things which I find beautiful and which I love—

He had scrawled a dash at the end of his sentence. Millie felt his meaning, and it made her cheeks burn. Why was he drawn to her? And, even more horribly, why was she drawn to him? Why could she not remove herself from her own emotions and see things with the clarity that was required, the clarity that the wise must possess?

She read on, mindful that the dates in the margin of the paper marked a long continuation of what he wrote over days and weeks.

There is tedium to this business of ships. We are always at the mercy of sea and wind. Sometimes we wait day upon day for the idle breeze, wishing we could get out and push behind. Then the wind will come up with a vengeance, as though sorry for its aimless loitering, and we are cheered at the thought of making good time. Yet it has happened that we dash on at a great rate, tack to the right and then to the left for two hundred miles or more, only to find, as the captain takes an observation, that we are twenty miles behind where we were when the vessel had lingered, becalmed.

There was another break, then a last entry where the writing was obviously careless and hurried.

On a day of calm seas we have encountered a sister ship heading the opposite direction, back to Boston harbor. They had come to a standstill (or whatever the proper term might be) and were conducting a sad and somber sea burial of a five-year-old child. The bereaved mother, pale and thin, would not be comforted, unable to bear the thought of her little girl lying under these wastes of green water. It was awful to behold, and to be helpless to assist her when I had the power to do so! I have the truth, Millicent, which would have comforted and gladdened her heart. Yet, I must write quickly, for I have found a friendly seaman who knows Gloucester and has agreed to deliver this letter to you. He is to be trusted, I am certain. So I must bid you farewell for the time being, and trust both our futures to that kind Hand which guides the affairs of his children here below.

Yours in fond friendship,
Nicholas Todd

Millie folded the letter and placed it back inside the envelope. What a peculiar young man to write such things. Without giving herself time to weigh or consider her own words, she drew out pen and paper and composed an immediate reply:

How can you say such things of God when you had just observed the terrible ordeal of that innocent mother and child? Was God watching over them, Nicholas? I see little justice in the world, and less of mercy. Is this God's way? I can accept it if it is, but I cannot have faith that he watches over all, yet allows some to suffer horribly and holds others up, secure and unscathed. That makes no sense to me. I do not understand this God you speak of.

She wrote others things as well, caring not what he thought of them. Let him sort out his responses to her. Had they not both been singularly honest with one another? With care she added this new sheet to the one she had written, wrapped up the packet again, and walked back into town.

Daniel Hawkins lived in the smallest cottage in Gloucester, which was tucked in under the eaves and seemed to rest against the walls of those on each side. He had never married, he had no family Millie knew of, and she could not even guess at his age. Her father used to tell her that he had seemed an old man to him when he had first signed on as a ship's boy under Daniel's tutelage. He still went out on the ships, and there wasn't a crew around that was not happy to have him. She knew he would be going out with the *Mary Anne* in a few days' time, and Liverpool would be the ship's first port.

When she knocked at his door he was there in an instant to open it, as sprightly on his short, bowed legs as most men many years his junior. He had no hair on his face, not even the suggestion of whiskers, and very little left on his head. But the thin, wispy strands remaining were faded yellow in color, with not one strand of gray. Chiseled on his face were the lines and wrinkles of a seaman, carved deep by the elements; no loose skin hung anywhere about them. Daniel's face appeared much like a weathered crag, and his deep-set eyes appeared to have receded into their sockets; yet they gleamed like glittering bits of live stone. His eyes had frightened Millie when she was a child. They still held a strange, almost mesmeric power, undimmed by weather and age.

"Come in, my child. What brings you down to the water?"

Millie gave him the letter and explained her request while Daniel poured a cup of hot tea for her and set out a plate of hard cookies and Scottish shortbread. Millie sipped the tea, letting it warm her insides.

"This young man to whom you are writing—what does he mean to you?"

It was a question Millie had not anticipated. She gazed at the silent, gentle face.

"So, you care for him. But he is not one of our kind, Millie."

Does Daniel know, too? Millie wondered with a start. *Has all the talk reached so far?* "Does that matter so much, Daniel?" she asked in a small voice.

He rubbed the smooth skin of his chin with a gnarled finger. "It may not matter at all. That is up to you to decide."

What strange talk. Millie sank back against the hard wood of the chair. "I believe he cares for me deeply, but I'm not certain why."

Daniel did not move, but his eyes and face were listening.

"Strangely enough, I care for him, too, though I fear what he stands for. And there is much in his life I am unable to understand."

"Then there is Luther." The old man startled her again with his words.

"Yes, then there is Luther. I know him inside and out. For many years our lives flowed in the same currents, and that ought to matter immensely, that sameness and understanding. But Luther doesn't really know me at all."

"That's because true knowing comes from deep in the heart, and many live and die incapable of it, ignorant of what they have missed."

His strange words led her to ask, "Did you ever love, Daniel?"

He did not hesitate to answer. "Long ago. She was a Gloucestermaid, one of the fairest, with eyes like the brown nuts in autumn and hair like your own, with every shade of sun and moonlight laced through it. She was very young, but I didn't know that. A man in love never does. We promised ourselves to one another and exchanged the most sacred of vows. I went out that season to the whaling a happy man, for I knew how rare were her gentle virtues and what a fine wife she would make. Indeed, that trip was the first time I experienced the sensation of loneliness, and it stunned me entirely. The companionship of my comrades had always meant everything to me, seeing as I had been at sea since the age of ten."

Millie leaned forward, entranced by the tale she was hearing, yearning over the lives it was unfolding before her gaze.

"But now that I had tasted that rare mystery of love between a woman and a man, all else left me feeling unsatisfied and unfulfilled. I came back eighteen months later . . ." He paused. His cheeks seemed to have sunk, and a hollowness had come into his voice. "I came back to find she had been six long months in her grave. Died of a fever, with my name on her lips."

Millie marveled at the strength of the pain his voice carried. How many years must it have been? Yet for him it had happened yesterday—for him it happened each day.

"Like a true woman she left me a note of comfort, urging me to remember her with gentle feelings and to go on with my life. 'I will remain a sweet memory,' she wrote, 'a soothing melody in the back of your mind.'"

Millie made a small sound of anguish deep in her throat.

"Yes, yes, it was hard," Daniel said, penetrating her eyes with his own. The force of his suffering kindled an agony of sympathy within her. "It was about as hard a thing as a man ought to be called on to bear."

He was sitting rigidly, every muscle in his body taut and aware. She knew the memory was stronger than the moment's reality as he struggled with it.

"Wasn't 'til the following summer that I learned from her younger sister how she really had died. I found the girl stretched out by Lucinda's grave, weeping bitterly. Her family missed her sorely, being the tender, lively lass that she was.

"'She is at peace now,' I said, trying to comfort her sister.

"'No, she isn't!' she cried. 'She did not want to die. She lay all that last night crying, begging God to spare her and let her be your wife.'

"I think my heart broke with those words. Truly, Millie, from that day on I was never the same."

Millie, clutching the arms of the chair, realized that her fingers were aching and loosened her hold.

Daniel continued his story. "'She worried for you,' the child said. 'Dear God,' she cried, 'my Daniel will suffer so if I die! How will he bear to come home and find I am cold in the grave?'"

Millie buried her face in her hands. She was trembling. "Stop!

Please!" she moaned. "I cannot bear more."

"Yes, 'twas hard, mortal hard. Grieve not, Millie, God has given me strength to bear it these many years—"

"How can you say that?" Millie cried. "It was God who took her from you."

"No, lass!" There was a force in the old voice, a rich timbre that made Millie stare at him. "You must never say that. Death took her from me; death regards no loved one's sufferings, as well you know. But in the end God restores all."

"Do you believe that?"

"I do."

"So does someone else I know." Millie mumbled the words as she wiped at her wet eyes.

"Your young man." Daniel was sharp. He tapped her letter against his empty tea cup. "That's to be considered, then," he mused. "Never make the mistake of mocking those who have found their way to a truth, just because you are still blind to it."

Millie did not like his words. She felt she would perish from grief in the close, small room. "Daniel, I must be leaving," she said, not surprised at how weak her legs felt when she rose to her feet. She walked over, bent down close to him, and kissed his cool cheek. She longed to say something, but no words would suffice. At last, she leaned her forehead against his and stood silently, loving him, yearning toward him and the gentle girl he had lost.

Outside the cool air felt sharp, stinging her cheeks and making her eyes water as she made her way home. She felt exhausted, overwhelmed, and friendless. And as night descended, the feeling grew worse. She longed for some escape from the oppression within her. When she heard a knock at the door she opened it eagerly and was happy to see Luther's large, solid form filling up the space.

"Will you walk out with me, Millie?" he asked. "There's a little shop on the pier that stays open late. We could get something to eat and a nice warm cider to drive off this chill."

She grabbed her heaviest cape and the fine calfskin gloves she had purchased in Boston. As they walked she held Luther's hand tightly, glad for the strong, warm feel of it, giving herself over with a sort of desperation to the saving forces of life.

*   *   *

"I do not understand . . . I do not understand you, Millie! I thought you and I were getting on fine." Luther leaned forward in his chair, his hands on his knees.

"Getting on fine is different from being married."

"These past weeks we have been together almost daily, and you have encouraged me!"

Millie knew he spoke the truth. Ever since that night at the end of September, when she had visited Daniel Hawkins and had been so upset by his tale, she had received Luther's attentions with a warmth that surprised herself. What did she fear? What was she running away from? She looked over at Luther's square, strong-jawed face. His brow was dark, and his eyes were brooding. One thing she knew: She did not wish to be married for the rest of her life to Luther. How unkind she had been to lead him, even unwittingly, to this moment.

He mistook her silence and edged closer, placing his big, lean hands on her shoulders. "I have loved you these many years, Millie, as well you know. It is time."

She shook her head. "I'm not ready."

He moved to kiss her, and she pulled away.

"Curse it, Millie, but you treat a man poorly. I am thinking of not going on a trading voyage this winter, but only over the road to Beverly and hiring out to one of the 'ten-footer' shops."

"You mean you would peg and cut shoes rather than fish?"

"'Tisn't so bad from what I hear tell, and the money is good. Weekends I could go out for haddock off Cape Cod, and there's always the smelt along the mouth of the river."

It was a good argument he made. Her silence encouraged him again.

"The money from both would be sufficient for a man to support a wife."

He had to stop saying that! "Luther, please! You must try to be patient. I cannot tell you yes."

"And why not?" The brooding had darkened his face and hardened the lines at his mouth and around his eyes. *Could Luther ever be harsh with a wife if provoked sufficiently?* The thought made Millie recoil inwardly and gave her the courage to lift her head and say plainly, "I do not love you as yet."

"You love me more than you know. You always have."

She blinked at him in honest wonder. Good heavens, he saw only what he wanted to see!

"It's only that you are loathe to give up the freedom of your own ways. 'Tis a shame, for your years spent in Boston did you no good in that."

"You do not know what you speak of. You do not understand me as well as you think you do, Luther."

"I understand that you must marry me, Millie. Live in my house with me, sleep in my bed, bear sons—"

"To go down to the sea with you?"

He shook his head, like some great, shaggy bear, in bewildered pain. "Millie!" He spat out her name like an oath. He had grown too angry to be reasonable. "What madness has gotten into you? Was it your brush with that Mormonite? Mother said he sent you a letter and you seemed most pleased to receive it. You must promise me to have no contact with him. Millie!" He cupped her chin in his hand and turned her to face him. "Do you hear me, Millie?"

Millie had grown angry herself at his overweening impertinence. She wrenched away from his hold. "Do not presume to tell me what to do with my life, Luther. You have no right!"

"Not yet, Millie. Not yet!" He put his hands on either side of her face and drew her closer to him, forcing his lips over hers, kissing her with a tenderness that surprised her, kissing her until she softened enough that he could leave her with some vestige of pride.

"I leave the first part of November, just over a week from now," he told her. "I want an answer by then. We could wait 'til spring to be married. In spring there are flowers, things a girl likes for a wedding. And we'd have some time before I had to fit out for another voyage."

He spoke these last words at the door, with the smell of the sea raw and cold at his back. She let him go. She had wanted to say, "You have your answer, Luther." But she let him go. The autumn sea broke on the shore with a sound as lonely as all eternity. What was it Daniel Hawkins had said at her father's wake? "The world is the less for every good soul who goes out of it." She sorely missed her father. What advice would he give? Would he see things the way Luther saw them? He had seemed to understand her need to get away, go to Boston, strike out in a life of her own. Would he have understood this? Would he have been able to help her now?

She would never know. She was alone in the world, with no one to counsel her. How she longed for the feel of her mother's arms around her once more. She secured the latch on the door and blew out all the lamps except one, which she set on the low table beside her mother's rocker. She would read for a spell before trying to sleep. A book was quiet company, but she was grateful to have it; she would have made poor company for herself this night.

Chapter Eleven

My dearest Millicent,

I am writing this on a dark day, in the midst of times such as you and I would not have been able to imagine before— cruel, benighted scenes belonging to the dark ages of man's ignorance and savagery. There is a state of open warfare here in Missouri. Troops have been raised to drive the Mormons en masse from their homes. Hundreds of men, thousands in some companies, thirst for the blood of helpless and innocent people. Can such a thing really be so? I see it, and yet my mind seems unable to grasp the horrifying reality of it. Until today. Today I have been forced to accept an abomination under the guise of law that has sealed our fate (I say "ours" Millie, for though not a baptized believer, I am one of these people, and their fate is mine). On this day, the 27th of October, 1838, Governor Lilburn W. Boggs signed an order stating that "the Mormons must be treated as enemies and must be exterminated or driven from the state." He authorized his generals and captains to increase their forces to any extent they deemed necessary. So, there you are. We are beset by cruelty and evil on every side. In DeWitt the people were shut up, held captive, as it were, by an armed mob of men. If their stock wandered outside the perimeters they were shot, as were any people who went too close to the outskirts of the settlement in search of food. Their provisions gone, some died of starvation and exhaustion. They were at last allowed to leave with what goods they could carry, leaving all else to the mob. They arrived here in Far West two weeks ago and have been welcomed into the city and cared for here.

But that is not all. Many homes in the outlying settlements have been burned, their contents ruined, their occupants forced out at gunpoint. Don Carlos, younger brother of the Prophet, is away on a mission. When his house was razed his wife, with two helpless infants, was driven out into the night. Somehow she made her way to a nearby settlement, carrying both children and wading the Grand River where the water was waist high. But now—oh, Millie! I tremble to think what power this order gives to our enemies. What shall they do now, with nothing to temper or stay them? And, how are we to leave, with winter coming on? And where are we to go?————

There was a pause, a long line drawn as if to stop the painful outpouring of Verity's soul. Millie shuddered. It was impossible to believe what she read. Her mind could not imagine the things Verity had described to her. What an evil day when Judith had invited the Mormon preachers into her house. *Come home!* Millie cried from the depths of her compassion. *Flee such madness and come safely home again! Surely not even the most sacred of duties could require this of you!* But the next words she read changed everything.

Leah is with child and is due to be delivered sometime in May, we think. Such joyful news—or so it would be under conditions of peace and sanity. But here, and now? Nor has she been well—honestly, Millie, can you fancy Leah a young matron preparing for motherhood? 'Tis but another charmed picture in the fantasy of marriage which she draws for herself. Mother abets her by spoiling her as outrageously as in the old days, or at least to the full extent of our now limited powers. And Edgar Gray does the same. But the toll tells on him. He worked long hours in the fields until the harvest was in, and he continues to work in the blacksmithing shop he shares with two other brethren.

Millie scowled at the picture Verity's words drew and at her friend's easy adoption of Mormon speech and Mormon ways.

Of course, Edgar fears for Leah's safety. But he will not burden his darling with that. All effort is made to keep the mother-to-be nurtured and protected. If I sound a bit bitter, I am. For it is me Edgar unburdens his fears to, and I must be sister, mother, and in some ways, yes, even wife to him—for is true companionship and comfort and sustaining not the natural function that husband and wife provide for each other? Oh, Millicent, I know not what to think. I am always tired, and I am always frightened. But Mother thrives! She becomes more and more Irish every day that we live here. What was it you used to call it, Millie—our "touchy Irish blood"? Well, it has become her salvation. She seems to thrive on the challenge and even the hardship. And now that she has Simon Gardner to order about, she is in her element. No, I am unfair. She is a good wife to him; she learned that well with Father, for he brought out all that was gentle and generous in her nature. When the refugees from DeWitt came, Mother set up a kitchen in one of the old deserted barns and organized the women, some to make soup, others bread, others to care for children to spell their tired mothers—she enlisted the young girls to do that. You know how she is; all ran smooth as clockwork, and she rolled up her sleeves and worked for twelve hours straight until several of the other women took her by the arms and marched her home. Brother Gardner laughed at her, with his hands on his hips, but there was such pride in his eyes! He does fuss over her at times, much in the same way that we all fuss over Leah. And she lets him! And, of course, it is good that she does.

Millie, I do not wish you to think ill of Leah on the strength of my petty and somewhat unkind report. She does possess her own virtues, as well you know. She has such a patience with children—perhaps, with that quality, she will make a good mother, despite her own immaturity. Several times she has tended little ones whose mothers are ill. She is able to soothe them somehow and lessen the loneliness they feel for mothers who lie sick in their beds and are unable to see to their needs. In such a way she blesses the lives of many. Indeed, her work is far more noble and humane in nature than mine. For the burden of my contribution lies largely with my skills as a seamstress, learned from you in that happier time which is lost to us now. I have callouses on all my fingers, and at times the light by which I sew is so weak that my poor eyes burn in my head. But I am doing my part, and that pleases me.

Dear Millie, I reach the end of my paper and other duties call me, yet it is painful for me to say farewell to you. For, while I sit here and write, in fancy I am with you once more, and we are innocent girls yet, untouched by the solemnities of life. Though you, poor dear, knew more of life's realities than we did. How gentle and kind you were, Millie, despite being motherless and, to some degree, fatherless, and thrust upon our poor mercies! There were times, I am sure of it, when we were most hard to bear. Yet how pleasant you were with us, and how patient! I shall never forget. I shall never cease loving you and praying for your happiness. Indeed, it does my heart good to think of you being safe and well away from this horror which has become our lot. I do try to pray to understand the purposes of heaven in trials such as these. The Saints have immense faith in this God they serve and, with childlike submission, take all things from his hand in humility—even in gladness.

The trapped, angry feeling, that choked resentment, rose up in Millie again. To hear Verity speak so! Verity, with her high spirits and clear, fearless mind! Obviously this oppression she suffered had subdued her fine spirit, perhaps irrevocably altering her. But then, even Verity had been unable to stand up to Judith, who was obviously the stronger of two and would manipulate others without qualm, which Verity would not. This was all Judith's fault. The Mormons had become her cause to fight for. She had never really belonged in Boston high society; her Irish blood was too raw and untamed for it. But Verity belonged. Verity had the gentleness of spirit and the disciplined perception to excel among the brightest and most privileged. Now she was wasting herself— indeed, endangering herself—because of her mother's eccentric and insensitive ways.

With indignation in her heart Millie read the last remaining portion of the letter:

By the way, Millie, I believe you would like Mormon men. They appear to be more sensitive to the needs and feelings of women than most and are admonished by the Prophet to appreciate the good wives they have. He is an exceptional man, this Joseph Smith, and he conducts himself with great dignity, despite the terrible calumnies which are forever hurled at his name, and despite the persecution he and his suffer.

I bid you a fond farewell for the time being, Millie. Pray for me and mine as I pray for you.

Love,
Verity

Oh, Verity! Millie could feel a blush spread over her skin. *What would you think if I told you of Nicholas Todd?* She collected her working gloves and big wicker basket and went out to the garden, mostly put to bed for the winter, though a few late marigolds— fading splashes of gold against the deep purple of the privet berries—gave a feeling of life to the scene.

As she gathered seed pods, which she would share with the birds, she still mused upon what Verity had written. Dare she tell her friend of her encounter with the young Mormon? She had a sudden, intense curiosity to know what advice Verity would give her. Surely she would never sanction a serious interest in a Mormon, which might lead Millie to share in her own wretched fate! After all, Verity had not adopted their religion nor married one of them.

Millie shaded her eyes to watch two golden flickers swoop playfully against a patch of blue sky. What was the point of all this, anyway? Nicholas was nothing to her. And, even if he had been, she could never live the life of a Mormon. So why torment herself further?

She stood up and stretched her back. A figure was walking along the high ledge above the sand through the hawkweed, which was shimmering in waves of pale yellow. She did not recognize the cut of the man, nor his gait. Even when he came close he remained a stranger to her. She pushed a few loose strands of hair behind her ear and straightened her apron. The man turned in at the stone walk and approached her.

"Miss Cooper," he said, touching his hat to her, "I am Thomas Erwin, the schoolteacher here in Gloucester. Might I kindly have a few moments of your time, ma'am?"

Millie invited him in, wondering at the reason for his visit.

"How long will you be away?" she asked after he had explained his errand. "And why did you come to me?"

"This is most probably my mother's last illness," he said, "and I should like to be with her until the end. That may be several weeks, or several months. But I have permission from the city fathers to sublet my teaching contract through the end of the spring term, if necessary."

"And why select me as your substitute? I have never taught school before, Mr. Erwin. I don't know if I can."

He smiled. He was a man of medium height, medium build, medium age, extremely ordinary in appearance, but he had a most winning smile that made his eyes sparkle and his face wrinkle into lines of pleasure. He would be good with unruly boys, for he looked much like one himself.

"Actually, your name was suggested and most highly recommended." He arched an eyebrow, assuming his words would please her. "And, in all honesty, Miss Cooper, your experience in Boston along with your excellent education fit you exceptionally well for the task."

Boston. Of course. She had been to the city, which few others had. And she had learned much from the lectures and plays she had attended while there.

"What do you mean, my excellent education?"

"Why, at the hands of your mother. She was a schoolteacher before her marriage, or so I am told. Those I have spoken to say she was not only educated but refined in her way. And she poured everything into the willing head of her daughter."

Millie was alarmed to feel tears gathering behind her eyelids. How long it had been since she had given any thought to that aspect of her mother's life! Through the years she had taken for granted the advantages her mother gave her, overlooking them in her constant yearning for better and more.

"Miss Cooper! I am sorry." Thomas Erwin was on his feet and had his large, nicely laundered handkerchief out of his pocket. "Allow me, please," he insisted, holding it out to her. "I face the loss of my own dear mother, and I know how tender your feelings on the subject must be."

Millie took it and blew her nose discreetly.

"Please consider the offer, my dear," he pressed. "Clearly your gifts are wasted here and, with all due respect, you must at some times be bored—at least in an intellectual sense." He smiled tentatively, and Millie got the impression of sun breaking through clouds in a thousand bright prisms. "It would fill the long, dark days of winter. Think of the challenge and satisfaction of it!"

"Challenge, certainly. Satisfaction is a less guaranteed conclusion, don't you think?"

"I do not. You will do superbly, my dear. And the children here are not ruffians or troublemakers. Indeed, most carry the quiet, solemn ways of their elders and could take some livening up."

Millie liked him. She could not help returning his warm smile. "I would like to do it," she admitted, "if I can overcome my fears and feelings of inadequacy."

With that the matter was settled. Mr. Erwin spent the next three-quarters of an hour explaining, instructing, and encouraging her, and promising more of the same. She would meet him at the schoolhouse every afternoon for the next three days. Surely that would suffice.

He was confident, and she felt strangely elated as she bid him good-bye at the door. After nearly reaching the end of the rock walk he turned and walked briskly back, digging his hand into his pocket and pulling out a thin envelope, which he handed to her.

"I'm sorry—I nearly forgot this," he said.

She reached out to take it, her heart beating in her chest.

"I was collecting my own post and asked if there was anything for you, since I knew I was coming your way for this little visit."

"How very kind."

He made her a gallant little bow. "Your charm"—his wonderful smile broke forth—"as well as the stimulation of our conversation made me forget altogether."

He started back down the path, whistling as he reached the end of it, cheering the very air around him. But Millie had already closed the door and forgotten him as she carefully opened the envelope with the Liverpool postmark, addressed in a hand she recognized.

Dear Miss Cooper,

It is with great pleasure that I take up pen and paper to in-form you of my progress since arriving in this city. The work in Liverpool is hard and discouraging, largely because life in this place is wretched and grinding for the many poor who dwell here. You, with the luxuries of Boston in your memory and the cleansing beauties of Gloucester before you, could not imagine the extreme poverty and hopelessness here. A worker in this city, and those like it, earns roughly five shillings to two pounds a week. This will buy about seven four-pound loaves, enough to half-fill the stomachs of a family with two or three children—although typically most families have more than that. This means nothing is left for tea or a little piece of meat to offset the constant bread and potatoes, and certainly nothing left to pay rent. In fact, potatoes are much resorted to, since they are hot, cooked fare and cost but a shilling for twenty pounds. Subsisting on a diet of potatoes leaves enough in the kitty for tea and an occasional piece of pie or sausage for the working man at midday, and perhaps stew and pudding for the entire family on Sunday. A great many people live on this meager diet, but also a great many die.

I do fairly well for myself, and when hunger o'ertakes me I have the luxury of remembered pleasures—the delicacies you made for us. What I would not give for a taste of one now!

Millie's brow wrinkled. This was too much—suffering everywhere! Did these Mormons attract suffering as honey does flies? If Nicholas knew what his own people were enduring in Missouri! With a frustrated apprehension she forced herself to read on.

Certainly the people here are sorely in need of what we have to offer them. But the only convert I seem to be making as yet is a little runt of a fellow named Gerry Hines. He has curly red hair growing all over his face and out of his ears. He owns a small grog shop near where we live and is always pleasantly intoxicated, I fear.

Though the work is slow, there are compensations. The spirit among the Saints here is sweet, and their simple, unquestioning faithfulness humbles me and makes me appreciate my blessings.

I think of you often and pray for you daily. Please believe me to be your true and constant friend and admirer,

Nicholas Todd

Millie was in a turmoil. She threw the letter down and paced the room. How could he say, "the people here are sorely in need of what we have to offer?" What a trap he was working them into! If they thought life was difficult for them now, what would they do if they were suddenly transported to Missouri, to the horrors of burning houses and bloodshed?

You are a fool, Millie! she told herself. *There is no conceivable reason for you to have anything to do with this young man, and every reason one could think of for you to shun him like the plague.*

It was not until later that evening, as she walked alone by the sea, looking out at the leaden gray expanse stretching beneath the cold stars, that another question came to her. What did Nicholas mean when he said, "The spirit among the Saints here is sweet?" The sentence had a nice ring to it, but what did it *mean?* She sighed aloud. Her mind was tired of puzzles and problems. Could life never be simple and straightforward, without exhausting all of one's resources? She pondered the question for a long time while the colorless waves washed at her feet.

Chapter Twelve

"I told Thomas Erwin I would take the position."

"You told him what?" Luther's mouth twitched up at one corner as he tried to control his anger. "Millie, what's in your head? What are you thinking?"

"I want a way to support myself, and teaching is a good one, one I believe I'll enjoy."

"Millie—"

"No, don't stop me, Luther. I've already told you that I'm not ready for marriage, not with you or anyone else."

"You'd rather be a schoolmarm and a thornback!"

Thornback was the most biting term for spinster that Luther could have used. It made Millie wince, for, in truth, she was nearly eighteen, pushing the prime of a girl's marriageability. Many much younger than she were already mothers once or twice, especially in these parts, where there was little else for a girl to be doing and where men wanted companionship and someone to cook their meals, keep a house for them, clean their fishing gear, and mend their clothes. Millie wasn't quite sure what the order of a man's needs was. Most did not seem to require as much companionship as a woman did. She wondered, as she often had, how many marriages were for convenience alone, and how thin must be the cement of true affection to hold many a man and woman together.

"Millicent!"

Millie recalled herself. When Luther brooded his whole countenance grew as black as his eyes. His anger seemed like a force emanating from him that she could reach out and touch.

"This is only a temporary position, Luther. It would be good for us both, and it would give me some time."

"Where did you learn to talk that way? From your fancy friends in Boston?" He took a step closer, hunching his shoulders like a disturbed beast lumbering toward her. "You've been different this last little while, and I'd like to know what it is."

"It is nothing to be concerned over. If I teach through the spring term—you yourself said we could wait until then to be married—"

"But I want to *know!*"

"I can't give you an answer. If you press me, Luther, then it must be no."

"I don't believe you." He straightened up as he came closer. He was a big man, and his presence made him seem even larger. He reached out with both hands and pulled her close to him. "I don't believe your words, Millie. I believe what I have felt when your lips touched mine." His voice had grown low and he was crooning to her, not as a mother croons to a child but as a man croons to the sea, to the mistress who enchants and mystifies him. "Trust me, Millie, and let yourself love me." With the tough gentleness of a seaman he wooed her, but when his lips covered hers she wondered for a brief, wicked moment what it would be like if it were Nicholas Todd bending over her. She wrenched away from his grasp.

"I'm sorry, Luther." She, too, spoke gently. "Please, give me some time."

He stared back at her, stunned. He was not accustomed to losing, and if he knew how to do anything, it was to persevere. "I've put off leaving for your sake as it is," he growled, the anger back again. "You want me off to Beverly, with things like this between us?"

It was as close to pleading as he could come. In sheer exhaustion and compassion Millie was tempted to give in. But only for a moment. She shook her head slowly. "I'm sorry. Please believe me, if I could make it easier for you, if it could be different . . ."

He backed away from her. "I'll take the coach out tomorrow, then. That's settled." He was still waiting. Millie did not dare make a move. Anything she did might start up things all over again, and she couldn't bear that. Nor could Luther, she was sure. He looked battered and bewildered as he stood across from her. A brief, painful thought skittered across her consciousness: *What if he loves me very much? What if this goes deep with him?* She had never loved anyone herself, so how could she understand what Luther was suffering right now? Yet sympathy for him would undo him and make him suffer all the more. Despite the terrible trembling inside her, she stood her ground.

"This is good-bye, then," he said suddenly. "I may not come back, Millie."

He couldn't mean that. "Don't be morbid. We can write, and see one another . . ."

He shook his head. "Too painful. I'll stay put in Beverly for the duration. When I come back in the spring it'll be to go out on a schooner . . ." He shrugged his broad, muscular shoulders. He was shifting the responsibility to her. She didn't like that. He was saying, *If anything happens between us in the spring, Millie, it will be up to you.*

"I hope things go well for you in Beverly, Luther, truly I do." She spoke the words gently, but they were his dismissal, and he knew it. He strode past her, threw open the door, and stomped outside without one backward glance.

She watched the great, fuming bulk of him grow small and fade into the evening mists that were rolling up from the sea. She was alone, with a new challenge before her, and not one human being in her life. Had she done the wrong thing? She had done the only thing she knew how to do. She did not understand her actions much better than Luther had.

When Luther entered his mother's kitchen he was still in a black mood. He did not mind telling her most of what had transpired. "She's gone crazy, that one," he muttered. "Clean out of her head. There be no reason for such behavior."

"Maybe . . . maybe not . . ."

The tone of her mother's voice made Luther glance at her sideways; he knew her too well.

"What have you in mind?" he growled. He was in no mood to be toyed with.

His mother cooed and simpered a bit, almost seeming to enjoy his discomfort. "More than one saw her walking the beach with that stranger"—Luther made a move as if to dismiss her, but she ignored him—"and since he's left she mopes about the places they walked together. I've seen her myself." Luther's head was up now. His mother's voice grew yet softer and took on a high whine. "I tell you, that's the trouble, son. She writes letters to him, she does—and I ask you, what good will letters do when he's halfway across the world, and a Mormonite—had you forgotten?" Her voice was laced with a satiny triumph now. "Perhaps he's bewitched her, he has. I tell you, that's the crux of it!"

"Shut up, Mother!" Luther's eyes had narrowed into slits like her own as he regarded her. "I'll hear no more of it."

"Then you'll hear no more of the lass, son, and you'd best look elsewhere."

His pride prevented him asking outright for help in the matter. She understood that.

"If he were removed from the picture," she said, "if letters no longer came to her with a Liverpool postmark . . ."

He knew at once what she was suggesting.

"If you can arrange it, do," he snarled. "But I don't want to hear of it."

Her eyes, small and deep in her head, took on an exultant shine.

"Girls of Millie's age are ofttimes foolish and need the guidance of those older and wiser than themselves"—she rubbed her thin hands together, making the sound of dry insect legs scraping against one another—"whether they know it—whether they want it—or not."

"I hope you're right, Mother."

"I know what I'm doing. You go to Beverly and do your work, and leave everything in my hands."

This was what Luther was accustomed to. If he retained any qualms concerning his mother's scruples, he was able to ignore them. Although he could not have said it in so many words, he wanted Millie, and he would do anything he had to in order to have her.

Almira Fenn was well pleased. Her first and foremost intention was to get her son what he wanted. But that Cooper girl was too uppity, always had been. And since her return from Boston she had grown worse. Someone ought to teach her that she had a limit. She had brazenly encouraged that Mormonite stranger and thought she could get away with it.

With a snort of satisfaction, Luther went out to the yard to oil and polish his churn boots while Almira gloated to herself and savored the prospect of bringing Millie down a peg or two to where she belonged.

Millie would have missed Luther if she had had more time. She confessed that fact to herself, though she did not to anyone else, least of all Luther himself.

There were fewer than twenty students in the school, but they were of varied ages and stages of progression. Millie's powers had never been so stretched in her life as she tried to assist, advise, instruct, drill, correct, and inspire all at once. She found herself bringing work home with her: correcting spelling lists, fussing over papers the older children had written, selecting materials she wished to use in her instruction. There was an excellent little volume on Thomas Erwin's shelf containing stories about the heroes of the Revolution. It caught her imagination; all sorts of ideas teased at her mind as she thought of ways to make history come to life for these young people.

Books began to entice her in a way they never had before. She realized that she could do with more learning herself; her knowledge was very scanty in an appalling number of areas. On the highest shelf in the schoolroom Mr. Erwin had a collection of books that were obviously texts from a college or academy of higher learning. She began borrowing these. Soon the short, dark winter evenings did not seem long enough for her; she found herself rising earlier in the mornings and falling asleep beside the fire with a book in her hands. So the days passed, and the weeks slipped away nearly as quickly as the days did, and suddenly Christmas was here.

The children had time off for the holidays, but Millie was hopeful that most of them would return and keep at their studies until their parents needed them for spring planting or fishing or marketing when the pollock and mackerel ran and the cod industry required heading, splitting, and salting skills. She was happy at this work. She felt alive, vital in some ways she had never felt before. But the holiday excitement, usually so infectious when in the company of children, had little power to touch her. She had nothing to celebrate and no one to celebrate with. Last Christmas she had been in Boston with Verity and Leah, and oh, the hostings and parties there, the shops and street vendors, the caroling on the Common, and the Christmas breads and cakes and puddings simmering for days in the great kitchen! Perhaps she should return. Perhaps this solitary life was not good for her. But to be in service was not ideal either, and households like Judith's were rare. Here she was her own woman, and that counted for something. And here was the sea, nearly at her own doorstep, and the green, silent woods, and the house that held all that was left to her of her own family within its walls.

On Christmas Day she baked a plum pudding and cooked a small goose, then added to their fragrance by lighting her best bayberry candles. As the afternoon shadows lengthened she sought her mother's rocker, with one of Thomas Erwin's books to keep her company. She had gone so far as to entertain hopes that Luther might come from Beverly. After all, it was Christmas, and surely his mother would be glad of his company. But for two days a terrible storm had enveloped sea and land in clouds of mists and snow. Travel would be too dangerous, especially with the raw, wet temperatures that accompanied the storm.

Now and again uneasy thoughts would stir misgivings within Millie. What did Luther do of an evening, with what time he had to himself? He was a grown, independent man, and men had their ways. Were there other women in his life? Did he amuse himself with the company of such women who frequented the taverns and alehouses where seamen caroused with each other? In truth, Millie knew very little about Luther's life. Though he wished her to marry him, she could not picture him sitting around pining until she made up her mind.

But it was just as well. She had no need of Luther's company this night. If her thoughts strayed, it was in a different direction. She thought of Nicholas Todd celebrating with the "Saints" in Liverpool, perhaps singing "My Truly, Truly Fair" to some pretty English convert, his blue eyes holding the warmth of the summer sky in them, despite what the weather might be, his voice vibrant with the exhilaration of his spirit, as contagious as laughter. Perhaps not. Perhaps he was huddled in some miserable room, shivering and hungry, without a proper coat and with holes worn in his shoe leather from walking the streets of the city in search of all those seeking souls who, as he put it, needed what he had to offer. Perhaps he was even lonely, as she was.

A gentle melancholy settled over her spirit as she gave way to such reflections. Perhaps—and she feared this would be most accurate—he sat huddled by a low fire, poorly fed but unmindful of the inadequacies of his condition because he was immersed in the Book of Mormon he was reading. The picture her mind drew brought an unwilling smile to her face, but at the same time it stirred the old, cold fears in her heart. *Why do I care for him?* she demanded of herself. *I would be miserable living the life he lives.*

She glanced up at the shelf. The Book of Mormon he had left for her sat there, bold as brass. She would not read it! What he did was his business, but not even to please him would she take down the book. Why should she? What difference would it make? She and Nicholas were nothing to one another, and all these contemplations were foolishness on her part. She selected a slim volume of poetry instead, and forgot the bleak night around her and even her own weary thoughts in the beauty and harmony of the verse.

Winter was tedium, there was no way around it. The days of January were one hueless expanse, as dingy as the stretches of winter fields and as blanched as the sea. But, trudging each day to the schoolhouse, Millie never failed to discover something of special interest or beauty to make the effort worthwhile, something that invariably reminded her of the tie all living things have to one another. One morning it was a kingfisher, handsome in his white collar and polished blue plumage. The clanking jar of his call echoed over the rimed water and seemed to spread into every fold and crevice of the cold, crackling space. One particularly gray morning she spotted a great osprey perched on the vane of the schoolhouse. At her interruption it soared and circled, then perched again, uttering strange, harsh cries, reminding her how much more at home it was in this wintry world than she, how mobile and adapted to the elements.

But once inside the tidy schoolhouse, with the fire in the potbellied stove stoked until it was roaring hot, Millie felt at home.

This was her element. Here she could function, here she could expand—sometimes she could even call forth wonder and beauty the way the kingfisher and the osprey could, and see it reflected back in her students' eyes.

One afternoon, as the last of the students scampered out of the schoolhouse, Millie saw a long, black shadow cast its wavering slant across her desk. With a catch at her throat she looked up to see old Daniel limping in through the open doorway. He seemed to be dragging one leg across the scarred wood floorboards, and she was shocked to see how much he had aged since setting out on this last trip.

"Aye, lass," he said, reading her thoughts with too great an ease, "the sea has taken her toll of me. These ten years and more when my rheumatic arms strained to haul on sheet and cable, and my eyes, faded and dim, strained through easterlies and fog to keep a proper watch, I should have retired from deep waters." His voice had a timbre to it that belied the words he was saying, but he went relentlessly on. "Yet, in truth, I'd rather grow gray in service of the sea than putter about with the other old men, lobstering and clam-digging."

Millie nodded. "You've done the profession proud," she said. "There will never be another like you."

He waved a thin, clawlike hand at her.

"It's true," she pressed, "and may as well be acknowledged." She could feel her eyes fill with warmth for him, as though her whole soul smiled out at his. "But I'm glad you've come home."

"I got off early—'jumped ship,' you may say—and came the short route by way of Amsterdam and back. I couldn't have stood another long stint to the East Indies, where the *Sea Hawk* was heading."

Millie pushed her chair back and rose, gathering her books and papers into a pile to take home in the leather satchel the schoolteacher had lent her. With a little pinch at her heart she wondered what it cost Daniel to say those words.

"You look right fine and proper behind that desk, Millie." Daniel's eyes, weak and faded as he had acknowledged, appraised her with enough healthy male appreciation to make Millie laugh lightly, and that pleased him.

"A pretty girl ought not to demur, my dear, or shun admiration. 'Tis the good God above who made all things that are beautiful, and I b'lieve he made them to be appreciated and praised."

Millie was speechless. She could only meet his eyes—wise, beautiful eyes, as deep as the sea they had gazed on. She could speak to him more purely and freely in that moment without the encumbrance of words.

"I near forgot the errand that brought me here." Daniel poked around in the depths of his pocket and drew out a creased, stained, much-traveled envelope. Millie had not thought of the letter she had asked him to deliver. She felt her pulse quicken.

"Yes, 'tis a reply to your letter, my dear." He handed it to her. "Does it please you so much, then?"

Millie dropped her eyes. Was she so transparent?

"He seems a fine young man," he said, sensing her misgivings.

"He's one of those Mormons," Millie said suddenly, surprising herself.

"Well, I know that. I like him, Millie, despite his religion. Don't we all have crazy notions of one kind or another that govern our lives?"

Millie nodded slowly, thinking on his words.

"He's certainly taken with you, and that's no exaggeration. Took a long time composing this here missive, and kept pestering me with questions about you. He's lonely, I reckon, out there away from his own kind."

He's with his own kind, Millie reflected. *Or at least, he's busy creating more of them.*

"It's a raw wind out there, raw and wet. Bundle up now before you walk home."

"I'll be careful," Millie promised. She leaned forward and planted a kiss on Daniel's cheek, where the skin was as shrunken and brittle as old parchment paper. But his clothes, even his skin, smelled of hemp and tar, wet canvas and tobacco. She drew the fragrance into her, and with it, all the memories of her childhood.

She tucked the letter carefully among the books in her satchel. Living at the edge of the old town as she did, her path home skirted the sea. All before her was gray: land and sky and ocean. Then, out on the colorless water, she spotted a fisherman in a white skiff. He made no sound at all as he moved about adjusting his lines, baiting one long silver thread with a shiny blue chunk of squid flesh. He was undoubtedly fishing for flounder in the still winter gloaming. He moved like a dream figure against the drained sky and the motionless sea.

Millie felt the hush of all creation settle upon her as she labored up the exposed incline, her feet sinking into the coarse-grained sand, rough with dank weeds and sea stones thrown up by the tide. Daniel had seen him and spoken with him. That made it seem less impossible to her that Nicholas had once walked here by her side. She spied a small, perfect cat's paw shell and scooped it up with her fingers.

By the time Millie reached her cottage the wind had undone her and she felt herself a mere raveling, a small, anchorless bit of flotsam that the sea of humanity had tossed upon the shore for the wind to have sport with.

She put her books on her father's desk but propped the letter against her mother's cruet set on the dining table, anticipating it, saving it as a child would a longed-for treat. After she had eaten her warmed-up broth and a slice of cold pie she reached for it, all at once impatient, her fingers clumsy as she unfolded the sheets.

The date at the top of the page read 10 December 1838.

Dear Millicent,

Can you imagine my feelings when an old seaman, bent with age and stiff bones, appeared at my door with your name on his lips and a familiar look about him? He placed your letter in my hand—a slim, light treasure, like yourself—and suddenly everything came back to me. I could smell Gloucester and hear the aged—ageless—men telling tales in their low, unhurried voices, and I remembered that Daniel himself had been one of them, and you were here with me as surely as he was, your hair as yellow as butter beneath the sun, your eyes as deep and patient and unfathomable as the sea.

Daniel and I spent a delightful evening in the brown belly of Brother Hines's Grog Shop. Yes, he has been baptized—precipitately, in my opinion. Oh, he's awfully sincere. But he goes about "business as usual" and has in no visible way altered his habits or beliefs.

Following the pleasure of time spent with Daniel, I turn to this even more welcome task of penning my thoughts and experiences for you. But the first thing I must address is surely not my adventures and mishaps, but yours. In the death of your father you have suffered an overwhelming loss. Now, with no one to care for you, no family of your own, my thoughts grow even more tender toward you, and I long to be able to comfort you—

"Don't say with your Mormon beliefs!" Millie muttered the words aloud, hesitant to go on and be exposed to his misguided zeal, which merely frustrated and disappointed her.

—and ease the suffering you are experiencing.

Millie sighed in relief. Did this mean he was willing to accept her as she was, and to not change her?

But if I am not allowed to help you, I have been given the opportunity to help those around me. Winter settles in here and one of the specters he brings with him is the dreaded diphtheria. The young and the weak are, of course, the first to succumb. It is terrible to behold, Millicent, and it troubles me deeply, for I hate nothing more than watching senseless suffering and being unable to offer assistance. But this once it has been different. There is a family who lives below us, a mother, two sons, a small daughter, and a drunken father. The woman, Laura Williams, is thin and hollow-eyed and suffers terribly at the hands of her brutish husband, but she does not wear the beaten, hopeless expression common to most of the poor here. She has listened to us, though she will not attend meetings in fear of the beatings her husband has promised if he should discover her. Yet she has taken a Book of Mormon, which she conceals but is able to read often since the man of the household is seldom about. All three of her little ones are ill, their condition worsening daily for lack of proper nourishment and care.

Sister Parker, whose house we live in, is a kindly old soul. At times she takes soup down to the children and sits by their bedside so that their mother might sleep.

On the very night of old Daniel's appearance, Mrs. Williams knocked at our door. The hour was late, but her husband was still off with his drinking companions, and in her desperation she approached us. With a faith that surprised me she asked us to administer to her children.

We went with her gladly into the dank, dim quarters where the sick children lay. As I looked into her eyes, where despair and hope struggled, I thought of my own dear mother, who had watched her children die before her eyes. It had been years until she found courage to try again and build almost a second family with my sister and me. I did not wish this gentle young woman to suffer as my mother had suffered.

Elder Howlitt and I placed our hands, one by one, on the heads of the restless, fevered children and pleaded with the Lord, through the influence of his holy priesthood, to spare their young lives. Mighty were the prayers I sent heavenward from the depth of my being that I might be worthy to serve as an instrument of his power and mercy, and not, through my weakness, thwart any of his designs.

Immediately upon our administration a change could be divined. All three children fell into a peaceful slumber, and the following day, when we checked in upon them, their eyes were less fevered, their throats more open and clear. Their father, just rousing himself from a drunken stupor, handled us a bit roughly and threw us bodily out of his house. But no matter. The good had already been accomplished.

I do not know how far we shall progress in teaching the gospel of Christ among these people. But in doing the deeds of Christ, I feel there is a great work we can do.

It was obvious he had forgotten himself. He was not preaching to her or attempting to exert an influence upon her, rather, he was pouring forth the feelings of his soul without restraint. Millie felt as though she had inadvertently stumbled upon someone in the midst of earnest and private prayer. Yet her presence was not an intrusion; she sensed that it wasn't. In some confusion she read on.

What luxury for me to speak to you thus, through the pages of this letter! As the sacred season of Christmas approaches I shall hold in my heart this gift of your friendship, and the influence of your guileless spirit upon mine. Do not despair. You write of injustice, of God and his ways, of faith, of doubt. God's ways never were man's ways, he tells us. Be still and trust him. This is our task. He will not only "reward us in the end" but will bless us along the way. I know it! Do we not learn and progress from that which we suffer? Do we not grow tender hearts in the process? What gives us power to keep striving—to rise above any and all things? His love. I pray for an abundance of that love to rest upon you, Millicent, today, tomorrow, and through all the days of your life.

God bless and keep you, dear Miss Cooper. More later, I promise.

Your friend,
Nicholas Todd

He had preached to her in the end. But it felt different. His words were a balm and a comfort, not a sting of contention. They could not conceal the faith and insight of his spirit. Before the force of it Millicent felt like a lost and bewildered child.

Chapter Thirteen

Luther came early. Millie could see the restlessness in his eyes when he first looked at her. She thought, *If I were to give him his desire and marry him, how long could I hold him before his own restlessness drove him away from me?*

"I cannot abide it," he told her, with a vehemence that did not surprise her. "One day longer cooped up in that building and I'd have gone mad."

"And you're here for your answer?"

"Well, yes, Millie, that's what I'm here for. But you need not be so blunt about it."

"I've had all winter to think . . ."

He didn't like the tone of her voice; she could see that in his eyes.

"And to get caught up in that schoolmarm business," he growled.

With an effort Millie ignored his remark and the irritation it caused her. "If I were to marry you this spring," she said, watching him carefully, "what would you do?"

"Do?" His eyes were as open and devoid of cognizance as a child's. "Set up housekeeping and have some grand times together before I go out to sea."

She knew what he meant, and just what he was looking forward to. "When would you go?"

"Billy Turner over in Medford is skipper of the *Suzanna,* an East India vessel. He'll be working on her rigging 'til May, most probably. With my winter earnings I can buy third shares in a little Chebacco with Pinky Jones and Andrew Hawley. That means we'd be after haddock and cod out at Old Man's Pasture and Spot o' Rocks 'til the *Suzanna* was ready."

"And then you'd go with her?"

"Course, Millie. Yes."

He did not understand her. He probably never would. But she understood him—too well for her own good. She had grown up learning that understanding as she learned to walk and speak. She had nearly forgotten that this was part of the reason she had left Gloucester in the first place.

"The Chebacco boat—that's nice, Luther. I'm happy for you. Go out with your friends and enjoy her. After you return from the *Suzanna's* voyage, we'll talk again."

"That will be months, maybe a year from now."

"Yes, I know."

"And you'd rather sit home a lonely and barren thornback than the wife of a seaman?"

"Stop it, Luther! Don't use that word! Don't be cruel. I told you I wasn't sure."

"And I told you what I thought of that!"

"So it wouldn't be wise for us to marry like this, Luther." Millie placed her hand on his arm. It felt so firm and muscular, so warm with life beneath her touch.

"Millie, I want to take care of you. I want to be with you."

She leaned her head against his great chest, suddenly weary. He made it sound so simple. Perhaps there was something wrong with her. But right now she could not help it. Right now she could not love him, not in the way he wanted, much least in the way that was essential for her.

"You're a good man, Luther," she said, her voice muffled against the rough cotton of his shirt. "More's the pity that you've fallen in love with me and not some sane, normal lass."

"'Tis you I want and no other," he said, wrapping his long arms around her. "Those you speak of cannot hold a man's interest. But you—you I could come home to for the rest of my life and grow old with."

His arms were insistent, his heart beating against her cheek, the words he had spoken still soft in her ears. He kissed her once, hard. "There's no other, is there, Millie?" He spoke the words roughly and, when she did not answer him, bent to kiss her again. But his question hung in the air long after he left her and, with the singsong persistence of a children's rhyme, ran over and over again through her mind.

*　　*　　*

It was spring. Millie's fingers were itching for the feel of needle and thread and the touch of fine cloth. For a long time she had been considering what she would do. Once she made up her mind, it took no time at all before her mother's kitchen was transformed into a sewing room, with butcher paper patterns, threads and trimmings, and snippets of cloth scattered over the floor for the mice to find. Many of the children in Mr. Erwin's school were poorly clad. Millie knew their families were struggling to make a living from land or sea. Now that warm weather was here she could not bear to see the little girls smothered in their heavy woolen skirts and stockings. She had brought yards of calico from Boston which she could make into small pantalets, and tinted muslins for aprons and frocks, with perhaps enough left to make shirts for the young boys.

Her fear was that the parents would be unwilling to accept such gifts from the teacher lady, or even be offended by what might look like charity. After some thought she determined to offer prizes for high achievement in spelling, history, and elocution, as well as rewards to those who would memorize the Declaration of Independence, Patrick Henry's "War Inevitable" speech, or some of the wise maxims of President Washington. At the same time she planned to approach some of the parents with the request that they allow her to sew frocks for their children, as a means of advertisement in hopes of securing clients for her seamstressing skills—although she knew there was scanty call for such work in Gloucester, where the folk dressed simply and every housewife possessed the basic ability to clothe her own family. But Millie was pleased with her own cleverness, and with the apparent success of her scheme. As she cut and stitched and hemmed night after night, after her lessons for the next day were completed, she took great pleasure in watching her small creations take shape before her eyes. If she was occasionally struck with a qualm, wondering if she ought to be sewing her own wedding gown, she was able to put such thoughts aside. Instead she wrote to Verity, boasting a little at how handsome her new clothes looked and lamenting the fact that she was not there to sew for the baby that would be coming. She was a little worried about Verity and the others; she had not received a letter since long before Christmas,

114

and heaven knew what sorts of things might be going on in that hostile wilderness where Judith had dragged them.

One midafternoon she walked to the post office to mail a letter to Verity. She carried one in her pocketbook for Nicholas as well. Ought she to post it? She had already answered the letter Daniel had brought her in February. Now the blustery days of March had drawn to a close, and she had not heard from either him or the girls. Would it be too forward to write him again?

She stood at the dusty counter waiting for Almira Fenn to come out from the back. Millie avoided encounters with Almira whenever she could, especially since Luther's return. The woman had a sour soul to begin with, and now that Millie had offended Luther, who was the apple of her eye, there was little patience extended toward her. Indeed, Almira usually refused to even speak to Millie when they passed on the street. But today it was Amos, Luther's brother, who came to wait on her. So Millie gave him both letters, asked politely after the family, and made her escape.

An hour later, when Millie was bent again over her sewing, Almira Fenn stood sorting her letters. When she saw the one for Far West, Missouri, she weighed it in her hand a moment, considering. "Better not tamper with this'un," she muttered under her breath. She tossed it into the mail sack. But the one following, addressed to Liverpool, England, she snatched with an exclamation of glee.

"I knew it!" She rubbed her thin, scratchy hands together. "The nerve of the hussy! For the life of me, I don't know why my Luther wants her!"

But she did know. She knew Millie was keen and clearheaded, and well trained in womanly skills. And she was pretty, the prettiest girl in Gloucester by far. If she had traveled to the city and put on fancy airs, well, even that added to her unspoken mystique and probable superiority—that is, granted that Luther could make her his wife.

With her thin, strong fingers Almira tore the envelope and the sheets it contained into little pieces and threw them into the fire, where they curled and charred and were consumed in a matter of seconds. Then she went on with her work.

* * *

Millie heard the happy peal of the church bells before she opened her eyes. They would sing out continuously for the next two hours until the schooners, white and shining, pulled away from the harbor. The *Suzanna* had been made ready in good time, and today Luther was to sail out on her, eager as a boy for the adventure ahead of him.

By the time Millie was dressed and ready the fish horns were blowing, a deep, throaty counterpart to the high, piercing clang of the bells. The wharves were crowded with families, the women and children sporting their best hats and pinafores. With a sense of satisfaction Millie noted several of her own creations among the bright throng.

They that go down to the sea in ships, Millie thought as she watched men gently tear themselves away from the clinging hands of wives and children. She noticed one little boy who would not release his tight hold round his father's leg, so his father allowed him to ride there, halfway up the gangway, before letting him go. Surely the bells and flags, and the pipes Blind Billie was playing from his seat on the pilings—surely all this was but to cover the fear and the anguish of parting.

Luther's family was here, crowded about him, Almira smoothing his shirt front and collar. He left them when he caught sight of Millie, walking with slow deliberation until he stood very close to her. The sea breeze lifted the light strands of his hair. The skin of his face was tanned a warm golden color by his weeks spent out past Eastern Point, and Millie could see the sea in his eyes.

He placed his big, warm hands on her face and pulled her toward him. He kissed her a long time before releasing her. She noticed several young boys snickering as they watched. She saw a line of white gulls dipping and rising from the glassy blue surface of the water.

"When I come back," Luther said, "there won't be any more asking." They were a seaman's bold words. But then he parted her hair and placed his lips against her ear and the soft skin of her neck. "When I come back I will marry you, Millie, and that is that." She closed her eyes and he kissed her again. She thought of her mother and wondered how many times this had happened for her and what she had thought when she sent off her man—*they that do business in great waters*—and walked back in silence to the emptiness of her house and the emptiness of her life.

Millie turned and walked all the way home as soon as Luther boarded his ship and was lost to her sight. She did not wish to see the lilting, graceful vessels file out of the harbor, round Mussel Point and Eastern Point, and head out to sea. She did not wish to be drawn into conversation with the other women who, seeing her with Luther, would assume that she felt as they did. Millie had no idea what she was feeling. But at least her life was not quite empty, thank heavens. She had the school, and books to read, and her garden. If she was aware that despite all these things she was still alone, with no child, no friend, no mortal soul to hold close to her, she did not acknowledge it. Only the foolish and thought-less acknowledged such things.

Three days after Luther left, Thomas Erwin, the school-teacher, returned, earlier than he had expected. He had buried his mother and was prepared to resume his duties. Millie was not prepared, but she had no choice in the matter. The immediate emptiness in her life was not of hours only but of purpose and pleasure as well. She was suddenly reduced to the bare essentials: herself and her garden. That was no longer enough. Last year at this time she was just returning to Gloucester. Last year at this time a stranger stopped to ask her directions, a stranger with eyes the color of the sea and hair like a raven's wing. But he existed no longer. The sea had borne him away from her, just as it had borne Judith and Leah and Verity away from her. Yet she dwelt cradled in the arms of the sea, knowing no other life, wanting no other life than this.

One week to the day after Luther's departure a letter arrived. It was postmarked "Liverpool" and addressed to "Miss Millicent Cooper." Almira Fenn set it aside until the place was clear of cus-tomers; then she tore it into small pieces and stuffed it into the cooking stove fire. She had promised Luther she would look after Millie while he was away, but she and the girl had never got on well together. She didn't know exactly what Luther had in mind when he asked her, but this was her idea of keeping her word to her absent son. That doing so brought Almira pleasure and a sharp awareness of her power was simply a bonus thrown in.

*   *   *

By early April Millie had planted sweet peas and spaded and prepared the ground for her various gardens. The soft spring rains had already coaxed out the fragile white snowdrops, with their delicate sea-green markings. By May the daffodils, jonquils, and tulips, the long purple bubbles of the crocuses, and the crimson splendor of the peonies all splashed the dull, sandy landscape with color and promise. As Luther left, the barn swallows and martins came, the bobolinks laughed in the spring sunlight, and the sand-pipers called, "Sweet, sweet, sweet," in the still, tide-brimming coves. Millie had always loved the cool days of May, full of work and warm possibilities. But Luther was out harvesting the sea, Nicholas was harvesting souls, and Judith and the girls were harvesting the bitter fruits of hatred and jealousy, while Millicent planted and tended, waited and hoped.

Chapter Fourteen

They told him it was May, and the mildness in the air seemed to prove it, though he still felt chilled to the bone and as weak as a newborn kitten. He remembered the past several months through a haze, fevered and painful.

At first he had refused to admit he could be ill. Yet if this was the price heaven exacted for the healing of the Williams children, he would not complain. But as the chills, headaches, and loss of appetite progressed into a raging fever and a throat constricted and on fire, oozing with yellow streaks of infection, he knew a wild time of sheer panic, when the nightmare seemed too large and too black for him and he struck out in sheer terror against his powerful tormentor. Only with eventual acceptance came the ability to fight back with intelligence: forcing himself to lie still; forcing himself to swallow when Sister Parker—who was accustomed to mothering him—or Elder Howlitt attempted to get liquids down his swollen throat; forcing himself to believe, through the chills, through the waves of heat that left his head ringing and his body soaked in sweat, that he could survive.

Then the first crisis passed, and with progress his youthful high spirits returned to sustain him. In foolish confidence, against the advice of both the doctor and Sister Parker, he got up from his sickbed to attend the baptism of Laura Williams and her three children, Ann, Paul, and Ben. He had to be there; it was only right. Wasn't it he who had befriended them, taught them, healed them? It was a wonderful day as the men testified of the divinity of the work, and all hearts felt the soothing balm of the Spirit and the quickening power of testimony. He would not have missed it, though he did not know at the time that it nearly cost him his life. In fact, he wrote an optimistic letter to Millicent Cooper, making light of the illness which had kept him confined for more than two months, and expressing his appreciation for the strength that had been given him to rise, to attend the baptism, and to will himself back to health.

After that the disease dug in its claws in earnest. Nicholas sank into a state of delirium. The doctor feared paralysis of the heart, and for many weeks the strictest watch was kept over him, day and night. He knew nothing of it; he did not despair, he did not even dream. When he awoke one May morning to hear the warble of a wren in the tree outside his window he had no memory of his illness or of the cold hold of Death that had clutched him so fiercely and nearly possessed him.

He was weak and exhausted and still in danger, for the doctor was concerned over symptoms of paralysis in his muscles. The general concern did not lessen. He was still carefully watched. The brethren in charge of the Liverpool area were consulted, and they pronounced their verdict: As soon as the young man was able to travel safely, he was to be sent back. The work did not require a man's life, surely, and with the state of things in Missouri he would certainly be needed at home.

So it was decided. When Elder Howlitt told Nicholas, his white face grew a shade more pale.

"I have done nothing here. Don't send me away a failure," he entreated through thin, chapped lips, as colorless as his skin.

He would not reconcile himself, despite arguments and importunings. He improved, but slowly, because the spirit was lacking. They had detoured around him; the work was progressing while he lay limp and helpless. He had no place here anymore, no plan, and no purpose. But he did not wish to go home.

The day before he was due to depart he wrote to Millicent, with a solemn promise from Sister Parker that she would see his letter safely and carefully mailed. He had little to tell; he did not wish to frighten her with the facts, and he hated to tell her that they were sending him home. The aura of failure clung to him, as distasteful as the toxins of the diphtheria. Now the slightest effort left him weak and trembling, but he would get on his feet; he would grow strong. Perhaps he would return to complete his mission more honorably. Perhaps he would travel East again, by way of Boston, by way of Gloucester, by way of a girl with hair like ripe wheat and eyes like the warm, honeyed browns of the earth, and a voice that held the sweet secrets of earth and sky and sea all together.

They carried him onto the ship. He was surprised at how many people were gathered to bid him farewell. Sister Parker wrapped her big, freckled arms around him and gave him a noisy smack on the cheek, her skin smelling of a faint mixture of rose water and the garlic she loved to put into everything she cooked. Without her he would not be here, flaccid, useless, and miserable as he was. How could he thank her? How could he thank any of them, tell them the depth of his feelings?

Joshua Howlitt had tears in his eyes. He had his part in wrestling Nicholas from death's grasp. Months ago, a lifetime ago, in that pleasant, dreamlike place by the sea, Nicholas had done the same thing for him.

Laura Williams, thin but not as pale as she used to be, was crying openly. She had a son by each arm—fine boys, with shocks of thick brown hair and large, intelligent eyes; boys well worth saving indeed.

Ann Williams, the ten-year-old daughter, came up close and pressed her forehead against Nicholas's arm. She felt like some frail, frightened creature trembling momentarily there. "We won't forget you," she whispered.

Nicholas could not control his own trembling. He must not give way to tears, he must not!

The faces blurred, growing more and more distant. This was not how it should be. This was not the farewell he had cherished in his imaginings these long, dreary months.

The ship's whistle sounded. Elder Howlitt let go of Nicholas's hand. He closed his eyes. When he opened them again there was nothing but an emerald stretch of sea, with the sun dancing in sparkles along its glossy surface. It made his eyes ache, deep in their sockets, to look at it. He closed them again and sat in a small pool of silence and pain for a long, long time.

Chapter Fifteen

In midsummer the earth slows to the pace of honey-replete bees and sluggish brooks; of boughs laden with berries, still and ripe and unpicked; of shady coves brimming with fish, sleek and silver and uninvaded. In midsummer the earth holds her breath and savors the wide array of her glorious wealth before the frenzy of autumn and harvest and the inevitable regression toward winter's denuding and decay.

Millie gave way to the sweet lethargy. She thought of nothing, questioned nothing, desired nothing. Then Verity's letter came.

It was dated July 7, 1839, Quincy, Illinois. Millie could feel the beat of her heart quicken in her breast. She sought her mother's rocker and sat down with deliberate care.

> Millicent, dearest, calm your heart and read what I have written without anguish or anger. I can picture all too well your beautiful eyes, golden brown like a fawn's, grow wide, and the lines around your sweet mouth grow tight. Please don't, Millie. We are delivered, we are well, we are in God's hands.
>
> Shortly after I wrote my last letter to you, on the thirtieth of October, a large mob force approached Far West. Our militia drew up in a line just south of the city and exchanged flags of truce with the mob. This allowed us to communicate with the enemy and learn their intent, which was to obtain three persons out of the city before they massacred the rest.
>
> That day, Millie, they had done just as they threatened to do to the little community of Haun's Mill. Our minds were incapable of imagining the scene: men and boys shot down mercilessly, wives and innocent girls defiled, children's brains

dashed out against the sides of buildings or their heads shot off in view of their suffering fathers and mothers—all in broad daylight! All under the protecting banner of law! Was this to be our fate as well?

At such a time one does not think or question; one prays and does what must be done. Hostilities were postponed until the next day, and during that dark night none of us slept. The men and many of the women worked to construct some fortifications, rude though they were, south of the city. Under cover of night, new groups of men, one group dressed and painted like savages, added their strength to the invaders. Comstock's men, their hands red with blood from Haun's Mill, boldly joined the rest.

How gray was that new dawn, Millie! Through the tense and interminable day negotiations went on back and forth between the mobbers, and we knew not our fate. Sanity lay in keeping busy. Sister Shumway requested that Mother accompany her to the home of several women who were in the delicate confinement of childbed; they helped bring three babies into the world—and under such conditions! Leah cried when she heard. "I don't want to have my baby here like this. I want to go home, Verity, I want to go home!" I could do nothing but comfort her, for I shared her feelings and longed to fly out of this place. When Mother found us in such a state you can imagine the scolding she gave us. But when she went so far as to say, "Count your blessings," Leah burst into tears again— bitter tears for one so young. "We are not yet as the Haun's Mill Saints," Mother said. "You have a fine, strong husband who loves you, and a child on the way to bless your union. God has not yet allowed our enemies to overpower us, and if he does, then we go to his rest."

"I don't want to die, even if I go to heaven," Leah sniffled. "What is it all for, anyway?"

Mother stiffened at that. "For the truth, for the sake of truth, Leah!" There was a light in Mother's face, Millie. I wish you could have seen it. "To live a purposeless and ignorant life and then die—that is tragedy, dear heart. To live and die for the truth's sake . . ."

She did not complete her grand statement; she never does.

We were duly subdued by her words, though Leah could not keep herself from sulking for the rest of the day. I nurse an anger, Millie, that at times turns to amazement. One moment I feel I despise my mother; the next I stand in awe of her. I never really understand her, despite her fiery Irish blood that runs in my veins.

I must proceed—I take up too much paper with my meanderings. Suffice it to say that Brother Joseph and some of the other leaders were betrayed that same evening into the hands of their enemies. The next day the mob was let loose upon the city. Our men hid us in the cellar and took turns standing guard. You will remember that both Brother Gardner and Brother Gray are large men and can be forbidding in appearance, especially with a gun in their hands. But our house is too small and humble to attract much attention, though it was ransacked like nearly every other building in the community, and the blacksmith's shop was burned to the ground. They killed many cattle just for the sport of it, robbed us of any possessions of value, and did worse things, far worse things, that I cannot bear to tell.

On the 6th of November the Missouri militia assembled the brethren and read them the terms under which we would be allowed to retain our lives: namely, to give up our leaders (which had been done against our will, as all things were), to deliver up our arms (which again was forced upon us), and to sign over our property to defray the expenses of the "war." It is ludicrous, yes, it is madness, but the final term explains it all: we were told that we must leave the state forthwith. I will quote you General Clark's words, as told to us by one of the men who were present: 'Whatever may be your feelings concerning this, or whatever your innocence, it is nothing to me. . . . The character of this state has suffered almost beyond redemption, from the character, conduct and influence that you have exerted." Simon had to hold Mother back physically when she heard this. She was not for enduring such insolent lies. It does make the mind recoil in horror and incomprehension. Oh, Millie, Millie, I could go on and on, but I am weary and my heart faints to recollect these dark things we have so lately suffered. I must be more concise and brief.

Suffice it to say that we prepared with the others—the best we could in our poverty and with a harsh winter settling over us to leave, as soon as the weather permitted us. Some did leave as early as February and March, but most of us tarried, for various reasons. Leah was ours. We kept lingering, waiting for the weather to become truly clement enough to risk her safety and that of her unborn child. But at last the decision was forced by the unmitigating harassment of the "citizens," and we took our leave of the city, on foot, dragging one small cart and carrying bundles on our backs.

I am not yet able to recount that journey, even in my own thoughts. We had the aid of two strong men, or we would not have made it through the mud and the wet snow and damp cold of early April. When we reached the Iowa side of the Mississippi River it was strewn with hundreds of homeless families and the remnants of their belongings. We lay down on the ground that first night to take our rest, and waited there for days before the men could arrange for us to be ferried across the river. We obtained a means of shelter because Mother still hoards a precious supply of funds from the sale of our home and belongings back on Walnut Street . . .

Here a smudge of ink obscured the next two words and Millie did not have to guess at the anguish her friend had experienced at the mention of her home, now forever lost to her. With a little cry Millie smoothed out the page and continued to read.

We secured rooms with a family where the wife is a semi-invalid due to an injury she suffered several years ago. I do sewing for the woman and her friends, and Mother has become maid of all work to help alleviate the costs of our keep in any way we can. Our men returned to help the poor and needy leave the state, under Brigham Young's able direction, so we were for some weeks alone. During this time Leah gave birth prematurely to a little girl. She was beautiful, Millie, with a fluff of fine red hair and a straight, well-formed nose, and the most perfect ears. She lived three days and expired peacefully in her mother's arms.

Leah said nothing. Her eyes grew wide and empty. She

held the baby out to Mother, who lifted her gently. Leah sunk back against the bed and closed her eyes. She refused to speak. She would not eat, she would not cry, she would not answer questions. At last, in desperation, Mother and I prepared the little body for burial, then took her in for one last time to her mother.

"We are laying Miriam to rest (Miriam is the name Leah had chosen for her) in a lovely spot beneath the protecting arms of a young birch tree. Will you come with us, Leah?"

I have never heard Mother speak so meekly, so tenderly. Leah did not move her eyes or otherwise acknowledge our presence. Mother sat on the edge of the bed and held her baby out to her. "Kiss your daughter good-bye," she said. Leah moved not a muscle. Mother leaned over and kissed the little one herself. Then she smoothed Leah's tangled hair back from her eyes with her long, capable fingers and kissed the smooth white skin of her cheek. "Verity and I will take good care of her for you, dear heart."

With that, we slipped out of the room. We buried Miriam's body on a little knoll above the Mississippi, in a sheltered spot beneath a weeping birch tree. When Edgar returned Mother took him to see where his daughter lay sleeping, "until resurrection morning," she told him. He is taking it very hard. Not to have been here, not to have even set eyes on his firstborn. He is such a simple, patient soul, and Leah's behavior stymies him. He tried to talk with her concerning their child but met with the same emptiness we had encountered. Then one morning Leah arose early and came into the kitchen, appearing rested and normal. Perhaps we were all staring at her stupidly; I don't know. She threw her head back and said, "Well, that's that. It's all over and done with. What's for breakfast, Verity?"

Yes, it will make you shudder to hear it. Edgar has become reconciled, at least to a degree. Strangely, it is Mother who grieves. Last night, knowing we would not be here much longer, I walked out to visit the grave. The path is narrow and shadowed, and I hung back, somewhat fearful. Otherwise I might have come upon Mother unawares. I heard her voice like a wraith's in the stillness. She was weeping quietly, and as

I drew closer I heard her say, "Poor motherless lass." I crept away and left her, my eyes blinded by tears— but I suspect not as bitter and lonely as hers. For the first time in a long while I thought of Father and the true meaning behind my promise to him, and how tenderly his spirit must yearn after hers when he sees her suffering so. I do feel at times that he is near us, Verity. Does that seem foolish to you? Perhaps he even understands her purposes in marrying Simon Gardner. I've always believed that he understood her more perfectly than she understands herself.

The page ended here, and Millie smiled through her own tears to see that Verity had written the remainder of her letter on the back of a bill of advertisement for Dr. Schiller's Foot Powder.

I have run out of paper, Millie, so this will have to suffice. I mentioned the fact that we are leaving. Next week we move to Commerce, which sits in a gentle horseshoe bend of the river not far from here. The Prophet Joseph has escaped his terrible prison in Liberty, Missouri, and is here among his people again. He has renamed the Commerce area Nauvoo, a Hebrew word indicating a beautiful place. The people of Illinois have been kind to us and seem to welcome us openly. It is generally hoped and believed that the Saints shall find peace here at last. Mother and Simon have bought a lot on what has been already named Mulholland Street. So when I next write perhaps it shall be from the comfort and security of our own house again. Pray that it may be so, Millie. Pray for all of us, but for Leah especially. I pray daily for you, that all is well with you, that you will find happiness in your own life, dear heart.

Your sister in spirit, with all of my love,
Verity

Millie felt sealed up in her own agony. After all Verity had gone through she could still pray! And she believed that Millie prayed, and that her prayers were efficacious. *I am not a minister's daughter,* she protested from the depths of her own turmoil. *No one taught me to pray. Your prayers are all I have, Verity. Keep praying for me, please. And pray for Nicholas Todd. Pray for him, lost and lonely somewhere on the streets of Liverpool.* Millie buried her face in her hands and dissolved into wrenching sobs that left her light-headed and shaken when she at last blew her nose and dried her red eyes.

Suffering was entrenching Verity more deeply with the Mormons and their cause than any argument or persuasion could do. She was becoming more and more removed from Millie and the life they had known together. And what of Nicholas Todd? The only clue Millie could possibly have was the information old Daniel had brought her, that he had blessed the sick children and been exposed to their illness. It could be very likely indeed that he took ill. It could also happen—she would not give place to that thought, to that possibility. He could not be dead! She would know it, she would somehow feel it. But if not dead, then why these long months of neglect? He had last written to her in December, before Christmas. That was over seven months ago. What other explanation could there be? Had he been forbidden to write to her? Had one of his letters gone missing? Had they sent him to the farthest outposts of Scotland where no one wrote letters and no mail service came?

She must have faith. But she did not know what faith was. She knew the power of blind and patient endurance. But that was not the same thing. Verity had faith. Millie could feel it. Through months of inhuman, almost incomprehensible suffering, Verity had known a peace and strength that was foreign to Millie. How, how did she come by it? What did it mean? With a terrible, fierce need Millie longed for some purpose, some pattern that would breathe dignity and meaning into her days.

Chapter Sixteen

Nicholas stepped off the boat at the Nauvoo dock and looked around him. His legs felt shaky, and the shrill whistle of the steam engine's valve still throbbed behind his temples. The city had looked a fair place when he gazed on it from a distance, approaching from the river. But now, passing slowly down Parley Street, the enchantment that distance had lent dissolved into the reality of poor houses, even more miserable hovels, and clusters of tents crowded with thin, weary people. Mud and the dank smell of the river was everywhere. *If I came home to get well, in mind or spirit,* Nicholas thought glumly, *this was certainly the wrong place to come.*

He inquired of several people on the street before finding one who knew his people and could direct him to them. To his horror he discovered that his family had only a tent of stretched calico to protect and house them. When his mother saw him, standing stooped and hesitant in the low, narrow doorway, she threw herself into his arms, buried her head on his shoulder, and cried like a child.

"I am all right, Mother. Everything is all right now," he soothed.

She lifted her head, and he was staggered by how much she had aged since he last saw her. Her cheeks were sunken, the skin of her face deeply lined and wrinkled, and her hair had turned gray.

"Where is Father?" he asked. "I've been so anxious to see him."

He read his answer in her eyes, but did not want to accept it. "Where is Father?" he cried.

His sister, Lizbeth, came up and placed her hand on his arm. "He died in Missouri," she said, "before we left."

Nicholas broke away from both of them and sat down heavily on the packed earth, all his strength drained from him. "Tell me about it," he said. He had heard snatches of the story of the events in Missouri from the other passengers on the steamboat. But that the Saints had been forced from their homes was not a new tale. And there had been such excitement and hope for the future in the voices and faces of the passengers as they talked among one another that he had dared to hope, too.

"Tell me about it," he repeated.

His mother sunk into her old, scarred rocker. Lizbeth settled on the ground beside Nicholas, hugging her knees to her chest.

"We were some of the last to leave," she began, "because Mother had been ill and Father refused to let her attempt such a journey in her condition. Finally the mobs forced us from our home at bayonet point, at first refusing to let us take the bundles and goods we had secured on a little cart Father had made out of parts of an old wagon. At last they relented, after much cruel taunting, and we started off. But after a few rods Father stopped and began digging through our belongings to find an old shawl to put around Mother's shoulders. It was bitterly cold."

Lizbeth shivered, as though remembering too vividly. Her eyes had taken on a glazed look, shaded and impenetrable.

"The mobbers must have thought he was looking for a gun, or some other weapon. One of them sprang on him and struck his knife into Father's shoulder, slashing cruelly. They laughed to see his pain and Mother's terror. 'That'll teach you,' the one with the knife said. 'Now get out of here while we've still a mind to let you go.'

"We joined the hundreds of Saints heading east. We were on the road over two weeks, though some made the journey in eight or nine days. But Mother's health did not improve, and Father's wound festered and made him suffer greatly."

She looked up to see Nicholas gazing fixedly at her with such naked pain in his eyes that she attempted a smile.

"'Twas not as bad as it could have been. Thanks to Brother Brigham and the Committee for Removal, there were relief stations scattered along the way which provided camp poles and wood for fires, and sometimes food. But the weather was raw, and we were always cold. When we reached the river bottom of the

Mississippi it took us four days to cross it through water and mud sometimes up to our knees. We didn't know how bad Father was. But the infection had spread in red streaks down his arm. When we reached the banks of the river he collapsed. We made a bed for him there, and he never rose from it again."

She paused, but the silence was more painful than her words had been. Nicholas could picture his father struggling to get his family to safety before he would let himself die.

He rose and stumbled out of the dim tent. But there was nothing to hide him. Instinctively he found himself heading down to the river. There, in a stand of old cottonwoods, thick with dead brush and mosquitoes, he dropped to his knees. He cried, cried with the abandon of a child, cried for all the anguish he had felt and seen and experienced—and not been there to prevent.

Six to eight weeks' effort, the brethren said, would erect a small cottage. Nicholas wondered. When he surveyed his handiwork, after working three weeks with hardly a stop, the structure did not seem anywhere near halfway complete. There was no one save his mother and sister to help him, for all else were in like condition. And he had noticed from the beginning that his mother's strength seemed broken—or maybe it was her spirit that was broken, and little was left after that. They were a pathetic trio, Nicholas thought. But he kept his thoughts to himself and tried to count the ways in which they were fortunate. They had been able to purchase land at a greatly reduced price, being counted as one of the families who had suffered the most during the Missouri persecutions, losing husband and provider. The discount was a blessing indeed. Despite their precarious health, not one of them had yet taken sick with the ague that was confining hundreds to their beds and claiming lives by the score. Lizbeth, though but fourteen, was an excellent seamstress and had obtained work that would bring in a small income, enough to live on until the cabin was completed and Nicholas, too, could find work.

There were many other reasons to give thanks. They had their lives and they had a future, God willing, here in this place. The prophet was alive and among them, and their enemies were over the river, separated by the broad brown expanse of the Mississippi. And for Nicholas there was another blessing. He had noticed from the first that his mother needed him, turning to him continually for comfort, strength, and advice. This had never happened before. After losing a whole family of daughters, she had sorely wanted another when she had decided to try for a family again. But he had come first, and when his sister was born her gratitude had known no bounds. She had a loving husband to care for her, and an infant daughter to fuss over. Though Nicholas knew she loved him well, she had not needed him as she had the others.

Now all that was changed. Nicholas was the first one his mother turned to, and he could see the joy that he brought her increase and soften her careworn features with each passing day. It was obvious to him that his life had been preserved for this purpose. And he was willing to serve, to give of himself to his family and to the kingdom. But in the back of his mind, after all this was done—the building, the planting, the growing, the settling in—surely there would be a place in his life for his own cherished dreams. The letter he wrote before he left England should have reached Miss Cooper by now. She would at least know he was alive and safe and that he had not forgotten her. Pray heaven she would understand and soften her heart toward him. If he were to recount the history of the Mormons for the past several months, she would not be pleased. She would not understand, and she would be frightened. He must move with care. As soon as this house was up and standing on its own feet, he would write her again, give her the Nauvoo address, and try to make her see the progress and promise this city offered. Nor would he be feeding her tales. There was something here in the very air of the place. Perhaps heaven had sanctified this spot for the Saints. Certainly the essence of brotherhood and compassion abounded here; he could observe it in practice on every side.

Each day as his strength increased and his house progressed Nicholas felt invigorated, and his spirits rose along with the rough-hewn log walls. His days were consumed with labor. At night he fell into a deep and restful sleep, free of anxiety and devoid of dreams.

Chapter Seventeen

It was a ceremony as old as the sea itself. Yearly, on a Sunday in late August, the folk of Gloucester gathered at the old church. With the minister leading the way they repaired to the water's edge, a more fitting place than within the four walls of a building, to pay tribute to those men who had been claimed forever by the sea.

This day the salt winds blew in over a green sea flecked with white. Millie stood with the others, listening to the grand words and solemn prayers. Her thoughts were with the maids of story and legend who watched and waited for vanished boats until they grew withered and gray and were buried at last with their wedding gowns for their funeral shrouds. Able seamen, she knew, know no fear and consider death not a great mystery but an ordinary part of life. Yet Gloucestermen, the oldest of all New England seafarers, sought their living upon the world's most dangerous waters: the Grand Banks, often shrouded with mist or sown with jagged icebergs; the Georges Banks, and closer coastal ledges, all treacherous, crowded with the ghosts of cold, drowned men, sightless eyes fixed in a stare, lips set in a thin, resolute line. There was no fanfare, no sense of heroics to the work these seafarers did, only a skill passed down through the ages and a heroism quiet and unremarked upon. Millie's father was one who had been taken by the sea and was now among those ghosts who haunted the dreams of the living, whose spirits forever hovered over their watery graves. Would there ever be peace for men such as her father?

Millicent shivered as a cloud, thick and black, rode across the sun's path and darkened the sky. What was the minister saying?

". . . Over two thousand Gloucestermen have gone down to the sea and never returned, and in our midst are their widows and children—two hundred and fifty-nine women and over five hundred orphans . . ."

I am one of them, Millie realized with a shudder. Voices all around her began singing the old hymn,

> A mighty fortress is our God,
> A tower of strength ne'er failing.
> A helper mighty is our God,
> O'er ills of life prevailing . . .

She looked about her at the faces, all turned seaward. How many of them sang from habit and how many from faith? How many truly believed in the words they were singing?

When the hymns were ended the minister offered a long prayer. The salt winds blew noisily and nearly drowned out his words. Then the children of Gloucester stepped forward, the young girls dressed in white, the boys in their Sabbath-day best. Their arms were laden with all the loveliest flowers of the woods and gardens and wayside fields of New England. Slowly they bent, graceful as young sea birds, and laid their fragrant offerings on the breast of the waves, and the receding tide carried them out—far out to the nameless graves that God alone knows.

Millie's eyes stung, and not from the salt spray. The tender, guileless faces of the young children haunted her. Nameless fears played across her cold senses like phantoms. She walked homeward against an east wind, which the old children's rhyme says blows good for neither man nor beast. The ancient rites were completed, but the ancient sorrows still shadowed her soul.

In September Nicholas's last letter written from Liverpool reached Gloucester. Almira Fenn disposed of it with hardly a second thought; her self-imposed calling had moved into the realm of everyday habit. Her mind was not given to reflection, and she spared no consideration for the girl whose course she had taken upon herself to manipulate and direct. Life was simple and straightforward to her way of thinking; one did what one must and let fate or chance or heaven take care of the rest.

Near the end of September Millie came back one morning

from a walk by the sea to find Thomas Erwin sitting on her doorstep. "You have one of the finest gardens in all Gloucester," he hailed her.

She removed the hat she was wearing to shade her fair skin. "Thank you. I work very hard at it," she confessed.

"Since the season is nearly over, could you be cajoled into working very hard at another task which you once appeared to enjoy?"

Millie held her breath. She scarcely dared hope.

"I do not intend to give up my school to you," Mr. Erwin hastened to clarify, seeing the expression that came over her face. "But I am in need of assistance with the lower grades. Might you be interested?" He paused only a moment. "Good." He did not need a reply when her whole face revealed her pleasure. "Good," he repeated. "I was hoping you would say that. The children miss you. They had grown most fond of you, you know."

Millie did not know, really, but she loved being told. She loved the children, she loved the teaching, she loved the mere association with books and learning, with slates and paper, with words and sums. But more than all that, this work would be her salvation. She faced a long winter alone. She had wondered until this moment if she would be able to bear it.

She sent the schoolteacher home with jars of her preserved jellies and a fresh apple pie. He was profuse in his thanks, but she kindly brushed them aside. He had brought her hope and a reason to keep going day after day; it was little enough she gave in return.

In October Millie carved jack-o-lanterns with the children and knit warm scarves and mittens to protect their tender skin from the biting cold that would soon blow in. She put her garden to bed and harvested her seeds, herbs, and spices, and dried racks of fruit to put aside for winter treats. She baked apple, pumpkin, and squash pies, and cranberry bread. She continued to borrow books from Mr. Erwin. She wrote long letters and read far into the night. Her days were full, and they had some meaning to them. And time slipped through her hands.

Before October was over Almira Fenn had destroyed two letters. The first one nearly slipped past her. It bore an Illinois postmark, which she associated with Millie's rich Boston friends who had lost their senses and joined with the Mormons, yet still had to be taken into account. But this letter bore a name that had become familiar to her, though in another setting. She disposed of it with her usual efficiency. Two days later she chuckled a bit to discover a letter from Millie, addressed to Liverpool, in her pile of outgoing mail. Then she knew her efforts were paying off for her and for her foolhardy son who thought he wanted the pretty little snit of a thing for his wife. Well, if he wanted her he should have her, if Almira Fenn had anything to say in the matter. And, of course, she had.

As the Christmas season approached Millie received a greeting from Verity that contained the most startling news.

Dear Millie,

I am to be married. He is the kind of man a girl dreams of, and he loves me as dearly as I love him. He is from New York and is a graduate of Harvard—he knows Boston and loves it, Millie! That is one of the best parts. He understands the very heart of me, something I never thought to find in another person while in this life. More later, my dear heart. A letter will follow after the holidays; I promise. I have so much to tell.

Millie had to be content with this tantalizing tidbit. But, oh, how cruel the contrast between her state and Verity's! The night before Christmas, while deep in sleep, she dreamed of Nicholas Todd. He was standing on a rock in the middle of a gray sea, surrounded by mists. A cold spray blew in his face and the mists rolled over him. He called out her name. He groped toward her with wet stiff arms, but a dense curtain of fog hid his face and then concealed him altogether. Millie cried out to him, but his voice did not answer. He was lost to her sight, beyond the sound of her desperate cries.

She awoke with tears choking her throat and lay awake in the cold darkness for hours, trying to make out the meaning of such a dream. Had the sea claimed this man she was so strangely drawn to? Or had death in some other form snatched him away from her, and her mind had sought the most natural symbolism for her—the sea—to express the dreaded horror? No! That could not be! Nothing so cruel and senseless and wasteful. Yet the thought of the fevered children he had cared for always sat like a cold stone at the back of her mind. Even in the sane, sun-washed air of morning she could read only one general meaning to the dream, whatever the particulars: Nicholas Todd was lost to her. But one thing maddened her senses. Through the caroling, the baking of cakes and cookies, the making of homemade presents, the school nativity scene—all the activities of the season that Mr. Erwin gently but firmly drew her into—her mind was consumed with one question: Was Nicholas Todd seeking her? Was he reaching out for her from some unknown place, as he had in the dream? Was he groping for her, searching for her as she was searching for him?

That Christmas season was one of great rejoicing for the Saints at Nauvoo. They were out of the way of their enemies. Under the Prophet's inspired direction they were building new homes and clearing land, creating a city where their children could learn to live the gospel in peace.

Nicholas was grateful. His house had been completed before cold weather set in, and his mother had made it homey enough with the little furniture that was left her. She and Lizbeth had woven colorful rag rugs for the floor, and Lizbeth sewed curtains for the two windows, though there was no glass yet to go in them. But with the whitewashed walls the big room had a pleasant air.

Nicholas's mother and sister had both taken to knitting gloves and mittens, which they sold to neighbors and to Lizbeth's sewing customers. Nicholas had also found work with young Frederick Rich and his father in their shoemaking shop. Every day things improved and looked brighter. Every day he could feel himself growing stronger, more fit.

But still he was haunted. At the end of the summer he had written to Millicent Cooper, but she had not replied. Surely his letter had reached her. Memories as clear and real as the things that were happening around him took his thoughts back to Liverpool and Daniel Hawkins's visit a year ago. What twists and turns his life had taken since that day! But the old seaman had seemed confident of Millicent's affection for Nicholas, as though he was privy to her feelings in ways Nicholas could not be. And Nicholas believed him. He believed, too, what he had felt with his own heart and seen with his own eyes. Such a sympathy of mind and spirit did not spring forth between a man and woman for no purpose at all. Why was she ignoring him? Had he offended or frightened her? Was she in trouble, or was she ill?

On a quiet day as the year drew to a close, Nicholas took pen and paper and sat at the back of the shoemaker's shop, encased in the pungent fragrance of leather, oils, and wood shavings. It was snowing outside, large, wet flakes that built up quickly so that sky and earth blurred into one landscape of white. He dipped his pen into the thick black ink. Was he a fool to be doing this?

Dear Miss Cooper,

I send this letter out of deep regard, and concern for your welfare—and in hopes that my attempt to communicate with you will not meet with your disapproval or offend you in some way I do not intend.

He started out slowly, but before he knew it he was pouring out his heart to her, and the mere doing so had a healing effect upon his own troubled spirit. Surely something would come of this letter, surely things would work out.

There were already certain young women of his mother's acquaintance who had expressed an interest in him. His mother was pleased, and anxious for her son to think seriously about marriage. "I want to hold my grandchildren in my arms before I die," she told him. She was older, since he and his sister were late children, and her privations in Missouri had aged her further. If Nicholas could please her, he would. If Nicholas could marry where his heart was . . .

He sealed up the letter, tucked it into his overcoat pocket, and walked out into the snow. He drew the cold, clean air into his nostrils. The smog and smoky fumes of Liverpool seemed like a dream. So did the tangy salt smell of the sea breezes drifting over a gray, weathered New England town. Nauvoo was new and just beginning; all things were possible here. This place, this gathering

138

of people, wove so many varied and radiant dreams into a harmonious pattern. Could not one more strand, diverse as it may be, find a congenial place here among the rest?

A new year, but no change in Millie's life, no expectations. Luther would not return until spring. In February the promised letter from Verity arrived at her door. She put down the book she had been reading and opened the envelope, a fluttering anticipation, not altogether pleasant, quickening her pulse.

Nauvoo, January 1840

Dear Millie,

Here is my unexpected news in detail, as much as I have time, space, and presence of mind to relate.

My new husband, Giles Winter, is a new convert, gleaned through the persistence of his older sister and her husband, who sent missionaries back East to assail him, with orders to persist and persist with him, until he gave way. He arrived in Nauvoo during those first terrible months in time to watch his sister and her new infant die of the ague, which has claimed lives here by the hundreds. At first his faith was sorely tried by this loss, and by the terrible injustice of the loss and suffering he saw around him on every side. In characteristic manner he went straight to the head—straight to the Prophet Joseph himself. As Giles relates it, Joseph listened sympathetically, with tears in his eyes. Then they discussed the various precepts of the gospel as Giles had been taught them, and the Prophet opened his understanding on many a point, and offered to give him a blessing right then and there, which he did.

Giles walked away from there, as he puts it, a changed man. I met him for the first time the following day as I was carrying lunch to Simon and Edgar at the blacksmithing shop. He spoke casually, a hello to a stranger in passing. But he told me later that as soon as I spoke to him, as soon as his eyes met mine, he felt that he had known me before. From that moment on he pursued me, and the sweet influence of his spirit made itself felt in my life.

You may well guess, Millie, that it was Giles who converted

me to the principles of Mormonism. Ever so gently he led my understanding, first on one point, then on another. It had to be so, for two cannot love and grow in unity when something so essential as religious belief separates them. My proud, determined reading of the Book of Mormon gave me some little foundation upon which he could build. I could open my heart to Mormonism, I suppose, because I was opening my heart to him, and in many ways that process was one and the same. Suffice it to say that I was baptized on the 18th of December, and nearly froze to death in the process, though the weather was thankfully mild enough for that time of year. Giles himself performed the ordinance. It seemed to me that we walked down into the water as separate people and emerged as one. Two days later we were truly united in the holy bonds of marriage. And Millie, dear heart, my life is made new! I am a different self, and the world I inhabit, though outwardly unchanged, has new dimensions because I see all things differently. Are you laughing by now? I would not blame you if you are. I have succumbed to the idealism of love with the guilelessness of a school girl. And yet, the realities of life here are so harsh and demanding that it is not as though I live in a make-believe world of love's perfection and pampering; it is not like that at all. Here I go, explaining and excusing myself to you! Let me get back to facts.

Giles is twenty-six years old, while I am nearly twenty-one. He is a shopkeeper, of all things, though he has the soul of a poet and contributes articles to the *Nauvoo Expositor,* which are published! We live in our own little house, half a block from Mother and Leah. And it is little, Millie. One room for cooking and eating, socializing and sleeping. But I don't really mind. This is the frontier, and I am kept busy making my own soap and candles, spinning and weaving, sewing and cooking— all the chores which were allocated to the serving girls back home. Giles says I will be surprised at how quickly Nauvoo will prosper. He predicts that within a year he will make a buying trip to New Orleans and we will see the latest fashions sported on Nauvoo's streets. Perhaps he is right; I cannot even imagine it. But for now I am content.

There you have it, Millie. Are you happy for me? You would be if you were here. We are so distant, so removed from each other. I grieve over that. I wish I could share with you all I have learned during these months, and I wish I could share with you my joy. I remain one who loves you and ever will.

Your friend,
Verity Winters

She signed her new last name with a flourish and underlined it with a squiggle of ink. Millie had to smile at that. *So I was right,* she said to herself. *Verity became one of them when she first decided she would throw in her lot with her mother and accept Judith's fate as her own. Her life is settled and decided now; it has turned off from the old life in a direction I can never follow.*

"*Two cannot love and grow in unity when something so essential as religious belief separates them,*" Verity had written, not knowing how thoroughly Millie would understand what she was saying. *That is the only thing that stands between myself and Nicholas Todd.* There. She had given place to the thought. *Could it ever have been with Nicholas and me,* she wondered, *as it is with Verity and her Giles?*

"Don't be a fool!" she said out loud, catching herself angrily. "There is nothing there to dream about, much less build upon. It was merely a relationship of days—a sympathy that both of us wished to extend, but circumstances, whatever they may be, have prevented us. And so, that is that. Let it be. It is over and done with."

She wanted to be happy for Verity. And, deep down in her heart, she was, despite the envy and the icy loneliness that singed the edges of her joy.

Chapter Eighteen

In January Almira destroyed another letter from Millie's Mormon upstart. In March Luther came home, and Almira was glad of it. Now this nonsense would stop. He would marry Millie, and the stranger could write every week then for what good it would do him. His intermittent letters were an irritant that only her son's marriage would be able to allay.

Luther came back looking hardened and older from his year spent at sea. The humble, almost imploring demeanor he had assumed with Millie was gone. His eyes, like glittering bits of black coal, bit through her reserve and would not allow her to feign ignorance, conceal her own feelings, or delay his intentions.

Millie looked at the whole thing a bit coldly. She was not in love with Luther, but she did hold him in high regard. He would be a responsible husband and a good provider. She enjoyed the physical touch of him. And he truly loved her; she had no doubt of that. Those were the positive considerations. The negative she ignored. What good would it do her to face them openly when, from this day on, her best defense would lie in concealing them carefully with what layers of pleasure, companionship, and confidence she could weave from this union? It would not do to be too vulnerable right now.

The only reprieve she could gain was to set the wedding for spring, the middle of May, when her garden would be in bloom and the martins and sparrows in voice. When she would have had time to grow accustomed to the idea. When it would be seventeen months since she had heard word from Nicholas Todd.

In a sort of daze she made the preparations, feeling oddly distant from all that was happening. From time to time she wondered what it would have been like if Verity were there, if she had someone to share things with, someone she cared for. If her mother were still alive, would she have any advice to give her daughter? Surely she had known all the secrets and sorrows of being a seaman's wife. And that was obviously the path fate had marked out for Millie. Verity had gone on without her, and all other doors had been closed to her. This was all that Life planned to offer her; perhaps Life knew best in the long run. She would try to accept it and do her best.

Three weeks before the wedding, on a mad whim, Millie left her cottage and walked in the direction of the old Copley estate. The few times she had gone by there in the past she had found no one at home and, indeed, little sign of activity about the place. If Jonathan Hammond was there, why, she would invite him to the wedding. What could be more natural than that? She would not admit to herself the childish hopes she was cherishing.

But it was of little matter. Her hopes were dealt a swift, indifferent death when she saw from a distance that the windows were boarded over and there was absolutely no sign of life. A sad derelict of a house, given up and deserted. She stood staring at it, a terrible burning behind the lids of her eyes.

"No one lives there any longer, miss." A fisherman docking his boat in the shallow cove close by had noticed her. He called out to her in a loud voice, but thankfully he was not near enough to see the tears in her eyes.

"Fellow who bought it went back to Boston. Didn't have the money he thought he had to fix up the old place."

Millie nodded her understanding and turned back toward home. *That is that,* she told herself for the second time. *What is the matter with you? It is over. Can't you forget and bury it?*

But for a day or two she was restless and walked the shoreline at night, alone with the stars that sat low in the spring sky and the sloshing sounds of the tide. It was here that old Daniel found her. At first he said nothing at all, merely matching his stiff gait to her girlish stride for as long as he could. Then he reached out for her arm.

"What is it, Daniel?" she asked him, not wanting to hear what he had to say.

"I hear you've set the date for the wedding," he wheezed. "You're to marry Luther Fenn."

"That I am."

"What of this other fellow, the one I left in Liverpool?"

"He may still be there, for all I know."

Millie could feel Daniel's consternation and sense the cogs of his mind slowly turning. "You've lost touch with him, Millie?"

"I have." She did not trust herself to speak much. Something within her had begun to stir and tremble.

Daniel shook his head slowly. "Then something's not right. He cared deeply for you."

"You don't know that!"

"I know it as well as I know I'm a man."

"Well, he doesn't care anymore. Either he is lying dead in Liverpool or he has come to his senses and realizes that what he needs is a good Mormon wife, not a hotheaded fisherman's daughter."

Daniel chuckled under his breath. "You speak truly there," he said, and his voice held the saucy grin that she could not see. "You're too much woman for Luther, Millie."

"I know that."

"Do you love him?"

"In some ways I do."

"Enough to make a life of it?" Daniel regarded her quizzically.

"I hope so. I truly hope so." Her voice was nearly swallowed by the sounds of the sea.

Daniel slid his hand down her arm and clasped her cold fingers in a grip that was amazingly firm, though Millie could feel how frail was the life that pulsed through his depleted flesh.

"Some of us must wrest what we want from Life; she will not give it up to us easily. You can do it, Millie, if you've a mind to. Don't flinch, and don't lose faith in yourself."

"I won't, I promise," Millie said, knowing this was the closest she would come to loving counsel as she embarked on this most solemn step of her life.

The planting was done. Seeds of hope and faith were sown into the rich black Illinois soil along with the wheat and corn. Nicholas had added another room to his mother's cabin. Converts were arriving by the hundreds, and some of the more primitive structures in the town were already being replaced by substantial brick ones. Everybody in the city seemed to need shoes or good strong boots to wear plowing. There was work in plenty to keep the Rich family shoemakers busy, and Nicholas was becoming adept at the cutting and stitching, the stretching and molding.

It was May, nearly five months since he had sent off his letter to Gloucester. He had heard naught in return. The silence seemed to shout at him and the void to swallow him up; he knew not where to turn. He prayed earnestly for Millicent morning and night. Was he a fool to keep trying when there was nothing to warrant it? Why couldn't he simply let go?

The spring weather, a tonic to so many, had not renewed his mother's energies. Instead, she seemed to be wasting away before his eyes. Jane Miller, one girl of several who seemed bent on attracting Nicholas's attentions, was in contrivance with his mother; he knew it. Through someone's good offices they were always thrown together, sometimes even found alone in one another's company. Jane was too forward for Nicholas—friendly and good-hearted, but she wasn't what he wanted. When he forgot himself and said as much to his mother once, she fairly bristled.

"I thought you liked a girl to have spirit," she said defensively.

"Spirit and aggressiveness aren't the same thing," he tried to explain, his unsettled thoughts with Millicent Cooper, who was far from forward yet had to be the most spirited girl he had known. He would write once more when he could grab a minute. It couldn't hurt.

The daylight hours were long now and he worked through them and past them, until at day's end he was so weary he could scarcely hold up his head. But a letter, a short letter—he could somehow manage that. Thinking of Jane Miller's smirking smile and pale blue eyes, he knew that he must.

In the end, the occasion was saved by the schoolchildren. Millie, a solemn and pale-faced bride, walked out of the church on Luther's arm to greet a flush of young faces, scrubbed and smiling, and calling her name. Singing songs of love and promise that Mr. Erwin had taught them, they led the couple along the sea path, scattering flowers before their feet. They were so lovely that Millie could feel salty tears begin to sting in her eyes. Here was something of love and joy for her to hold onto!

At Stage Fort Park a long feast table had been set. Later there would be bonfires and dancing, toasts to the new couple, and merrymaking of all kinds. But Millie would remember best the faces and voices of the children as they skipped beside the sea, fresh as young colts, with the unborn dreams of tomorrow bright in their eyes and the sea wind lifting the locks of their silken hair.

The day following her son's wedding Almira Fenn fished a letter written by Nicholas Todd out from her stack of incoming mail. The accursed thing! She took its appearance as a bad omen and nearly laid the whole matter out before Luther, but in the end her cooler judgment prevailed. The deed was done; the knot was tied. In time the letters would stop coming, and Luther would never know all she had done for him, that he might possess his desire. But then, had it not been thus between mothers and sons since time began?

From the very beginning it seemed awkward, almost unnatural, for Millie to share her parents' bed with a husband. Luther knew no such qualms, but he was tender with her, and patient in his own way. The married state pleased him well. A softness crept into his speech and showed itself in half a dozen little ways. Millie wondered if it would last beyond the first blush of sexual passion and domestic pleasures. She kept a tight, shipshape house. She was a good cook. She provided bright conversation to enhance Luther's hours at home, which some seamen complained of as being dull. There was nothing dull about Millie. After long years at sea, Luther reveled in his bliss. Millie responded; it was impossible not to. At times she even believed that what she was feeling was happiness; it must be. The power to please another is a rare and valuable gift and increases one's self-worth and well-being. Millie glowed under the effects of it.

Luther stayed close to home that summer, fishing for cod and mackerel along the Georges Bank, which was only a hundred miles east of Cape Cod.

"The mackerel are much more elusive and hard to catch," Luther explained to Millie after an especially good haul, as she helped him remove his high yellow churn boots and his wet calfskin trousers. "But they bring in over ten dollars a barrel, where they were stuck at five only ten years ago." He glowed with the success he and Pinky and Andrew had experienced in their little Chebacco. "Cod has risen, too," he continued, "but not nearly so much."

Millie was glad. Success at fishing meant peace in the household and a chance to plan for the future.

The sweet days of summer came and went with a gentle sameness that was soothing. Millie gardened and baked and visited more with her neighbors, now that she had become a respectable married woman.

One night, as she and Luther were getting ready for bed, he pulled her toward him and blurted out a bit awkwardly, "How do you feel about children, Millie? I should like to have me a son."

Of course you would! she said to herself. She should not be surprised. Seaman lived on through their sons—their fine skills, their ancient knowledge, their legends and dreams. Without sons it would all dim and then vanish.

"Not quite yet," she hedged. "I'm not quite ready."

"Course you are," he said, drawing her yet closer. "A child would keep you company while I'm off on the long stints."

She did not like how he told her what she was thinking, ignoring anything she said that he did not want to hear. "What if we had a daughter?"

"A little girl who had sunlight in her hair, who looked like you? I wouldn't mind that. Then next time a son."

He was not teasing her; he was in dead earnest. If only it were as simple as that.

But he had put the thought in her mind, and, surprisingly, she felt herself drawn to it. It wasn't a matter of judgment, it was a matter of some deep, primal response that his words had called forth from her and that, as the days passed, would give her no peace.

Bless Verity! Millie had at last given in and written to tell her and the others about the wedding, but she had never expected a reply this soon. It was a slender envelope, but any word from her friend was welcome.

Dearest, dearest Millie,

I cannot describe to you the joy your letter has brought us. When I told Mother of your marriage tears actually came to her eyes. She was more attached to you than any of us realized. I believe she admired your sprightly ways, while I admired mostly your gentle spirit (as well as your thick golden hair). Anyway, all happiness to you, my dear heart. I hope Luther is worthy of you, and I wish I were there to lecture him every now and again just to keep him on his toes. Mother says husbands require a great deal of management and a woman who is not willing to work at molding and training her husband should not expect to complain. So like her, isn't it? I do not understand her ways. Thank heaven Giles takes very little management, or I do not know what I should do.

Illinois has the blackest, richest soil I have ever seen, and we look forward to a rich harvest to reward all our exhausting labor. Perhaps this year it seems more difficult to me because, you see, I am expecting a child. It will be born in October— thank heaven not in the heat of this terrible summer. I have been ill and weak, more ill than I remember Leah being. But then, one notices differently when something involves one's own self.

I must here add that poor Leah has suffered two miscarriages, which must be very hard on her. She shows little of her feelings. And yet, Millie, I strongly suspect that she does not wish to have another child. I think she is afraid and yet will let none of us help her, just living in her own quiet shell. Edgar frets about her like an old fishwife, but to no avail. Now that I have a husband of my own I can see how dangerous her behavior might become. But she has locked all of us out, even Edgar to too large a degree. He has work to keep him busy, at least.

This city is bursting at its poor, half-sewn seams. People pour in every day on the steamboats—interesting assortments, mainly from the isles of Britain. Mother sniffs out the Irish and makes a big to-do about them. Oh, Millicent, would you believe, Mother has wormed her way into Giles's business, advising him on which styles of bonnets to order, how many bolts of fabric of one kind or another. She has rearranged his whole store and claims sales have risen because of the enticing new ways she has contrived to display things. Giles believes she is right and indulges her frightfully. But alas, if any item sits too long on the shelf and fails to show signs of selling, Mother whisks it away and finds some poor needy soul to bestow it upon. Leah says she behaves like a minister back home would and fancies herself the same. There is some truth in that observation. Anyway, Father would be proud of her, I am sure. Perhaps her behavior stems in part from the poverty of her own childhood in Ireland. She must feel something for the suffering of these people that you or I could not feel.

The spirit of Joseph lights this city, and we have peace here. Everyone works so very hard. I try to do my part, but I love it when Giles pampers me, as he often does after a difficult day or when I have been particularly ill. Not for three months but for nearly five my stomach refused to hold anything. I was weak and dizzy and sick several times a day. Now that has passed, but the heat makes my feet swell, I am beginning to feel big and cumbersome, and it hurts every time I bend down. See what is in store for you, Millie? I wish you were with me. Leah is no comfort at all. I avoid all mention of my state and its hopeful conclusion: a live, well baby. Will that prove too painful for her? I tremble to think of it.

The days pass quickly and the work never ends, so I must close this letter and attend to the tasks that await me. But remember, dear heart, that I am with you in thought. I can easily picture you in your cottage by the ocean, and sometimes, in truth, I desire escape from the hustle and bustle that is ever present around me and long for the peace you must know. Beautiful Millie, be happy, and think of me as I think of you, with fond memories and devotion that time cannot dim.

Your Verity

Autumn seemed to sneak in overnight and snatch summer away from them unawares. Millie missed its going, though autumn meant she could help out at the school again and brought a lightening of the grueling labor of the planting and harvesting months. Luther tried to talk her into going to Beverly with him, but she would not consider it.

"I can make more money there," he argued.

"Not much more," she reminded him. "And this school is

149

important to me. You've never understood that. From the beginning you've made light of it."

"What you need is a child of your own."

Millie concealed the sting she felt at his words. They had been married over four months, and there was no sign of a child yet. "It's the children, yes, but it's more than that," she tried to explain. "It's the books and the learning within myself. I like how that feels. I find so many different ways to give, Luther, and there is so much to discover." She watched him as she spoke, but there was no comprehension behind the stare of his gaze.

"Work on the winter sea is harsh, Millie." He would not relent.

"But the harvest is good on the Georges in winter, and you have a boat and trusted companions." She argued too well; his irritation was mounting. "I'm not going. Go yourself, if you'd like."

"There's too much about being with you that I'd miss, love."

Millie knew what he referred to first and foremost, but she let it pass. Her mind and spirit were of little consequence to him, though he meant well enough in his own way.

Religion does not separate us, she realized with alarming clarity, *but lack of shared sympathies does.* Yet she must not think of such things, not ever. It would do her no good. She must find ways to compensate—she must have a child. Though she knew instinctively that a baby would not prove a cure-all, she felt very honestly that it might be her salvation, and Luther's as well.

October is called the yellow month from the fading of the leaf; all things old and dying wither and fade in October. That was how Daniel Hawkins died. He grew brittle and weightless as the leaves that layered the woods where Millie walked to pick late blackberries and gather sprigs of hawthorn and dogwood to display in a jar on her kitchen shelf.

Amos Fenn ran to tell her; she met him walking down the long slope, her arms sagging with the weight of the tangled, woody branches. She thanked him, fed him a large piece of apple pie in a bowl of rich cream, and hurried him back to his mother. Amos was a good sort of boy, and would be better if he could be got away from Almira's influence. She taught a stinginess and self-interest through her example that belied any words she might speak. Luther had fared all the better because he left home when only a youngster and took to the sea.

It was indeed difficult to hold onto the boys in a town like Gloucester. As soon as fishermen's sons could walk they swarmed over every banker boat or Chebacco that came into port. They became expert at hand-lining for cunners, the small fishes that swam in close to shore. They were always seen hanging about, begging the older boys to teach them to row. By the age of six they were able to aid in curing the catch, and a fishing village was one of the few places in the world, Millie supposed, where a boy eagerly helped his mother with the kitchen work in order to qualify as a sea cook. Boys as young as nine did the cooking on Marblehead and Gloucester fishing boats. The next step was to become an apprentice and learn at last the secrets of luring codfish to hook and the art of heading, splitting, and salting with quick precision.

Millie admired Thomas Erwin more than she could say. In his determination to educate these boys who had only the sea in their eyes and in their heads, he employed every resource he could muster. If Millie had sons they would know history and poetry and literature, and not only that of the sea. She would open their eyes to other possibilities that the wide world held.

She sighed. So Daniel was gone, dying an easy, natural death, the way all things in nature die—an unnatural death for the likes of a seaman. Except for the sense of her own loss, she could not really feel sad. All his comrades had long since gone the way he was going, so the best of company awaited him. And after all the hard, lonely years he was going to *her*, the girl who, in memory, dreams, and perhaps even spirit, had been with him all his life. *I don't even know her name,* Millie thought with a sharp little ache. What was it Daniel had said? She could not remember, but she had written it in her journal. For some reason she felt she must know, and she dug through the pages until she found the entry: "*But now that I had tasted that rare mystery of love between a woman and a man, all else left me feeling unsatisfied and unfulfilled. . . .*" "All else" in the mouth of a man like Daniel included the sea, and if he had truly felt that way about this woman—Lucinda—he had been a rare man. But perhaps day-to-day living would have drained out the magic, even from a love such as his. Verity seemed to think she could hold onto the glory she felt with

Giles. Was it possible? Millie herself had no answer, not being one of the few who had known the rare mystery of perfect love between husband and wife.

Be that as it may, she had a good life, a good marriage by any standard except the ideal. A grateful heart, she had always been taught, is not only a blessing but a duty. She would try to be grateful. With the passing of Daniel she had lost her last tie with Nicholas. If she still saw his face in the sea spray down by the rocks, if she still heard his voice in the echo of the surf, then that, too, she must wrench from her heart. Death was a letting go—with Daniel's death she must let go, too. She must. Or this love would become a poison within her heart.

Chapter Nineteen

As the year 1841 began, the Saints had every reason to celebrate. In December of 1840 the Illinois legislature had incorporated Nauvoo as a city. Joseph had framed a liberal city charter that made Nauvoo similar to a city-state in many ways. There was a university in Nauvoo, a playhouse, a newspaper, a library, and several schools. In February 1841 a military unit called the Nauvoo Legion was organized, which required all males between the ages of eighteen and forty-five to perform military service. Nicholas was happy to join. He had come to be friends with many of the brethren in the city and looked forward to this strictly male association. If business continued to prosper, in another year at the longest he could build a new house. It was time to get on with his life, and he knew it.

Walking beside the river one day, looking over the skim layer of ice that coated the surface, a sudden thought came to him: he would write a letter to Daniel Hawkins, the old seaman. Perhaps he could help. Nicholas had no address for him, but his name was well known in Gloucester, and a letter was bound to reach him. Nicholas remembered his quiet sympathy and the wisdom in the words he had spoken. Certainly he was a last resort; certainly, if anyone could help him, Daniel could.

He walked back to the shop and sat at the low bench with his feet to the fire. The day was far spent. If he stayed here too long his mother would send Lizbeth after him. But this had to be done now, before he looked too hard at the matter and lost his courage.

At the same time he jotted a short note to Millicent. It was two years almost to the day since he met Daniel Hawkins in Liverpool. Two long, straining years. Perhaps with the tide of success in Nauvoo his own fortunes would turn. Money, security, a bigger house—none of that was worth anything unless he had someone he could share it with, someone he could love. Even in prayer he could not turn his thoughts away from her. Until something changed, he must continue to try.

More than any other time, it is said, spirits haunt the year's last dying hours, sobbing and sighing along the scratchy black branches, the bare, empty beach. The air is hushed where they pass, and anyone who encounters them will feel the chill of their presence, and the whole soul will grieve.

In the dank days of December Millie felt the presence of such spirits as she walked the wet beach. They seemed to rise on the misty spray of the water, and she almost fancied she could feel their breath brush over her skin. Who were these presences? Her father? Old Daniel? What did they desire of her? This year, now dwindling to a close, had seen her relinquish her girlhood for the status of wife. Was she the same person, walking this stretch of shoreline, that she always had been? In what ways had she taken into herself characteristics of Luther's, mingling them with her own? If only she could walk here knowing that new life, an extension of her own soul, her own being, moved within her. She felt less than a complete, worthy woman because she could not produce a child. This, above all else, would lend her true merit in Luther's eyes. It was not fair, it was not just, and yet it was so.

She walked for a long time, hugging her arms to her body, drawing the taste of salt and cold down into her lungs and feeling her soul spin out of her body on the long, haunting note of the curlew's call. She felt as thin and insubstantial as the mist that rolled up from the sea, bound only by her mortal longings to this frail spot of earth. Perhaps these spirits that whispered wordlessly to her meant only to comfort her sorrow and lend her some strength as she bent before the sweep of the sea wind and the strong forces of life.

At the end of an afternoon of shopping Millie stopped in at Almira's post office to see if there were any letters for Luther or herself. Almira regarded her through close, squinted eyes. Just four days earlier she had disposed of two letters from Millie's stranger, one addressed to her and one to old Daniel. She had chuckled at that. "Dead men tell no tales," so the saying goes. She had been vexed at the time. But Millie, slender in a dark green coat, her face flushed from the cold, with tendrils of golden hair curling round her cheeks, looked uncommonly pretty and somehow vulnerable, even to Almira's begrudging gaze. The sense of discomfort that came over her was not quite guilt or remorse, but close enough for Almira to seek someone to blame. It was Millie who had caused deceit in Almira and trouble for all of them. So thinking, Almira asked sharply, "When are you going to have good news for us, Millie?"

She peered at her daughter-in-law closely and noticed the girl's cheeks pale.

"Luther's been patient, he has, 'specially when his cousin over in Beverly, married less time than yourselves, has been these three months with child. And for that matter—"

"Have you letters for us, or haven't you?" Millie cut her off with a look that stopped even Almira's tongue. She handed Millie an advertisement from a shipping firm in Boston and a letter from Verity. As soon as her hand closed upon them Millie turned and was gone. She would never let Almira see tears in her eyes, never; she would choke on them first. But all the way home her sight was blurred by them, senseless and futile as they were.

Nauvoo, November, 1840

Dearest Millie,

I am writing this in hopes that it will reach you by Christmas. At last I have been blessed with the birth of my child. She was later by nearly three weeks than the doctor had predicted. How long that time seemed! I was so uncomfortable and, I must admit, fearful that all was not well. But she is here, and she is perfect. We have named her Katherine Rose. Her hair is a cloud of auburn fluff, and so far her eyes are blue. She has a lovely chin and a full, strong mouth like my mother's. But thus far her behavior indicates a much milder temperament; perhaps her "touchy Irish blood" is sufficiently diluted! Oh, Millie, I wish you could see her, I do! No one could have told me what joy motherhood is; one has to experience it to realize how it opens up the heart and unlocks the music of the universe for your ears to hear.

A trembling, starting from deep inside, shuddered through Millie's frame. She skipped the remaining passages telling about little Katherine and picked up where Verity began:

> Leah is expecting again, so we are all careful of her. It is not as though she pampers herself; I fear I often give a wrong impression of Leah. She helps where she can. In fact, she has become a fine cook and delights in baking treats for the poor families whom Mother fusses over. Just yesterday I left Katherine with Mother for a spell and, arriving back earlier than I had expected, found Leah rocking her by the fire, looking as pale and sweet as a young angel with her offspring. It tore at my heart. The most difficult thing is that she yet remains aloof, as though gazing at life from a distance, shrouded and protected, not really a part of it.

Poor Leah. For the first time Millie's sympathies truly went out to her. *What wretched creatures we are,* she conceded to her own conscience, *that only through our own suffering can we develop tenderness for others. Where the mind has not been, the heart cannot follow. But why must it be so?*

> Well, enough of gloom. This is a happy season and, thanks to Mother's enthusiasm as a businesswoman, a profitable one for all here!
> Blessings on you, dear Millie. May the Lord's peace surround you and may you know of his love for you—that is my prayer for you at this blessed time.

> Your own fond friend,
> Verity Winters

Millie's first Christmas with Luther was less sweet than it could have been because of the cloud that hung over them. He was kind to her, even at some times attentive, but he could not hide the fact that, in this one essential way, he believed she had failed him as a wife.

During the long winter evenings, reading by candlelight, Millie gave it much thought. Could Luther not look upon the two of them as a family until a child came? What intrinsic elements constituted a family anyway? He knew that she longed for a child as much as he did, yet she was unable to convey to him the sense of emptiness and unfulfillment that her barrenness brought. They were not united in their desires; each walked his or her own path. They might want the same thing, but for totally different reasons. Was that common with a man and a wife? Was she making mountains out of molehills? She did not know. She had no one to seek wisdom and advice from, and once again the ugly feeling of resentment against the Mormons rose up in her. It was they who were responsible for all the woes in her life, in Leah's life, even in Verity's. She found herself cursing the day she had ever heard of them, cursing the hour she had first looked up from her fragrant garden to see Nicholas's face. If he had not existed in her life, if he did not still dwell in her heart, might she have been more content from the outset with Luther? Did much of the fault lie in her?

With renewed energy and an attempt at real tenderness she tried harder: listened to Luther more carefully, praised him whenever she could, saw to his little needs in ways she knew would please him, and, hardest of all, opened her own heart and allowed him to gaze inside. For weeks she tried, sometimes hating the effort, chafing at her own confinements, sometimes mindless of anything but the sheer joy of giving and the inner peace that it brought. But with Luther himself she had to admit at last that she noticed no significant difference. He appreciated her, he was more amorous, less quarrelsome or moody. But her trembling heart, open and exposed, remained lonely, unapproached by whatever lay concealed within her husband, concealed by layers of habit and convention, indifference and fear.

April came, wet and windy, beset by gales that should have blown themselves out with February's passing. May was much the same. Millie felt always a little soggy and subdued. It was nearly impossible to work in the garden or to set about spring housecleaning. Even the children drooped, unable to stretch and run about and play at their sports.

Luther stayed, working close by, though Millie sensed the restiveness in him. It had now been a year since the minister had pronounced them man and wife, in the same church and at the same altar where her mother and father had taken their vows. She had spent a year living as a wife in the same house her mother had lived in. Had life been this hard for her—this heavy upon her heart?

The silences told her nothing at all. The winds blew and the old walls creaked, but no voices whispered through them. And in the still, fire-lit house she felt no traces of her mother's spirit, nothing to show her the way.

The winter days lengthened into spring. Spring along the Mississippi was always a wet and muddy affair. But oh, it was green, and the smells of sweet grass and prairie flowers and the black loam were heady! At such times Nicholas wished he knew more about farming and could simply work the land and be out-of-doors in all kinds of weather instead of cooped up in the shop. The days softened, there was love and new life everywhere. But no word came for Nicholas. A sort of numbness set in to assist him. It was three years since he had met Millicent in her garden in Gloucester. He could look back on it now as some sort of dream. Now, for the first time, every memory of her was not tinged with pain, every thought not colored with an urgency that churned up his mind.

At the beginning of the new year the Prophet had received a revelation commanding the Saints to build a temple. Later the basement was dug and walled, and on April sixth, the anniversary of the organization of the Church, the cornerstones were laid. Nicholas, as part of the Legion, marched to the bold height over-looking the river, where the new temple would stand. The military band played, and cannons boomed out boldly. The ladies of Nauvoo presented the Prophet and his officers with a United States flag woven of silk. Sidney Rigdon addressed the Saints; he was outspoken, almost flamboyant, and imbued them with a sense of the destiny of what they were doing this day. Nicholas felt it already, deep inside the quiet recesses of his heart. He was one of the first to volunteer as a worker on the edifice, willing to do any-thing the more skilled laborers asked him, aware as he was of how mediocre his own skills were. But what a privilege to work for the Lord and for the benefit of generations to come!

Thus, there was plenty to occupy Nicholas's time, and even his thoughts. He could feel the growth and progress that came from his efforts, yet it seemed to have nowhere to go. Some self-imposed boundary, tied to his feelings for Millie, prohibited his spirit from filling its true measure. He needed a wife, he knew it; but the realization left him cold and indifferent inside.

Chapter Twenty

Nauvoo, August, 1841

Dearest Millie,

On August second Leah gave birth to a fine, healthy son. They have named him Joshua Hyrum—Joshua for Edgar's father and Hyrum in honor of the Prophet's elder brother, who is Patriarch to the Church and the gentlest man God ever placed on this earth. So he is well named. And well loved, as you can imagine! Edgar is like a man in a dream; he holds Leah in awe, I believe, for having produced so perfect a being. I do believe Leah has been able to let go and accept this happiness, for the old gentleness plays about her mouth and there is a softness in her eyes that I have not seen since Missouri.

I hope all is well with you, Millie. You do nicely at writing newsy little tidbits, and your descriptions of the scenery are so vivid that I can hear the thundering of the tide and feel the salt spray on my face. But you say little about *you*. And that is what I wish to know. That is what I miss. Can you entrust more to me, dear heart, the way we used to in Boston in that world long ago, which I still hold in my heart?

My Katherine grows and changes daily. Her hair is a thick, tangled auburn, and her eyes remain blue. She enchants everyone. Even Mother can be coaxed away from her mercantile or philanthropic interests by Katy's entreatings and forget all else in watching the joy with which she learns and discovers the world about her. I believe it is best that Leah gave birth to a son. A little girl might have stirred the old memories and brought back all the heartache, but Joshua Hyrum can carve his own place, fresh and new.

I suppose I must tell you that I, too, am expecting a second time. This child will be born near the end of November, so Katherine will be a year old and walking and, hopefully, I can manage it! I find it difficult already to carry Katherine about for long spells, or to bend over to pick up after her or do work in the garden. And with time that will only grow worse. I hope I can find room in my heart for another child this soon. I am yet too enamored of my Katherine; she seems all I could ever possibly want.

Simon and Edgar are building a new house for Leah and Edgar and their family; Mother and Simon will remain in the old cottage for a time yet. It is strange how Mother doesn't seem to mind a bit. Perhaps because she is seldom home anyway. This spring there were a great many sick with the ague, and she went from house to house nursing and encouraging—and freely distributing Giles's store goods. He is, in truth, more patient with her than I am; I believe he understands her in a way that I can't.

Giles is such a hard worker and his business prospers, so I am free to concentrate my efforts on being a mother and a homemaker. He never fails to enter our home without coming in search of me and giving me a gentle kiss and a kind word before he turns his attentions elsewhere. Even Katherine cannot charm him away from this pattern. I cherish the sweetness of his love for me.

You may well ask how fares my mother's marriage with Simon. It weathers her eccentricities and independence of spirit quite well. Simon farms a large number of acres and works weekly on the new temple and seems content to let Mother fly about on her own business. And he dearly enjoys listening of an evening to her recounting of the day's adventures. He takes great pride in her work and in the vibrant sort of beauty she has managed to keep, despite her years. How evident is that pride when he walks out to meetings or parties with her on his arm! 'Tis an endearing sight, Millie, and I cannot be cold to him knowing how sincerely he loves her and seeing the indulgence that flows from his generous heart.

I've no time for more, dear heart. I am to go berrying with some of the neighbors this afternoon, and Leah, who has been watching both of our children, informs me that Katherine has just fallen and bumped her head and is crying for me. She begs forgiveness for being the cause of shortening my letter to you and sends her love—wishing to know if you are still as beautiful as she remembers you three years ago!

With love, your "less beautiful" and matronly friend,
Verity Winters

Despite the constant pain caused by her own inability to produce a child, Millie found she could rejoice, more and more as time passed, in the joys and successes of her dear friend. *Perhaps I am growing up,* she thought wryly. *Perhaps age is producing some fortitude in me, at least.*

She was to need it. As September brought cool mornings and the first hint of yellow in the green trees that topped the hillsides, Luther came home one day from the fishing and announced that he had signed on for a voyage to Singapore.

"How long will you be gone?" Millie asked, struggling to keep her voice even. It still bothered her that he made decisions without consulting her. They were two people who lived together, but they seldom functioned as one.

"Before summer's over. It's a short trick, really. We need the money, Millie—" He glanced up from the fish he was cleaning. "Maybe we need the time away from each other, too."

"Why do you say that?"

"You know, this thing about a baby, not having children, well, it's worn on us both. A separation might lighten the pressure and make it easier when I come back."

Half a dozen different retorts came to Millie's mind, but she only nodded and tightened her lips. She was learning that one skill which seemed requisite for a woman: to keep her mouth shut. But she had not figured out how to do so without also closing her heart, feeling a terrible tightening in her chest and the loneliness that followed.

She did not go to the harbor when the town turned out en masse to bid Luther's vessel godspeed. She could not bear the glances and whispers of the other women, of Almira in particular. Some may feel sorry for her, others disdain her, but they all knew she was unable to hold her husband because she could not produce the son he desired. They all knew she had failed.

To her amazement Luther seemed to understand. He did not press her or begin an argument when she announced her intentions. When he was ready to leave he drew her close to him, his big hand cupping her chin and covering half of her face.

"You're still the prettiest woman in all of Gloucester," he told her, his voice gruff with feeling. "I shall miss the sight of you, Millie." He kissed her for a long time; she could feel his reluctance to draw away from her. He sighed as they parted, and in his eyes she could see, like a shadow, the quiet loneliness of sea days and sea nights.

"I want to carry this lovely face with me," he said, "so that when I close my eyes I can see you. When I look out and there is only gray wave following gray wave, your warm mouth will smile at me and I can feel the touch of your lips pressing mine."

With that he hefted his sea bag and walked from the house, never looking back at her; that was considered bad luck. But Millie watched after him until he had disappeared from her sight. Even then she stood at the door, her eyes burning with unshed tears, her mind pitifully echoing and re-echoing Luther's last words.

Nicholas did not attend general conference meetings to socialize, as some did. He loved the concentration of power he perceived there as the Saints united in purpose and faith. Sidney Rigdon was an impressive orator, but Nicholas would far rather listen to Joseph Smith speak. No one could make the gospel seem as rich and alive as the Prophet could; no one else emanated such tender, unqualified love as one could feel in the Prophet's gaze when he looked over his people.

At first Nicholas did not even notice the commotion beside him as he concentrated on the words of the speaker. Then, as the sounds began to pierce his consciousness, he heard a voice call out, "Catch her! She's fainting!"

He turned just in time to open his arms and cradle the young woman's body as she fell. He lifted her effortlessly—she weighed no more than a child—and carried her to where his wagon rested in a small stand of trees. There was shade here, and quiet. He doused a cloth in water from the nearby river and bathed her forehead and pale, slender arms until he saw her begin to revive. Her eyes, when she opened them, were the softest brown he had ever seen.

"Where am I?" she murmured. There was such a mingling of fear and confusion in the brown eyes that Nicholas placed his hand over hers, which felt soft and smooth as a little white lily.

"You fainted in the press of people," he told her. "I brought you here." Then, as the confusion remained in her gaze, he added belatedly, "I am Brother Nicholas Todd. What is your name? Where are your people?"

"I have no people," she replied, her voice barely more than a whisper. "I am here all alone."

"But you must live somewhere, with someone . . ."

She sighed and struggled to raise herself. Her thick hair, which hung in soft curls to her shoulders, was the same warm shade of brown as her eyes. "My name is Helena Miller. I came over from England three months ago. My father had been a tin miner in Cornwall, but he died when I was a child, and my mother took sick our first day on the riverboat out of New Orleans." Her eyes seemed to grow larger as she spoke, and to take on a distant, almost haunted expression. "She lived long enough to see Zion with her own eyes, but died two days after we arrived."

"Have you no other relatives? No brothers and sisters?"

"No, there is no one. No one at all."

Overwhelmed with pity for her, Nicholas gazed into her eyes and was surprised to see in their rich depths a quiet confidence—a faith, really—that reached out and spoke to his own.

"What have you been doing to take care of yourself? Where have you been living?"

"That was three weeks ago. One of the sisters on the ship has a family of nine children. I live with her and help with the care of them."

"In a two-roomed cabin?"

"One room, actually." Her small mouth tightened resolutely; it was a lovely mouth, gentle and kind. "We get by."

"That is hard to believe!" Nicholas was becoming worked up and struggled hard to control himself. He demanded with sudden insight, "Have you enough to eat?"

"Not always."

"That's why you fainted, isn't it?" He grabbed hold of her

hand. "This must be ended. You're too frail for such treatment. I'm taking you home with me."

It was a resolve of the moment, but as soon as he had made it Nicholas felt the rightness of it flow through him. He drew a deep breath to calm himself. "My mother is ailing and could use help about the house, since my sister is largely occupied with her work as a seamstress." He paused. She was watching him, silent and wide-eyed. "They will welcome you, I assure you." He smiled and gently smoothed the hand he held. "There, that's settled and done."

For the first time he could ever remember Nicholas left meeting early. He drove the young girl to the new house he had built for his mother. He fixed her something to eat, then insisted she lie down to rest in his own room while he went back for his mother and sister.

When he explained what he had done his mother made no objection. In fact, her eyes took on that pleased, almost glazed look with which he had become so familiar. *Prospects for Nicholas again!* He could hear her mind churning out the thought. But, for the first time, it did not offend him. For the first time he had thoughts of his own that coincided with hers.

From the beginning Ellen Todd liked the slim, quiet English convert; in fact, she was wont to say that the first time she set eyes on Helena, walking a bit bleary-eyed and unsteadily into her kitchen, she knew this was the girl Nicholas would choose for his wife. Nicholas did not begrudge her the obvious triumph she felt, because he knew it was laced through with joy. She was not well, and the relief she felt at his marriage was understandable—in fact, it pleased him to be able to make her happy at last.

Five weeks after Helena's arrival in their household, where she fit in so beautifully and harmoniously, the two were married by Apostle Heber Kimball. Helena wore a truly elegant dress fashioned by her young sister-in-law, Lizbeth, and everyone who saw her agreed they had never set eyes upon a lovelier bride. A party was hosted in the bowery following the ceremony. The warm Indian summer weather held. Mellow and fragrant, the evening spun itself out until the tired couple sneaked away to the small cabin Nicholas had fixed up as their home.

Watching Helena move about in the cozy, lace-curtained room, Nicholas felt a warm confidence regarding his choice, the same confidence he had felt from the very beginning. Growing to know her better had not dispelled any of the aura of gentleness and kindness that clung to her. She had no great faults, no obvious weaknesses, nothing he had discovered to mar the beauty of her spirit. He felt himself a fortunate man. And he loved her tenderly, though he felt his affection did not match her own. Time would amend that, and would complete his healing. It had to; heaven would be merciful to him and grant it so.

Several days following their wedding, sometime past the middle of November, Nicholas was out walking alone by the river, a habit he still enjoyed whatever the temperament of the weather. His mind was empty of all thought or reflection as he enjoyed the beauties around him. Suddenly, a picture of Millicent Cooper came into his mind, a picture so vivid that it startled him. With it came an impression that she was in need of assistance of some kind, an impression urgent enough that he found himself searching for a secluded, overgrown place where he might lean against a tree, close his eyes, and offer a prayer for her.

He prayed a long time, but when he opened his eyes again a sense of peace flowed through him. He shook his head in wonderment at what he had just experienced, and picked his way back to the main path. However, he did not think it strange that a prompting should be given him concerning the girl in Gloucester. It seemed a natural order. For who else was aware of her and concerned for her welfare? Surely this meant that his prayers for her through the years were acceptable in the sight of heaven.

He went on his way thoughtfully, no longer aware of the landscape through which he walked as he contemplated life's entanglements and purposes which seemed so strange and wonderful, so above his own ways.

Millie heard the wind, like the keening of dying spirits, shiver around the sides of the schoolhouse. Shivering herself, she urged Thomas Erwin to dismiss school early and send the children home. A New England northeaster was blowing up, and this late in November it promised to be wicked indeed. Millie herself wasted no time in hastening home and battening down the hatches, protecting what she could from the gale force of the wind that was building, building, gathering strength as it churned the sand into spiraled eddies that whined with voices of their own.

All day the wind built and the sky became a deep, green-tinged black, with eerie lights playing through it. No living thing should be out in such weather, yet Millie knew there were ships out in the Georges or fishing off Sable Island that would be limping through the slashing seas toward a safe port. Her skin went cold at the thought of them, and she uttered a little wordless prayer in the back of her mind.

The sun did not go down; it had been blotted out long before nightfall. The storm possessed the sky and in its fierceness drove all the elements before its cold breath—a breath that had the smell of death in it. Millie, sitting alone with a book and a cup of hot tea, felt the house rock to the rhythm of the blast. She looked up from her book, straining to hear the sounds that the storm made, a dread sensation creeping over her that she was not alone.

"What is it?" she said aloud, and was flooded by a memory of the autumn morning beside the sea. Was it the spirits of the dead calling from their watery graves to her? Here in this house she had never felt a sense of the other world so strongly.

Something as powerful as an audible voice spoke the words, "Norman's Woe." Without hesitation Millie bundled up tightly, took her father's lantern, and walked into the black night and the storm.

She fought her way up Hesperus Road to the feet of the rocky promontory where lay the reef of Norman's Woe. Long before she drew near she could make out the swinging lights of many lanterns and hear the muffled warning of the fog bells sounding over the rock-bound coast. Scrambling on her hands and knees she slid and stumbled down the rough slope until she reached the broad shore, where the white water, whipped by the wind into boiling towers, rose before her like a living barrier. She felt herself shrink inwardly but forced her feet to move forward.

The sand and the shallow pools by the rocks were littered with debris from the wreck of a ship whose slanted, sinking hulk Millie glimpsed once imperfectly, then again as lightning parted the sky and the green lights glowed. Dozens of dark, silent shapes moved over the beach, bending and swooping like awkward gray birds as they scooped up the spoils. Millie called out, but she could not hear her own voice, and she knew no one else could. The wreckage of the dying ship would be picked as clean by these cold shapes around her as the bones of the dead are by black-plumed birds of prey. Millie turned. There was no reason for her to be here. She tightened her hand on the dancing, wavering light she carried and headed toward the slope. But a sudden sound made her freeze and then turn slowly around again.

In a shallow pool not three yards from her feet a large wooden chest was lodged between two rocks. The sound was coming from there. Millie moved closer, her eyes wide and cautious in the weird light, her heart beating with fear. The sound came again, and she knew with certainty this time that it was the distressed cry of a child.

Using a length of wood as a lever, she pried the battered lid open and, lifting her lantern above her, peered inside. Two big eyes stared back at her, dark and frightened, framed by hair as wet and stringy as seaweed.

Millie reached out slowly. "I won't hurt you," she said. The child could not hear her voice, but she saw her lips move and felt Millie's compassion reach out to her. She raised thin, shivering arms, and Millie secured the lantern, then lifted her out of the coffin and wrapped her long cape around the slight, trembling form. She could not have said how she managed to drag herself up the incline, balancing the swinging light and the weight of the child in her arms. By the time she reached her own cottage her whole body felt numb with the cold and the strain.

Once inside, she collapsed on the floor, and the child huddled near her, both drawing deep, ragged breaths but speaking no word. When her strength returned Millie carefully removed the child's sodden clothing, rubbed her down with a clean towel, and dressed her in a soft muslin frock that she dug out of the big chest where her mother had long ago stored her own outgrown clothes. She spoke as she worked, explaining what she was doing, humming under her breath as a way of soothing the child.

The large eyes moved about, watching Millie, and at length the terror in their gaze subsided. Millie warmed broth and coaxed her to eat a few bites. Seeing the girl's weariness, she lifted her and tucked her into the bed under the eaves where Millie had spent her own childhood.

The blue eyes fluttered and closed, protected by thin, blue-veined lids. The white face was almost translucent in the yellow glow of the candle. *A fairy child,* Millie thought, *given up by the sea.*

Studying the sleeping girl, Millie judged her to be three, perhaps four years old, no more. *She was sent to me,* she realized, a great shudder running through her. *Some power called me out into the storm.* The words "Norman's Woe" had come distinctly into her mind. But why her?

The wind continued to rage through the dark night, and a deluge of icy rain soaked the land and slashed the bucking seas in long silver streaks. In a stranger's bed the lost child slept the sleep of exhaustion, but Millie kept watch, cooing and crooning to her through the lonely gray hours before daylight.

The next morning the torn and battered land shivered beneath the cold sun. Bleary-eyed, the people of Gloucester turned out to view the wreckage and assess what damage the great storm had done.

Millie woke late, her muscles cramped from sitting for hours in the rocker. She felt drugged and light-headed. The child still slept, so thin and motionless that Millie's breath caught in her throat and she feared the little one might have died in her sleep. But reassured by the gentle rising of her chest, Millie washed and dressed and did half her morning chores before she heard the child wake and stir.

Millie was amazed anew at the deep blue of the girl's round eyes set in her pinched, white face. She spoke to the child, who made no attempt to respond. Gently and unhurriedly Millie dressed and fed her, explaining all the while that they two must walk into town and see what they could discover concerning her family and the ship that had carried her here. The docile child, her eyes nearly free of the alarm that had clouded them the night before, did all Millie asked.

Millie went straight to the wharfmaster, who knew of the drowned ship, but they had not recovered a ship's log or even a list of her passengers, route, or destination. He was not even sure of her name.

"We think she was the *Lady Elizabeth* out of New York heading for Portsmouth, but we can't be sure. There were no survivors as far as anyone knows." He peered down at the child.

Millie explained, and he shook his head back and forth as he listened. "I'll send out a bulletin right away," he assured her, "and we'll see what we come up with." He rubbed his chin. "May not be much. Can you keep her till then?"

Millie nodded.

"What's her name? Has she told you?"

"I can't get her to speak."

He slowly shook his head again. "Shock, I suppose. 'Tis a pity, and a great wonder that you discovered her, Millie. Well, leastways she's well off with you. I'll keep in touch." He touched the brim of his hat with thick, tobacco-stained fingers.

"Should we put an advertisement in the New York newspapers?"

"You might do that. Cost a pretty penny, and what can you tell of her, save a description? But you might do that if you'd like."

"Do you think the trunk might still be there on the beach? I'd like to look through it again. I don't remember seeing anything last night, but—"

"Nothing's left on the beach, lass. It's been picked clean as a bone. Take the child with you, and don't go expectin' no miracles."

Millie smiled up at him, a hard lump in her throat. She was hoping for a miracle, though not the one he spoke of. She was hoping against all hope that if the child's parents had perished in the wreck of the ship, no one would come forward to claim her. She was hoping that the storm gods had indeed sent her as a gift—a precious, unsought gift from the sea.

Days passed, then a week, then two weeks. Millie had paid for carefully written, meticulously thorough advertisements in both Boston and New York papers, but she heard no word at all. She began to let hope flutter within her like a fledgling bird. But she was also dismayed. Not once since the night of the child's arrival had she spoken a word. Millie knew trauma could do strange things to the mind, and she tried not to worry. Surely in time something would surface in the girl's thoughts, some inner resource rise to aid her. But meanwhile, her silence merely increased the mystery that clung to her. "Child of the sea," Millie whispered often, at times almost believing that she was some sort of a changeling, different from Millie and the children she taught at the school. Her eyes were as wide and blue and fathomless as the sea, and her hair was fair, almost white, like new sunlight on the first days of spring. She looked as if she could be Millie's own child, and that haunted Millie, too. She began calling her Adria, which means "woman from the sea."

When a letter from Verity arrived a week before Christmas telling of the birth of her second daughter, Millie didn't mind. For the first time she had something warm and tangible to wrap her own heart around, and talk of daughters did not fill her with pain.

> We have named this one Emmeline, and she is as different from Katy as she can be. Where Katherine is precocious, constantly teasing or begging, Emmeline seems quiet and docile and content to look on. Of course, I know it is far too early to tell, but one senses these things. Already there are signs that Leah's Joshua will give Katherine a run for her money once he figures out how to walk on his stout little legs. I predict he will be as big and burly as his blacksmith father, and I hope half as gentle and kind.
>
> Are you well, Millie! I hope you will be blessed during this season when we celebrate the brightest, best gift ever sent to this earth. I pray that God, who cares for all his children, will bless you with love.

She meant with a child, of course, though she was fearful of stating the words directly. Millie looked over to where Adria sat, playing with a rosy-faced doll Millie had made for her. "Your prayers have been answered, dear friend," she whispered. The air around them was sweet and melodious as the sea when the colors of sunset brush its surface with gentle shades of vermillion, burnished gold, and orchid as pale as the blush on a fairy's wing; when the evening birds raise their hushed lullaby to the sky, and the tide, with the same hushed murmur, caresses the shore; when one can almost hear the rhythmic breathing of nature in that great, glowing space.

> Some say that ever 'gainst that season comes
> Wherein our Saviour's birth is celebrated,
> The bird of dawning singeth all night long;
> And then, they say, no spirit dare stir abroad,
> The nights are wholesome, then no planets strike,
> No fairy takes nor witch hath power to charm,
> So hallow'd and so gracious is the time.

Millie read the words from Shakespeare's *Hamlet* aloud. Three years ago she had not known such beauty of language existed. Six weeks ago she had not known that life could be so hallowed and gracious as this day was. Her little sea woman sat by the fire drying her long, corn silk hair, the soft shadows playing along her white skin. Millie began to hum the words of her favorite carol, "Silent Night." Before she knew it she was snuggled on the long settle with Adria wrapped up in her arms, singing every Christmas song she could draw from her memory from long, long ago when her world was a child's world, made up of sea and sunlight and warm, moist sand, and dreams were as real as tomorrow's sunrise, and all things were possible because she believed. What had happened to that child? At this moment, with her own child soft at her side, she could believe again, if only a little. She could hope without fear. She could open her heart to tomorrow, whatever may come.

Chapter Twenty-one

The blustery month of March stirred up the land with an almost wicked glee after a mild, quiet February. Millie had been taking little Adria to school with her and she had become quite a favorite there, especially with the older girls, who enjoyed fussing over her, and the boys, who, with unexpected solicitation, protected her from every danger and saw to her every need. The child remained gentle and unassuming and never appeared to consider taking advantage of the kindnesses shown her. She answered to her name quickly and seemed to accept it. She still had not spoken, much to Millie's sorrow, and at times her silence became a weight. Millie longed for the spark of active communication the sound of the child's voice would bring. More than that, she longed to know what thoughts and feelings flitted across her young soul. She seemed to understand everything. If speech were restored to her, what might she reveal of the knowledge and experience she had gleaned these past months?

For Millie time had never gone by so quickly, or so enjoyably. Every day held new discoveries, seen through the eyes of this child: the coming of spring, with the arrival of the swallows, sand martins and finches, their voices shimmering through the warm May haze; the planting of sweet peas, poppies, forget-me-nots, and tender tea roses. Walks by the sea meant filling baskets and pails with sea stones and shells and bright bits of coral. The days warmed and lengthened, the sea stretched herself out like a sleek, lazy cat, and Millie found herself almost wishing that Luther would be late in coming, so as not to spoil the gentle perfection of these days she shared with her pale little will-o'-the-wisp by the sea.

* * *

21 June 1842

Dearest Millie,

So much has happened these past months that I do not know where to begin. We prosper, and thank heaven for it. I talk like a Mormon and have almost forgotten to wonder what effect it may have on you. I do wonder what you will think when I attempt to recount the experiences I have been having. Yet you are the first I think of, dear heart, to share my most sacred feelings with.

The brethren have begun conducting proxy baptisms for the dead in the temple—the living standing in for their ancestors who in life had no chance to hear the truth and accept the gospel. Hundreds are availing themselves of the opportunity. Sister Rockwell (whose son Porter is the Prophet's boyhood friend) has set a record, with forty-five baptisms for her own forebears. Mother must be a close second! She has organized all the records on the Boyles and Flynns and O'Brians and herds us all into the temple to do our part. I felt a bit squeamish about it at first, I must tell you. After all, who are we to say they want us doing this work for them, though I know the principle is that they are free to refuse if they like, but cannot progress without proper ordinances.

One afternoon in the temple I was sitting off alone by myself on a bench in the corner. I closed my eyes and began to think about what it was we were doing here and just where it might lead. Suddenly I was aware of the sound of sweet music sounding faint in my ears. Then my father's figure appeared before me—Oh, Millie, I know you can imagine what this would mean to me! Without thinking, I opened my eyes. He was still there. He lifted his head and turned slowly until his eyes met mine. The expression of his gaze pierced me like a shaft of pure light. I felt like singing out loud and at the same time weeping for joy. He smiled, and without moving or seeming to utter a word he *spoke* to me, Millie! I heard the rich tenor of his voice, vibrating with such tender affection that I did start to weep. *Do my work, daughter,* he said, *that we all may be united one day.* My mind sent the question out to him, *Then you approve of this gospel and of what we have done?*

His smile deepened; he seemed to nod his head gently in affirmation. Then his image seemed to fade away from before my gaze. But oh, the blessing he left! The sense of unity and peace that thrilled through my soul!

When we left the temple I could tell that Mother was watching me, though she said not a word. Later that evening, when she knew the children would be sleeping, she came to my house. "What did you see in the temple today?" she asked bluntly; you know Mother's ways. When I hesitated she said, almost matter-of-factly, "You saw your father, didn't you? My Anthony appeared to you."

For a moment I wondered if she would be angry with me. I had not sought the vision. I told her what he had said to me, and her wide, intelligent eyes filled with tears.

"It is as it should be," she said, with that rare tenderness in her voice that cuts to my heart. "If it had been me, none of you would have believed it. He had to choose you; all the more so because of the promise you made him."

She saw my eyes fill with amazement, and she chuckled softly—you know, the way she does under her breath. "Oh, I knew he was worried about how I would behave once he was gone, Verity. I knew when he called you in to him that he meant to lay the burden of my well-being on you."

"And you took advantage of it!" I replied, momentarily angry. "You knew you could get me to follow you here because of that promise and because of the love I bore Father!"

She admitted it freely. "Yes, I knew. I also knew your heart and the fine tenor of your mind, dear heart. If once you gave the principles of this religion a chance, I knew you would embrace it."

I dislike how right she always is, even when it works to my advantage. You may be asking, as you once did, "Do you really want this, knowing how she manipulated you? Is this your own free choice, even now?" Dearest Millie, if I could somehow make you feel the beauty and dignity of this religion! The testimony of truth is a fire that must burn in one's breast. If you felt it as I have, then you would know why I do not doubt.

Millie did not want to hear this. She had been feeling truly happy for perhaps the first time. She did not want thoughts of Nicholas to mar that happiness. She skipped a little ahead to where Verity wrote:

I hesitate to tell you, but must. Both Leah and I are expecting again. Just barely. I would say both children should come by late February or early March. I never fancied myself the motherly type, yet here I am, Millie, with a baby a year. I shall have to find some way to slow this thing down or I will have no energy left with which to care for those I already have. It is lovely to think of Leah and me having little ones so close together. I only pray all goes well, as I pray for you and the beautiful gift God has given you.

Your friend and loving sister in spirit,
Verity

Perhaps I can relax now that I have Adria to care for, Millie mused. *Perhaps now my own child will come.* But lately it didn't seem to matter as much as it used to. She had a child she could love, a child she could care for with all the tenderness and compassion of her woman's heart.

A checkered pattern was beginning to emerge that perhaps some were not aware of. But Nicholas perceived it with a sense of unease. During the first part of the year Joseph Smith printed installments of his translation of the book of Abraham in the *Times and Seasons.* It excited much attention in the East. The *Boston Daily Ledger* called the Prophet "the greatest original of the present age." The Church was earning respect in the world at large. But closer to home the stirrings of their old enemies were beginning to make themselves felt. Just as the Saints had begun to believe that all was truly peace and prosperity, Joseph Smith was arrested in connection with the attempted murder of Governor Boggs. And intelligent, charismatic John C. Bennett, mayor of Nauvoo through the Prophet's good graces, twisted the truths Joseph had taught him and, with all the power of his nature, turned against the Church with vehemence. There was unrest from enemies both without and within, and the Prophet was in hiding because justice would never be a luxury he could claim. Nicholas felt the Saints were taking one step backward for each step forward, just as in Missouri and the last days of Kirtland. It frightened him.

In August, when Joseph was illegally arrested, Nicholas became part of a network of brethren who were organized to scout for trouble and, if necessary, even at a moment's notice, to protect the Prophet from his enemies. Nicholas would never forget these days—feeling the comradeship of the men but the tension as well, knowing as each did that he may well be called upon to give his own life for the safety of the Prophet and for the sake of the work. The finality of the commitment was a cleansing of a sort for Nicholas. All that was insignificant in his life fell away and he was able to perceive the pure essence of what was essential, what was necessary, even noble in his life. The insight altered him. Each time he returned from a tense night of riding, waiting, and watching, his eyes and ears straining to detect the least motion or sound, Nicholas felt he had become more sober about life, yet at the same time more appreciative, as though all his senses had been fine-tuned. When he had Helena in his arms and smelled the fragrance of her hair against his cheek he was overcome with the beauties and blessings that were his.

In August his sister, Lizbeth, married her sweetheart, Frederick Rich. It was a good match; the two families had already proven to be compatible in most every way. He wondered if Lizbeth might end up producing the first grandchild for his mother. It had been nearly nine months since he and Helena were married, and there was no sign of a child as yet. Save for his mother, he was of himself in no hurry. Once children came they were always with you. He was enjoying the days alone with Helena—the quiet tranquility of them, the exclusive pleasure of having to answer to no one but each other.

September was often as hot in Illinois as was August. The first sign of autumn was the corn drying on its stalks in the fields and the dead insects drying in the boggy marshes of the low river lands. Working outside on the temple in such weather was pleasant for Nicholas, who was usually cooped up indoors. The sun was warm on his neck and the back of his head as he bent over his work; he could feel it prickle his skin underneath his thin cotton shirt.

Reaching into the barrel for a handful of wooden nails, he noticed a man walking toward him—a squat little man bristling with red hair and good humor. Nicholas froze, not believing his eyes.

"Gerry Hines!" He shouted the words so loudly that half a dozen heads raised to look at him. The little Englishman paused and scratched his craggy cheek with a stubby finger.

"Me lad!" he suddenly cried, recognition flooding his eyes. "Fancy meeting the likes of you here. I thought you were done for, I did, when they sent you home looking more like a corpse than a living man."

Nicholas laughed out loud in his pleasure. "Heaven knows how anyone lives in your miserable English climate, Gerry, but here I am."

"Aye, and here I am!" Gerry beamed, sticking out his round barrel chest and rubbing his hands up and down his shirt front. "Took me awhile, lad, but here I am."

There was little work done for the next half hour as the two talked over the happenings of the past years. Nicholas was tickled to learn that Gerry had taken a wife. "A gentle English lady," he boasted. "I've settled down right and proper, if you can believe that."

So his work had borne more fruit than he had expected, Nicholas mused. *How hasty we are to make our own conclusions and counsel the Lord. How unpromising my first convert, the drunken owner of a grog shop, had seemed.*

"It's been these twelve month and more since I've tasted liquor," Gerry assured Nicholas. "Eat my wife's good cooking instead." He patted his ample belly as if in confirmation. Nicholas smiled, remembering the substantial girth of it back in England, thanks to stout and cheap ale.

Nicholas worked the remainder of his shift in a glow of pleasure, anticipating what joy it would be to tell Helena of his chance discovery when he returned home that night. But, walking through the city as the sunset burned the sky with flames of orange and yellow and masses of smoldering red, he thought of the sunsets over the ocean in Liverpool—and in Gloucester—and of the girl with hair like sunlight who had walked by his side.

* * *

Luther stared at Adria too long and too hard. The child trembled beneath his gaze.

"She's a pretty little thing, isn't she?" Millie urged.

"Send her out to play, Millicent. I want to talk to you."

Adria had skipped past them and was out the door even as Luther spoke.

"I don't know, Millie." Luther scratched his tanned forehead. "I don't know if I can live in the same house with somebody else's child. She watches us, Millie . . . I don't know what she's thinking or where she's been. I thought it would be just the two of us, you know, alone, when I came home. You can see that."

Millie let him wear out all his feeble excuses. "Adria was sent to me." She spoke the words slowly and firmly. "She *is* my child. If there are others, I shall be as happy as you will be, Luther, but do not think you can harm this child because of your own pride and selfishness."

He blinked back at her, bull-angry and uncomprehending. His eyes were growing dark, taking on the brooding look she so hated to see.

"She belongs here," said Millie. "She feels safe and loved. I won't have you spoil that."

His silence was exactly the answer she was dreading.

"She'll do you no harm." She made her voice come out gentle. "She's been a blessing so far. Let her be, Luther. Give her the bit of space she requires."

It was little enough she was asking him, and he knew it. He growled low under his breath to show his displeasure and to cover what they both knew: that in the end he would acquiesce. But that was not what Millie wanted—what in the long dark stretches of the night she had dared to desire. She wanted Luther to embrace the child. She wanted to see Adria draw tenderness from him, to unite the three of them into something they had not been before. She could if Luther would let her. But Millie shouldn't have hoped. She should have known better. She should have planned for the reality, not the dream.

A few minutes later Luther marched down the rock path, heading back to town to have some of his nets fixed and to check on the condition of his Chebacco boat, which his partners had been plying these last months without him. Millie watched him

179

with tears in her eyes. He had come home nearly as restless as he had been when he left her, and Adria's presence had not helped any. The summer was nearly worn out. There was school to look forward to, and the last push of harvesting, drying, and preserving before winter set in. The endless round of season following season was much more meaningful now that she had Adria to share it with. But what of this man? What of the harmony between husband and wife? The depth of her loneliness could not be cured by a child's love; well she knew that.

She dried her wet eyes on the sleeve of her frock and turned to go back in the house. Seemingly out of nowhere Adria glided across the garden and threw herself at Millie, wrapping her arms around her legs and nearly upsetting her balance. "Mother!" she cried, hiding her face against Millie's apron.

The word seemed to hang in the air. Millie placed her hand on the girl's head. "Adria? Dear, it's all right."

The child had never seen Millie cry. She lifted a tear-stained face and repeated the exclamation. Millie gently disentangled herself and knelt down by the child, drawing her into her arms, where she burrowed her face against Millie's shoulder.

"It's all right, dear heart," she crooned. "I *am* your mother, and I love you and will take care of you always. Don't be afraid."

For a long time they knelt on the stone path together, rocking gently back and forth in each other's arms, Adria saying, "Mother, Mother," over and over again.

That was the beginning. Once Adria's voice came back to her she used it almost incessantly, except when Luther was in the house. Then, like a small, timid bird, she would retreat under the protection of Millie's wide apron, or find some book and disappear into a corner. If the weather was mild, like as not she would go out by the sea and play on the long, sandy shore. Millie often found her there when she was not playing in the garden or beneath the shady trees on the hill slope with her toys and her dolls. She was a solitary child, and the sea seemed to draw her, harboring no nightmares and terrors of the dread night she had spent there. That all seemed wiped away, or never to have existed at all.

Luther relaxed a little into a routine that revolved around

Millie and the running of the household foremost, Adria next, and himself last of all. Such it was in all seamen's houses, as well he knew. But he had an excuse for resenting it because of Adria's presence. And the old excuse returned again, uneasily at first, then scarcely disguised.

"I've been home nearly eight weeks now, Millie," he began one night after Adria was safely in bed. "End of September the mackerel stop runnin' and I've got to decide what to do."

He had been trolling and chumming with small bait from his Chebacco boat up and down the whole coast, and doing well. But he was right; it was time to make a decision.

"What would you like to do?"

He ran his fingers through his hair. His eyes grew cloudy. "It's not easy to say. I could work the coastline all winter if I thought it would be worth it."

Millie swallowed and clenched her hands into fists to stop her trembling. "Is that the only reason to stay home, Luther? In hopes of making a baby? What about being with me?"

"I didn't mean it that way."

"I think you did." Her words fell into a silence that was as dense as a stone. She hated these silences. "I can't do anymore about it than you can. Maybe it's not even my fault."

Luther's head came up at that. But at least she had got his attention.

"Why don't you realize how much I suffer, Luther? Do you think this is easy for me?" She wanted to mention the dozen ways in which she suffered, but knew that would both tire and anger him and serve no point. He was not one to be moved to sympathy by whining and complaining. As was to be expected with him, in the end it was her beauty that softened him.

"Ah, Millie," he sighed, reaching out for her and stroking her hair. "You look hardly more than a child yourself. You're the loveliest thing—the loveliest thing—" His lips found hers, and he kissed her with a tenderness that brought tears to her eyes. "A woman pretty as you shouldn't have to worry about anything. You're just about right as you are."

The following morning before going out to the boat he announced his decision, a decision that would dictate both their lives but which he had made, in his customary habit, alone.

"I'll stay close this winter. Maybe work the Georges a little later, see what happens, take it step by step."

He expected her to be pleased, and she was. But only as far as it went. The veil of her loneliness still separated them; she wondered idly as she watched him walking away if he lived within his own lonely vacuum or if, largely unaware, he gave it no thought at all.

Chapter Twenty-two

"Yes, Mother, we are certain. The child should be born sometime in September."

It was a good way to start the new year—a gift for Nicholas's mother that brought a frail but tender light back into her eyes. She had been failing; perhaps the bitter winter weather was taking its toll. Now Nicholas knew she would want to hold on until this child was born.

There were other good omens. Judge Pope of the Supreme Court in Springfield dismissed the charges against the Prophet. Free again, Joseph held a feast at his house in honor of his release. The Saints dedicated Tuesday, the seventeenth of January, as a day of fasting, prayer, and thanksgiving to God. Nicholas had much for which to be thankful. He only prayed that the Lord would be merciful and allow the Saints to live peaceably with their non-Mormon neighbors, though deep in his heart he knew that truth has always been beset by opposition, and the agency of man is not tampered with, even by heaven. It was so difficult, though, to want to live as other men—to reap what one planted, to raise one's children in peace and safety—and be denied.

City of Nauvoo, March 7, 1843

Dearest Millie,

They are here! Two perfect girls, who arrived within days of one another. Mine is called Julia, and Leah's, Jenny. One would think they were twins—one would think Leah and I were giddy girls, for all the delight we take in them. I am so grateful, Millie! Life has been good to me.

There are nearly a dozen wards in Nauvoo and over 15,000 people, many of them converts who keep pouring in. Why can't you be one of them and come help me care for my babies? Katherine is more filled with vim and vigor than ever before, now that she can run anyplace at her fancy. Emmeline, thank heaven, is a mild, patient little thing. What should I do if I had two like Katy? Mother is the only one who can control her, and she enjoys the contest, as I think Katy does, too.

Oh, I miss you! Shall we ever see one another? Can it really be years that have separated and changed us? I cannot write more at this time, but know, dearest Millie, that you are still in my thoughts, despite the press of duties that fill and crowd my days. Do not forget that I pray for you always,

Your friend,
Verity

Millie received Verity's letter near the beginning of April, which was really an ending, a closing, a dying for her.

Sable Island was set among shoal waters that afforded ideal feeding ground for halibut, cod, and haddock, fish greatly desired by Gloucestermen. Nowhere was the fishing better than close in on the two long bars that formed northwesterly and northeasterly, making the island a full, deep crescent. Yes, nowhere was the fishing so good or so dangerous as here. The island had earned well its name of Graveyard of the Atlantic. Two hundred-odd wrecks of one kind or another had settled into her sands, and they say that the bones of hundreds of men lie scattered and bleaching along her shores. Yet of all the men who sailed the sea, Gloucester fishermen were the only ones who did not give the island wide berth in winter; even less so when March had blown itself out and they could feel spring stirring.

It was here that Luther had gone aboard Billy Turner's schooner the *Suzanna* as part of a seining fleet. In the early morning hours of the tenth of April a gale struck in force. The curtain of night had not yet lifted, and whirls of snow, as frozen as small chips of ice, beat down upon the ships until sight was impossible. The world closed in upon them and became no more than the white madness that circled their heads.

Inch by inch some of the ships limped out to sea, and by late afternoon the first of the fleet nosed into harbor in Provincetown, Yarmouth, and Marblehead. One vessel did not return. Some reported having seen it driven ashore on the long bars and feared for its fate, but no mortal eye watched the disappearing hull of the *Suzanna* who lived to tell the tale. She did not return with the others. She and the men who went down with her had become part of history now.

It was Jim Trollop who came to tell Millie. She swayed a little, and he swore to the men later that her pretty young face had turned gray. After he left her she sat alone in the blackness; she could not bear the thought of lighting a lamp. She needed the darkness to cover and hide her. She pulled her knees up to her chin, rocking and keening softly. *You are gone, Luther, with no word between us, no last kindness, no understanding before this swift end!* Perhaps time would have helped and befriended them, perhaps a child would have come, and the tenderness that could soften Luther's eyes when he succumbed to Millicent's physical beauty would have blossomed and grown into what she had longed for. Perhaps—perhaps! But there was no perhaps. She had become a mourner for the second time in her life, and Luther had become part of a legend that belonged to the sea.

The sudden commotion at the back of the room made Nicholas tense his muscles and turn his head sharply. Brother Clayton! Why would he interrupt a meeting in progress? The man walked the length of the hall until he reached Hyrum Smith, and the instinctive fears of nearly every Saint in the room were confirmed. Joseph was in trouble, perhaps hurt, perhaps dead? No, never that! The Lord would protect him; the Lord had always protected him.

Hyrum dismissed the meeting and requested the brethren to meet with him at the Masonic Hall, but so large a number rushed to answer his request that the building couldn't hold them. They adjourned to the Green, where they were told the story of Joseph's capture by Constable Wilson of Illinois and Sheriff Reynolds of Missouri. Nicholas realized that many about him appeared to remember these men. Murmured threats, like the sound of a wind rising, spread through the crowd.

Volunteers were organized, part to ride overland, part to travel by river to Joseph's aid. The air was electric with the fears and tensions of over three hundred men. Nicholas was assigned to ride overland toward Peoria in a group of 175 men.

When he went home to pack a few things and tell Helena what had happened, he expected to meet with some opposition. She only tightened her mouth into a thin line and was silent. He pulled her gently close to him. "You are such a good wife," he said, "What would I do without you?"

She sighed in his arms and nestled closer. He loved her with a tenderness that increased every day he lived with her. "Take care of yourself while I am away," he made her promise. "It shouldn't be long."

"I will pray for your safety," she said, and her voice trembled a little. As he rode off to meet the others he tried to hold onto the warmth of her, the beauty of her eyes smiling after him, the strength of her love.

They must have been a singular sight: 175 men riding across the prairie, dark shadows against the crimson-streaked sky. The following day they divided so as to make their way in smaller groups through the country. After all, they were Mormons, and Mormons excited not only attention but suspicion when they gathered in any size group at all. In the morning their captain, Brother Grover, met Stephen Markham, who had been sent by the Prophet to instruct the brethren to join him at Monmouth. Joseph had obtained a writ of habeas corpus in Dixon which allowed him to obtain a hearing in Nauvoo, whose municipal courts had a right to try cases under such writs. Over the next several days Joseph's brethren arrived in small squads. His two captors grew more and more nervous as they found themselves surrounded by the same men they had bullied under protection of the law and driven from their homes. Nicholas thought they were a sorry, sniveling sight, the two of them. But he was not surprised at the directions Joseph had given that no one was to injure a hair of their heads or cause them any discomfort.

By noon of the thirtieth of June the Prophet's company of 140 men approached Nauvoo. Word had been sent ahead, and the whole town came out to meet them in a long train of carriages, with the brass band playing and the cannon firing in time with the tune. Joseph mounted his horse, Old Charley, and rode straight through the town to the Mansion House, where his little ones crowded about him, welcoming him with the unreserved delight that is the special province of children.

Nicholas, watching the scene, had tears in his eyes. Never had he been prouder to be a Latter-day Saint than at this moment. The dignity and purity of this man, Joseph Smith, impressed him anew, and he rode to his own house feeling nothing but gratitude for the privilege he had of walking and talking with such a man.

Dearest Millie,

I take up my pen with reluctance, for what I must tell will, I know, meet with censure and misunderstanding. So I pray, dear heart, that you keep as open and merciful a mind as you can.

The Lord has made known, through revelation to the Prophet, the practice of plural marriage—the taking of more than one wife. There has been rumor about such things existing or coming in the Church for some time. Not a soul I have talked with—male or female—is anything but troubled by the idea, but as Saints we are taught to follow the Lord's command, as were the Lord's people in ancient times. I do not understand it myself! But some have been called to live this principle, and Mother's Simon is one.

When he first told her of his directive, as gently as he could—how can a man tell a wife gently that he is going to supplant her or diminish her station by taking another!—Mother said nothing but walked straight out of the house and over to Brother Hyrum Smith's. "He would know how to explain it," she told me later, "better than anyone could."

I guess he converted her, or at least placated her, for never a word of complaint has escaped her lips. "This is a hard thing," I said to her myself, "a hard thing to ask after all else we have been through."

I think she came close to agreeing with me at that time, but instead she said—gently for her—"The Lord has his purposes. He has always asked the most difficult things of his people."

"Why?" I persisted, my heart sick within me.

"To fit them for heaven, my dear heart," she replied. "We

are mortals, and we tend to live for mortality and altogether forget that we are here to grow and to prove ourselves for something better. If we only could see!"

I did not think polygamy "better" then, and do not now, but I held my tongue. I did not wish to torment her, brave as she is. I wonder what it has cost her inside. Something terrible. At times I glimpse in her eyes a pain, almost a desperation, that goes straight to my heart. Many whisper that this will be the undoing of us—all the excuse our enemies need to wipe us off the face of the earth. I try to reason calmly and have faith. But that is not easy when just last month, a constable from Hancock County and a sheriff from Missouri came and arrested the Prophet for "treason" while he and Emma were visiting relatives over by Dixon. These men are bold and cruel and will stop at nothing if they believe they can get away with it. They did not this time, but actually ended up being arrested themselves. And what did the Prophet do, after they had bruised and bullied him and even threatened to kill him? He and Emma provided a good supper for them, seated them at the head of their table, and Emma served them herself! Could you or I do that, Millie? I wonder, at least concerning myself.

You may be thinking that Joseph is a monster himself to suggest such a practice as polygamy, but that is not so. A more modest and Christlike man you could never know. 'Tis not his idea, but comes from God, and Joseph has resisted for years. But now there is no way to escape it.

Oh, Millie, pray for us. If our enemies rise up against us again, what shall we do? Where shall we go? They have already pushed us to the edge of the civilized world. And to leave Nauvoo! All who are here have poured our life's blood into it, and we love it well. To walk away—again—leaving all behind us . . .

Millie could feel Verity's pain reach out and wrap itself around her own heart. She could not even imagine life as her friend described it. How could they endure this life she described?

She pondered that question on and off all day long. When she tucked Adria into her bed, warm and cozy as a little nest, an answer came to her unbidden. *To love something good and noble, to give your life to it—that alone brings joy, that alone brings peace.*

She scorned the thought, wondering what had put it inside her head. Restless, she walked the night beach, alone with the sound of the breakers gently rolling to shore, alone with the sky, so endless and mysterious over her head. Did Luther really exist somewhere up there still? Did her father and mother? What could heaven possible be like if it was merely a hodgepodge of people in various conditions of sinfulness and goodness, much as it was here? Did Luther miss her, if thought and feeling were granted him? Were there things he regretted and wished he could come back and change? If he were to appear—to walk across the gray beach toward her this minute—would she be willing to change herself, too?

She hated the questions, the eternal questions that had no answers. She missed Luther, more than she had ever dreamed she could, knowing he would never return. His death had closed her up in another vacuum, much as when she first returned to Gloucester. In part that was Almira's doing, who, in her perversion, would blame even his death on Millie. People listened to her. And she was not only good at telling the worst things but at altering and rearranging the facts to fit her purposes.

Millie couldn't fight back. She didn't know how, nor did she have the heart for it. She looked after her own business, tended the house and garden and Adria, helped out at the school. Beyond the confines of her own little world, there was no life for her.

Adria was a quiet child, but she was eternally curious. Sometimes when there was little for her at school Millie would let her go down to the wharves and visit the old sailors who sat around telling stories and mending nets. She had asked Blind Billie to keep a watch on her, which to some might have seemed strange. But Billie knew every sound and breath on the waterfront and could identify half a dozen people or more by their footfall along the boards.

The child quickly became a favorite among the seamen. They taught her their ditties and songs and rehearsed for her tender ears the old legends of ships and sirens, maidens and their sailor lovers. She was a good listener, and quick to remember all they told her, at times correcting one of them solemnly when he got any of the facts in a story wrong. They took to teasing her by making mistakes on purpose, and it tickled them to hear her painstakingly retell it the way it should be. "She's a rare one," they whispered among themselves. "Long as she's alive and well the old ways won't die."

One afternoon she came skipping home along the sand, singing loudly at the top of her lungs, "My truly, truly fair, truly, truly fair, how I love my truly fair . . ." Millie paused at her work in the garden to listen. "There are songs to sing her, trinkets to bring her, flowers for her golden hair."

Millie put her hand to her hair and lifted it lightly. What was it the stranger had said? *Like the colors of a young fawn when the sun dapples his coat*—those were the words Nicholas had used. It had been a long time since she had given a thought to him. Yet now it all rushed back to her with the words of the song. She closed her eyes, wanting desperately to remember—wanting desperately to forget.

Adria came up to her, and she put her arm around the child's waist.

"Do you like the pretty new song I learned, Mother?"

"Yes, dear heart, I do." She pushed the child's damp golden hair back from her forehead and then bent to her work, while Adria sang the verses over and over again for her to enjoy.

For the first time Nicholas wasn't sure he agreed with the Prophet's decision. Run for president of the United States! Not one man in ten thousand would understand. Nicholas knew the logic behind it. They had learned these past few weeks in the congressional elections that both parties resented, even hated them, yet courted their favor, hoping to secure the Mormon vote en masse. Joseph had written letters to five candidates for the presidency concerning their views regarding the Saints. Three of the candidates replied, but they seemed to have little sympathy for members of the Church. So, how could the Saints as a body, or individually, support any of them? It was a powerful statement Joseph was making by putting himself forward as a candidate. A necessary statement, perhaps. But an anti-Mormon meeting had already convened in Carthage, calling upon all good and righteous men to assist in humbling the pride of that "audacious despot,"

Joseph Smith. Nicholas was fearful of the emotional consequences that may result from this move.

Late in September Helena gave birth to a son. Her labor was long and difficult. Nicholas was amazed at the joy in her face when the midwife at last permitted him to go in to her.

"I've given you a son," she said, smiling weakly.

He loved her so much at that moment that he felt tears choke in his throat. He leaned his head against hers and whispered his love for her until she blushed softly and pushed him away.

They named the boy William Abel—William after her father. But everyone called him Abel, everyone except Helena, who liked to laughingly refer to him as Abe. Nicholas's mother fussed over both of them; watching her Nicholas wondered where her strength came from. Ever since the onset of the past winter she had become thin and frail, her small frame shrinking upon itself visibly. Helena gave up the child to her no matter how often she requested. When Nicholas attempted to praise her for her kindness, she grew serious.

"I really don't think she will be with us long, Nicholas. I've seen too many signs. Sometimes I believe this new love for Abel is the only thing that sustains her from day to day. As much as she is ready to go on to the husband who awaits her, I know she hates the thought of tearing herself away from him." There were tears in her eyes. "And when she is gone he will have no grandparents, Nicholas, no one but you and me."

"Then he shall have all a child requires and more, my dear." He kissed her pale cheek, so cool to the touch of his lips.

She smiled, knowing he tried to comfort her. But it was a sorrow to both to be bereft of parents and family, to feel they stood alone against the world, especially in times such as these.

As fall hardened toward winter, reports of violence filtered in from the solitary farms and homesteads along the prairie, which were the first and easiest prey. And before the year had sighed itself out, Ellen Todd let go of life herself, with one long, gentle sigh.

She could not be buried beside her husband, but Nicholas found a choice spot in the new cemetery heading east on Parley, just outside of town. A slender linden tree standing on a small rise sheltered it. There would be a good view from here, and the violent storms of winter would be softened by the strong, growing tree.

Through the heavy weight of his sorrow, one comfort gnawed at the edges of Nicholas's consciousness: she rested in peace. When the persecutions came again, as Nicholas felt they were bound to, she would be beyond their power, and safe.

Summer was an easy time. Millie could be consumed from sunup to sundown by her garden and be all the happier for it. But best of all she liked the early days of autumn, warm still with the last fruitfulness of summer, and ripe with the smells of harvest and the age-old customs of gathering, gleaning, and garnering all the bounties of earth. She and Adria got by. She sold some of the produce from her garden on marketing days, and did an occasional piece of sewing for various people in the town. Luther's friends were good to her, remembering her with choice fish when their catches were good. And, of course, she had her little bit of income from her work at the school. They seldom felt a real pinch. As Christmas approached she knitted scarves and mittens and sold them to help finance the gifts she planned for Adria.

She noted the November day that marked two years since Adria had come to her. She had considered the idea of using this date as a birthday for the child, but thought better of it; she was superstitious about such things. Instead she selected the second of February, as the long, dark winter was beginning to break up and spring seemed a possibility. This gave them a real cause to celebrate and to forget for one day, at least, the dreary sameness of the harsh, frozen landscape and the short winter days.

She could only guess at the child's age, thinking for the thousandth time how strange it was that she seemed to come from nowhere, with no past, only this beautiful, clean surface upon which she and Millie together began to etch the experiences and impressions of her new life. The tightness Millie had lived with for months, the trembling of her hands every time she had searched through her mail, seemed but a memory now. By rights of the heavens, Adria was hers.

She decided Adria had been four when she came out of the sea, feeling it safer to err in that direction than the other. The child's native brightness would compensate for any error. That would make her six on this birthday, a very big girl indeed. Millie gathered her courage and invited some of the little girls from the school near Adria's age to come out to the house. They played "Blind Man's Bluff" and "Hide the Thimble" and "I packed my trunk to Saratoga and I put in"—a bonnet, or a parasol, or even a crocodile. It was delightful to see what the children came up with. Adria had the best memory of all and never lost track of the items or left one out when it was her turn. When they had had enough of the games, and Adria had opened the little gifts the children had brought, it was time to enjoy the goodies Millie had set out for them: warm raspberry tea laced with lemon, scones with rose petal jelly, strawberry rhubarb tarts, and lemon lace cookies.

Only the lengthening shadows forced Millie to end the festivities, bundle up the little girls in their wraps, and send them scampering home. She and Adria walked into town with some of the younger ones, stopping to visit Blind Billie, who sat in his rags on an upturned log playing thin, eerie tunes on his Irish pipe.

The lilting melodies stayed with them as they walked home hand in hand through the gray evening, and seemed to enchant the very air which they moved through, seemed to hallow the day. Millie trembled with gratitude and clung to the little fingers that wrapped round her own.

Chapter Twenty-three

Millie had been almost sick with worry these past months. When she stood at Almira's counter and saw Verity's familiar writing, she snatched the letter right out of Almira's hands. Almira scowled at her, looking so much like a nasty witch that Millie had to suppress a sudden giggle.

"Thank you, Almira," she called gaily, waving the letter.

Almira muttered under her breath and shuffled into the back room, leaving her alone. Today Millie didn't care; today she had Verity's letter. She waited until she was home in the garden, which smelled of buds and new grass, to open it up.

My dearest Millicent,

Here it is April of 1844, a new year; the long winter is over and past. But it very nearly was the last of this world's winters for me. I know you must be worried and wondering why I have neglected you, but these past months I have been beyond thought or care for anyone or anything. I have been in the grips of the terrible typhus fever, and close to death. Leah also was ill, so Mother and the men had their hands full caring for us and keeping the children away from their poor mothers, while at the same time seeing to all the little ones' needs. By the time Julia and Jenny celebrated their first birthdays we were able to sit with them and be in some small way a part of the festivities. How grateful I was to feast my eyes on my beautiful children again and be spared this time from death's grip, granted the privilege of loving them and raising them up to the Lord. Certainly this is the heart of life, isn't it, Millie? When I think of you and your precious Adria I know of a certainty that God sent her to you. And what a fortunate child she is to learn life from your wisdom and example!

Millie let the letter drop to her lap. She felt uneasy and inadequate when Verity praised her. What wisdom, what depth of understanding and feeling did she have to transmit? Certainly little when compared with Verity, whose faith was so strong, whose merciful nature extended to all, without question or qualification. True, she was not bitter and narrow-minded like Almira, but was she all that she should be—for Adria's sake?

You will be interested to learn what has happened with Mother during this time. Simon's second wife is a woman by the name of Margaret Brady, a young widow, actually, not many years older than I. When she first came into the household Mother was polite, but she largely ignored her, working 'around her,' so to speak, with her usual efficiency. Now the girl is with child and ill, and she seems pathetically ignorant of how to care for herself. Mother has begun to fuss over her; you know how she is, Millie. It bring tears to my eyes to see Maggie's simple gratitude. I believe she adores Mother and now, like an eager child, does everything she can to please her. Bless Mother. I don't know if I could do the same in her place. But how right and beautiful love and mercy are, under any conditions. Don't you agree?

Do I? Millie wondered. Uneasily she thought of Almira. She may be harsh and uncharitable, but Millie had used that as ample excuse to close her own heart to the woman. Since Luther's death she had not once invited Almira to her home, she had not once been kind; civil, yes, even respectful, but nothing beyond that. How did Verity have this power to pierce to the core of her being and make her want to be good?

Thus we are getting by now, better than before, and we are grateful for God's mercies. I shall write again, as my strength returns to me and I begin to pick up the threads of responsibility which are mine.

Stay well and happy yourself, my dear heart.

Your Verity

Millie raised the letter and pressed it to her lips. A fleeting vision of Judith, with flaming eyes and a gentle mouth, passed through her mind. What would she do without the friendship and example of these extraordinary women?

She folded the letter and placed it carefully in the deep silk-lined box with the others. This box had been her mother's, and one day it would be Adria's. The natural order of life, at this moment, seemed a marvelous thing to her. She would do better. She had much to be grateful for, too. She walked back to the garden humming a tune under her breath, feeling strong and happy inside.

Nicholas heard the commotion outdoors and wondered why it sent a chill along the surface of his skin. He walked to the front window and looked out to see Porter Rockwell riding down the middle of the street, shouting like a crazy man. He hurried to the front door and threw it wide open.

"They have killed Joseph! They have shot the Prophet! They have killed Joseph!"

He kept repeating the words over and over again. Each word was thick with the man's own tears and anguish. Nicholas, feeling suddenly weak, leaned against the door frame. His whole body was trembling. This could not be so! God in heaven, what would they do without Joseph!

But it was true. A mob consisting largely of the Carthage Greys stormed the jail where Joseph, Hyrum, John Taylor, and Willard Richards were being held. Governor Ford, who had pledged his protection personally to the Prophet, departed from the city without him, literally leaving the prisoners to their fate.

A depressed stupor sat on Nicholas's mind. The streets of Nauvoo were shrouded with a dark sense of gloom. As a member of the Legion Nicholas chafed to be called out to ride in vengeance to Carthage, but when Brother Richards brought back the bodies of the Prophet and Patriarch he urged the Saints to keep the peace. Addressing them outside the Mansion House, he said, "I have pledged my honor and my life for your good conduct—knowing your hearts as I do."

"Be still, and know that I am God." The phrase kept running over and over again through Nicholas's head. The worst had happened. Where in the world could they go from here? How could they go on without Joseph's spirit, which had strengthened them all?

On Saturday the third of August, Sidney Rigdon arrived in Nauvoo and the next day spoke to the assembled Saints, telling them they must appoint a "guardian" to build up the Church to the martyred Prophet. That did not ring true to Nicholas. He knew the Twelve were hastening back from their various missions to be with the Saints. By Thursday the eighth, the date that William Marks, Nauvoo stake president, had set for a general meeting, the majority of the Apostles were in the city. Nicholas felt that Joseph had made it pretty clear that the Twelve held the keys, the necessary authority to continue the work. As he stood listening to Brigham Young speak he wondered suddenly if the sun was blinding his eyes.

"We have a head," Brigham cried, "and that head is the Apostleship, the spirit and power of Joseph, and we can now begin to see the necessity of that Apostleship." But this was a voice like the voice of Joseph! Nicholas heard it distinctly. It thrilled through his whole frame. And Brigham's face—no, it was the face of the Prophet gazing over his people once more.

Nicholas glanced at those around him. He could tell from the expressions on their faces that they saw what he saw, and he heard murmured whispers and exclamations of wonder.

God is still with us, Nicholas thought. *He is telling us the work will not fail. The truth Joseph gave his life for is still in God's hands.*

It was time to gather in the summer's harvest. But after that, what? Those who had thirsted for the Prophet's blood—had they had their fill? When the Saints did not retaliate after the murders of Joseph and Hyrum, the vermin who were responsible slunk back to their homes. They were not brought to answer before the law for their actions; that would be asking too much. But would this content them? Would they leave the Saints in peace now?

Nicholas was surprised by the advice Brigham Young gave the people. "Stay here and sow, plant, build, and put your plowshares into the prairies," he said. "One plowshare will do more to drive off the mob than two guns." He told them to let all "enjoy plenty, and our infant city may grow and flourish, and be strengthened an hundred fold."

If only, if only—Nicholas did not dare to hope that it could be as simple as that. But work on the temple was stepped up, and he threw in his might with the rest. Here, within these walls, would be power. Here he felt strongly the influence of Deity in the Saints' daily lives.

Millie's life was slow-paced and predictable, but she didn't mind. After Verity's last letter she had decided that she had all she needed to make her happy, and be happy she would! Such a resolve was not difficult with the summer sea at her feet, the fragrance of blossoms and sweet herbs strong on the air, and the wonder of Adria's life unfolding before her eyes each new day.

When she received a letter from Verity so soon after the last she felt a stab of alarm rather than pleasure. Something had driven her to write; Millie sensed it. Something not good! She opened the envelope almost reluctantly and smoothed out the creased page.

July 23, 1844, Nauvoo

Dearest Millie,

This must be brief in the telling, or else my heart will break. On June twenty-seventh the Prophet Joseph and his brother Hyrum were shot and murdered by a mob in the county seat of Carthage, not far from here. You cannot imagine the stunned grief of his people—the sense of loss and confusion that pervaded this place. Since then Brigham Young and the Apostles have organized the Saints and taken over the authority of the Church, as Joseph Smith wished them to do. But in this oppressive and bitter summer the scarlet fever has struck and claimed many little children as its victims—my dear Katherine as one. Katy, so full of life and energy! I cannot yet believe it is true. The house is like a silent, echoing tomb without her presence. Oh, Millicent, this is too hard! Everything else I have tried to bear with patience—but this! Pray for me, Millie, for I am unable to pray for myself.

Your sorrowing friend,
Verity Winters

Millie let the letter fall to the floor and sat stiff and silent. Adria found her that way when she came in the house nearly an hour later. She had to coax her to notice her, to coax her to move, and at last to speak. And she wondered why it was that her mother cried softly the whole time she set the kitchen table for the two of them and prepared their simple meal.

Nicholas waited anxiously with the others in the cold lower room of the Seventies Hall. Every now and again he would blow on his hands and rub them together to keep them warm. At last they heard the sounds of a rider approaching. Someone threw open the door and the breathless messenger burst into the room, scattering a sprinkling of snow on those nearest him. He did not need to speak; as he lifted his face to meet theirs they could read the weight of his message.

"The state legislature repealed the charter of Nauvoo—the city, the Legion, they are no more."

No one spoke. The silence was more than the man could bear, and he added in a low voice, "They have snatched everything away from us with one stroke of a pen." He shrugged his shoulders, a hopeless gesture. "We stand utterly exposed."

Nicholas was one of the first to leave. Some would linger, he knew, until talk was stirred up again and they could tear the dread news to pieces, but he couldn't bear that. He walked home through the frosty January morning, too stunned to think. Whatever course Brother Brigham advised from here on, this was the end, and everyone knew it. Would they really go west, as Joseph had prophesied? He couldn't imagine it; his mind simply went blank when he tried. He entered his house and tried to form a smile as Helena approached him, her whole face a question. He shook his head.

"The worst," he said. "They have stripped us of our charter—they have stripped us of any future we might have had here."

March 11, 1845

Dearest Millie,

Yes, I am still alive and surviving. Here horror follows horror, and we are not granted the luxury to sit down and grieve. In January as the new year began, life in Nauvoo as we know it came to an end. The legislators in Springfield repealed the city's charter, which leaves us at the mercy of our enemies, as well they all know. I believe we will be forced to go west, as Joseph intimated. I dread the prospect. I dread everything lately, it seems, and without Giles and his patience I could not go on. I pray someday I may repay him and give him strength in his weakness, as he has given so freely to me. This is the sanctification of the union between man and woman—to go down into the vales of death and suffering together and bear each other up. I look back at the tender, untried love of our youth and courtship and treasure those days. But this, this oneness of service and sympathy, has been dearly bought and shall be dearly kept.

Maggie, Simon's second wife, has given birth to a son. He has the distinction of being one of the first infants to be blessed and receive his name in the new City of Joseph, for so we have renamed our city, almost by common consent. Mother is as devoted to the child as Maggie is; it is really lovely to see. By the time you receive this, I myself will be five months with child. I fear I do not rejoice in this state as I did in the past. I am somewhat numb still from the loss of Katy, and when not numb, afraid. And fear is the worst enemy of peace and productivity—that I know.

Enjoy your peace, precious Millie, and live your life fully—for all our sakes.

Love,
Verity

Millie thought of Verity's words. They sunk deep down into her heart and sat there like little hot stones. The following morning when she rang the big iron bell to call the children into the classroom, she looked at them carefully as each went by. She knew them well by now, knew which were orphans to the sea, which were children of farming or merchant parents, which had fathers who liked drink too well, which had slovenly mothers, which had mothers who beat them—the list could go on and on. But as she looked into their strong, eager faces she thought, *Not one of these has problems that he or she cannot surmount.* And thinking so, Millie realized that the brightest and best were those who had struggled the hardest, who had fought for one small victory following another, asking no special favors but taking life as it came. So God had designed it. Perhaps in wisdom; she wasn't sure. But she was prepared to consider the idea seriously for the first time.

When Joseph died at the end of June, 1844, the temple walls were but one story high. By the following May the capstone was laid, and Brigham Young, addressing the assembled Saints, said, "I pray the Almighty in the name of Jesus to defend us in this place and sustain us until the temple is finished and we have all got our endowments."

Nicholas said amen to that in his heart. He had given as much of his time and labor to the building of the temple as any man in Nauvoo. Helena was with child again, and he was glad that the date for their endowments had at last been set. When this child was born it would be under the covenant, to parents who were united to one another beyond death, through all the eternities to come. When this child was born, God willing, they would still have a house to bring it home to.

Dearest Millie,

I have given birth to my firstborn son, and all is well. He is as beautiful as any of his sisters were, and a wonder to me. We have named him Anthony Giles, after his father and mine; fitting names for so sweet a spirit. I bless the Lord for his goodness to me, and wonder, looking into Anthony's eyes, if he did not see and converse with his sister before coming here—if he does not bring us her love and her greeting, though he is unable to express them except through the love and peace of his gaze.

It is now October, the time of gathering in the harvest and expressing gratitude for our bounty. But our bounty increases, and we gather a richer, longer-lasting harvest: the harvest of souls. Converts keep pouring into the city, large numbers from Wales—dark, quiet Welsh miners who sing with the voices of angels. Over five thousand Saints attended the conference held in the temple. Brigham told us, "We want to take you to a land where a white man's foot never trod, nor the lion's whelps, nor the devil's!" and he had the Saints covenant as a body that we will take all the poor with us to the extent of our abilities and means. Then, in his characteristic way, he promised, "If you will be faithful to your covenant, I will prophesy that the great God will shower down means upon this people to accomplish it to the very letter."

What manner of people are these? Millie wondered, reading the letter. *Do they glory in trial and persecution? They certainly don't shrink.* For the first time in a long while she thought of Nicholas Todd and the things he had said—about faith, and knowing for oneself—high, idealistic things. But Verity and the others had been living those ideals as realities these many years. Had Nicholas Todd? Was he buried in Liverpool, or did he return to Nauvoo? Was he a polygamist with two or three wives? For some reason she could not picture that. Her mind was blank when she thought of him; he was like something she had dreamed, no kind of reality at all.

Every available building in the city has been converted into a wagon or harness shop. You can imagine how busy Edgar has become! Daily they prepare more and more timber for the wagons and scour the country for iron. They say it won't be long until every blacksmith, wheelwright, and carpenter will be busy literally day and night. Brother Brigham wants the bulk of the Saints out of the city by April—how can that be? Giles says we must sell the store and its inventory early while we can still get some kind of price for it; otherwise we will be forced to give it away. With Mother as his agent I think we will fare better than most! But this is not the real reason I am writing.

I wanted to tell you about our endowments in the temple. For you see, Millie, through the authority the Prophet was given and the ordinances the Lord revealed to him, we are able to be sealed, husband and wife, past the separation of death as an eternal family, with our children sealed to us as well. Does that not *feel* right? Think upon it. To me it answers some deep inner need and speaks peace to my spirit.

As Giles and I and Leah and Edgar prepared to receive our endowments, Mother grew unusually quiet and withdrawn. When word came that a time had also been appointed for herself and Simon, her face bleached of all color, she set that wide, powerful mouth of hers, and went off all alone. When she returned she requested a private interview with her husband and told him bluntly, "I wish to be sealed to Anthony. I have given it much thought and prayer. He is the husband of my youth; I could never love you or any man the way I love him." ('Tis Simon himself who told me this story, bless his heart, with tears in his eyes.) "You have Maggie now, and a fine son, and the promise of more family, which I cannot give you. Please understand and release me to be sealed to Anthony. He may not want me, after all, and then I shall have to take my chances—"

She could not go on. He caught her hands up and kissed her cheek, hardly able to talk for the tears in his throat. "No man could ever wish for a better wife, Judith, than you have been to me. If you are yet willing, we shall live together and help one another throughout the rest of this life. But I would love you less than you deserve if I did not grant you my blessing to be sealed to the man who, I am certain, cherishes you still."

So, dearest Millie, is that not the most bittersweet of stories? What a good, noble man we have found in Simon Gardner—despite our spiteful, indignant hatred of him back on Walnut Street.

It was painful for Millie to look back, because, in some ways, all the years between ceased to exist. Life had been too easy and too sweet then to have lasted; she should have known that. But that time was a treasure, a bright pearl on the string of life's experiences that could never be taken from her.

A few weeks after Verity's last letter arrived Millie was glancing through the *Boston Globe;* Mr. Erwin always kept a current copy on his desk. She was halfheartedly looking through the advertisement section for seeds and bedding plants when something caught her eye.

LDS Meetings held every Sabbath in Boylston Hall, corner of Washington and Boylston Streets, ten o'clock in the morning. Visitors welcome.

Just a small advertisement stuck ignobly in with columns and columns of others, but Millie was impressed. She had not realized there were Mormons in Boston still, though that only made sense. Not every single one would have gone to Nauvoo. She remembered a Mr. Tewksbury who had attended some of the meetings Judith held at the house. He had a prominent business on Commercial Street. Chances were that he had remained. She wondered about Jonathan Hammond; could he be in Boston still? He would remember her. How singular to think of the terrible chaos and falling apart of Nauvoo, yet missionaries were still sent out, and people still joined with the Mormons, forming small, faithful congregations. It seemed most strange to her.

Well in advance of Christmas Millie helped Adria compose an invitation, with a pretty picture drawn upon it—Adria's handiwork alone. Together they took it to Almira at the post office. In substance it read: "Millicent and Adria Fenn request the pleasure of your company (Amos and Matthew included) at a Christmas Day dinner held at the Cooper Cottage promptly at two in the afternoon. Please come! There will be good food and presents for all!" The last line was Adria's idea, and she insisted on keeping it in.

Millie hardly dared to think what Almira's reaction would be. But two days later Amos hand-delivered her reply: "Pleased to accept your kind invitation. Will be there at two. Will bring rolls and my cranberry pie."

Almira was known all along the coast for her cranberry pie. And while Millie liked baking bread, Almira knew she had no patience for small, fancy-shaped rolls. It was only natural that she would insist on contributing; most women would. So it was quite a kindly reply, all things considered.

As the great day approached Millie stewed and fussed enough that Adria noticed, and in her own way tried to reassure her. "If she doesn't like what you cook, it's all right, Mother. You still have me."

After that, it *was* all right. Millie remembered her blessings and realized, with an intuition she should not have lost sight of, that Almira would be feeling nervous and fidgety, too.

When she heard the boys scrambling up the stone path, spraying snow in every direction, she threw the door open wide. Amos grinned at her; he was still a good lad. When Almira came close Millie ducked in quickly and planted a kiss on her cheek, then pulled her in and helped her remove her scarf and her cape, and her audacity was covered by the confusion of the moment.

The duck was roasted to perfection, the potatoes were fluffy, the pudding moist and tender. In essence, the meal succeeded, and the young ones kept the conversation going. And somehow, after the exchange of small gifts, they were still there, drinking tea and munching on shortbread and singing the old folk songs and carols that celebrate the birth of the Savior of men.

When Almira was ready to leave and had her hand on the doorknob, she suddenly turned. "It was a Christian thing you did, inviting us, Millie, and I thank you, I thank you kindly. We all had a wonderful time."

The boys chimed in with enthusiasm, and Amos, with a wink, threw his arms round Millie's neck.

"I'm lonely, too," Millie said softly, "and I have been selfish these past years. Let all that be in the past, Almira. I should like it if this marks a different future for you and me."

When they had gone she gathered Adria into her arms and held her tight against her. The tears in her eyes were for her own foolishness, not for Almira's stiff pride. And when she knelt by her bed that Christmas night to pray, it was Verity's wide, lovely eyes that smiled at her out of the darkness. *'Twas you who gave me courage to do it,* she whispered, as though Verity could see her, as though Verity could hear.

Chapter Twenty-four

Nicholas's wish, at least, had been granted. When his daughter was born they were still living in their own house, made all the sweeter by her presence. The following month he entered into negotiations to sell all his property and put what little cash he received into food and supplies for the trip west.

Frederick and his father had sold the shoemaking shop, as well as their own homes, and with the proceeds purchased wagons and oxen. The smell of new wood was everywhere in the air. By Thanksgiving some fifteen hundred wagons had been completed by Nauvoo's artisans, and it was calculated that nearly two thousand more were under construction. The Church was buying cattle and mules anywhere they could find them. The Bill of Particulars, specifying the requirements for the journey for a family of five, listed animals, tools, seeds, clothing, and bedding to 500 pounds, with 20 pounds of soap, 1,000 pounds of flour or other breadstuffs, and salt, spices, beans, and dried foods. Nicholas promised Helena he would make room for his mother's old rocker. But there would be so many other things, precious and hard-earned, that they would be leaving behind.

Heber Kimball, addressing the Saints, had said: "I am glad the time of our exodus is come; I have looked for it for years. . . . There may be individuals who will look at their pretty houses and gardens and say, 'It is hard to leave them'; but I tell you, when we start, you will put on your knapsacks and follow after us." He and his wife Vilate had just completed their own very lovely house less than five months ago.

Perhaps a little of that feeling was beginning to come to Nicholas. As he walked through the city the streets looked sad and already seemed to wear a deserted air.

It was the spirit of the Saints that gave life to this place, he thought. *And their eyes are already turned elsewhere. Perhaps a part of our hearts will always remain in this city, to hallow this ground. But wherever the Saints dwell, there will be progress, and there will be joy.*

He went home, bent over the cradle of his new daughter, Emma May, and kissed her soft, fragrant cheek. Abel ran to him, and Nicholas lifted him onto his shoulders. "Come with me to the blacksmith's lad, and we'll check on the progress of our wagon."

Helena walked into the room. She had grown thin after the birth of this baby, and her ivory skin stretched tight and pale over her high cheekbones.

"Be careful with him, Nicholas," she said, smiling at her son's excitement.

"Never fear, my dear," he assured her. Then, coming closer, he smoothed back her brown hair and rested his hand on her cheek. "Things will be all right, Helena. For the first time I feel it."

"I'm glad," she responded, relaxing at his touch, and he knew she was thinking that if he could let go, if he could go forward with confidence, they would all be all right.

He walked out into the brisk morning with his son riding his shoulders, and the slim, lovely temple standing silver against the pale winter sky. He had put so much of himself into the building of that temple.

"We must leave it in God's hands," he said out loud. Surely the spirit of Joseph would ever rest over this place, and God would sanctify the efforts and faith of the people who must leave it behind.

February marked another birthday for Adria. Could she really be eight years old? Outside the sea stretched like gray, rippled steel beneath an ash-colored sky, and the wind rattled the brittle vines against the sides of the house. Inside, as the short day waned, the fire burned bright and the lamps shed rosy fingers of light into the cozy room. Drawing the curtains against the night, Millie shuddered, thinking of Verity and the others and what they might be facing right now. She tried to comprehend it, but could not. It seemed at times like a horrible fairy tale, the horrors that Verity wrote. And she was so helpless here to do anything for them!

Verity always wrote: "Pray." But Millie knew she wasn't very good at praying, at pouring her heart's feelings into a void that seemed unfathomable to her mind.

The wind picked up; she could hear the high whine of it under the eaves. She turned and called Adria to her, longing suddenly for the sound of another voice, the warm touch of a loved one's hand.

4 March 1846, City of Joseph

Dear Millie,

One month ago today, on the fourth of February, the first wave of Saints left the city. Brigham warned us that we must have all in readiness, for if we waited many more days our enemies would hedge up the way. A temporary camp has been established at Sugar Creek in Iowa, just over the bluffs we are accustomed to looking at from our side of the river. Brigham himself left the fifteenth of February. The river was frozen over for a time—something we have never before seen here—and so some of the wagons did not need to be ferried over, but worked their own way, like a long white snake, along the gray stretch of ice.

We departed today. I am writing this in the wagon and shall post it in one of the Iowa cities we shall pass by on our first stretch of the journey. We are as well outfitted as most. Giles has painted the wagon boxes a bright, jaunty blue, and our oxen are large, good-looking beasts. The men have thoughtfully arranged warm, quilt-piled nests in the backs of the wagons for beds.

Mother has convinced the little ones that it will be an adventure to look forward to. "Each night you will have a new, different bedroom," she tells them, "with new things to see outside your canvas windows, and there will be bright prairie flowers to pick in the spring, and lots of fresh air and singing round the camp fires at night, and then, one day, mountains—have you ever seen a mountain?" Of course, none of them has. She shows them pictures and tells of the rolling hills in Vermont and the mountains back home in Ireland. She has made it all right for them. For myself, it is like wrenching part of my heart out to leave Nauvoo.

I stood this morning on the corner of Parley Street and watched the wagons roll by. The women all had their faces wrapped in scarves and shawls against the bite of the moist wind, and most of their eyes were downcast. How did any of us dare meet one another's eyes and reveal the pain that was there? "Tear Drop Lane," that is what the Saints have come to call Parley Street, where we turn our eyes from the city and take our last walk away from Nauvoo. It is cold, very cold. The reeds and willows along the river are frosted, and the ice is thick.

"Three cheers for Zion!" Giles just shouted, peering in here and seeing the set of my face. "Three cheers for Zion!" Our line of wagons has taken up the cry, and I can hear it in a hundred voices, and the tears are choking my throat. Zion— "the pure in heart." That's what Joseph taught us. Zion, the Lord's chosen people.

Giles told me this morning as he walked beside me and caught up my cold, chafed hand in his, "We go with God, Verity. He will watch over us, and all will be well." *All will be well*—I cling to those words, Millie, and try to remember my faith. Spring will come, and in time the journey will end—but I can't look that far! It builds a longing in me that is far too painful. One step at a time, one step after another, with Giles smiling encouragement to me, and my child in my arms, and those words in my head: God goes with us; all will be well

> Your little pilgrim who loves you dearly,
> Verity Winters

These Mormons! The Lord's people! That is what Millie had so hated about them at the first. Who did they think they were, setting themselves up above others? *They have paid for it,* a little voice said as she tucked Verity's letter away with the rest. *"Never make the mistake of mocking those who have found their way to a truth, just because you are still blind to it."* Old Daniel had said those words to her. Now, what made her think about that?

Irritated, Millie marched out to the kitchen and began to beat up a big batch of muffins. She had some dried blueberries left in the pantry that she could mix in. The Mormons had taken Verity and the others away from her. She could stand in her kitchen and pretend she was mixing up these muffins so she could take a warm plateful over to Verity; she could pretend all she liked. But the truth was, Mormonism had brought her life nothing but trouble and woe. Heaven knew how long it would be before she heard from Verity, to know whether they were dead or alive. Wherever this Brother Brigham was taking them, they would be beyond civilization, and certainly beyond the postal coach route—beyond all communication, all hope, all love! It was good she knew the receipt by heart, for her eyes swam with tears as she bent over the bowl and stirred the muffin batter and tried to forget.

Summer was so full of sweetness that Millie almost felt guilty enjoying it. Thoughts of Verity and the others and what they might be suffering sat just under the surface of everything she experienced. Almira continued to be friendly, and Millie continued to woo her. They had picnics together out by Bass Rocks or on the beach at Briar Neck, eating their fill of flounder, whiting, and tender swordfish. If Millie thought of Verity off in the middle of nowhere, with nothing to eat except weevily flour and beans, the food would clog in her throat. But life must go on, and in Gloucester during the summertime, life was good.

As though not to spoil her, summer ended abruptly, with a dark squall that tossed whitecaps far up on the beaches and rattled the gray roof shingles and spattered cold rain in the streets. It was never really warm again after that. Adria, used to roaming the wharves with the old seamen who coddled her, ignored Millie's warnings to stay inside. The first day of bright sun she skipped down to the waterfront. The old men were happy to see her again. They treated her with tasty tidbits from the lines they were fishing and regaled her with tales. Millie, who had walked over to Thomas Erwin's to return some books and take him a warm pie, cut her pleasant visit short when she noticed the sun disappear behind a solid gray bank of clouds. When she returned home she found the house empty and the sky churning gray. With a sinking feeling in the pit of her stomach, she started back toward town.

Storms can blow up of a sudden along the coast. As soon as the sea started to moan and heave the old sailors sent the child on her way with a gentle shove and a warning not to dawdle. Adria meant to obey. But as the wind piled the sand into shifting dunes she saw a little white dog, all dirty and bedraggled, trapped on the rocks above the sea ledge, whimpering piteously. Her child's heart did not stop to reason; she knew she must rescue the poor, helpless thing. The wind frightened him; he crouched low on his belly and, at the sound of her voice, crept toward the edge of the rock. There was no way but up; she must scale the small outcropping to reach him. She crooned to him reassuringly as she groped for foot- and handholds, all the while thinking of what fun it would be when she got home and told her adventure to Mother, who would clean and dry the poor dog and give him a bowl of warm milk. And she would be a heroine of sorts, to be fussed over, and surely Mother would let her keep the little dog for a pet.

She may have made it if the rain had not struck and made the black rock instantly slippery. The dog inched back from the edge. The pelting drops stung Adria's face, and she could not see where she was going. She quickly repositioned one foot, thinking she had wedged it in properly, but when she lifted the other foot everything started to slide all at once, and she couldn't grab hold. With a little cry she slid down the face of the rock, striking her head as she fell on the jagged base of the promontory. She lay sprawled and quite still, with her face in the sand. The white dog wormed cautiously forward, laid his nose on his paws, and began to whine.

Millie frantically scanned the path that winded its way by the sea as she hurried to town. When she reached the main street of Gloucester she alerted Almira and Amos to help her, while Matthew rounded up others who would be willing to scour the beach in the storm. It was Amos, with his young ears tuned to such noises, who heard the dog whine and followed the sound to the base of the cliff. When they carried her home and laid her across her own bed, she was still unconscious, and hot to the touch. Dr. Thatcher shook his head, looked her over carefully, then shook it again.

"Keep her warm and dry, Millie. Watch for choking and convulsions. If she wakes up, call for me. If she gets any hotter, cool her down with cold cloths. I'll come again in the morning." He patted the top of her head with a firm, gentle hand. "There's nothing else I can do."

Almira kept watch with her that night, and Amos stayed, too, and kept the fire going and ran little errands for them. Millie couldn't go wild with grief the way she wanted to, not with Almira right there.

The morning dawned gray and empty. The doctor came again as he had promised, but he could do nothing for her. His face told Millie what she did not want to know.

All through that long night and the leaden hours of morning Millie had tried to pray. Her mind pleaded with the unknown God of power to save her child's life. *She is all I have, all! Don't take her from me, I beg you, I beg you!* She said the same words over and over again.

After a little while Almira went home to see to her duties. Amos, who had scooted off along the sand as soon as the doctor appeared, came back with the little dog on a leash and tied him securely at the back of the house. He talked Millie into lying down for a spell, surprised at his power to do so, and made a solemn promise that he would sit every minute beside Adria's still form. He broke his word a bit by sneaking a bowl of water and some scraps out to the starving, shivering puppy. Then, to make up for his duplicity, he stroked Adria's white cheeks and sang out loud, very softly, every song that he knew.

In the next room Millie fell into an instant sleep, from which she woke an hour later, feeling strangely refreshed. Something had awakened her, but she couldn't say if it was real or if she had dreamed it. Of course she had dreamed it, for, clear in her mind, she had seen Nicholas Todd in a room in Liverpool, low-ceilinged, almost bare of furnishings, its small-paned windows coated with a thin layer of ice. He and another man were bending over a low, cot-like bed, on which huddled three small children, thin as wraiths and as ghostly pale. The men placed their hands on the head of the first child and closed their eyes. She heard Nicholas's voice, but only as a murmur that soothed her, bathing her with a feeling of light. They repeated the process on the second and the third child. Then Nicholas looked up, across the cramped, cold room, and met her eyes. At that moment, she knew. She knew exactly what she must do to save Adria's life.

When Almira arrived at the house later that afternoon, she learned from her son that Millie had been gone these past three hours. She shook the truth out of poor Amos, despite his pledge to secrecy. But it made no difference now. Millie had taken the coach to Boston and would hopefully return before the next day. Almira was furious, as angry as Amos had ever seen her, and, being her son, he knew why—because she had come to care deeply for that snit of a girl who had snared her Luther and then not been able to give him a child. And nearly as much, she loved the sea-borne girl who she had swore would never be accepted as kin of hers. All she could do was sit by the bed of the still child and wait. But she did that with a grace that would have surprised Millie and warmed her sore heart.

Millie remembered the name; it came to her as clearly as everything else had. The train took her to Boston in just over an hour. She located Boylston Hall with ease, and stumbled up the narrow steps in her haste. The first floor of the building was a market, divided into stalls for the sale of all kinds of goods. The unexpected din and press of people disoriented Millie; she stood momentarily frozen, uncertain, then hurried up the stairs to the next floor, where the confusion was only a vague echo in the back of her head.

This floor was apportioned into four large rooms. The door to one was open, so Millie walked boldly in. The gentleman sitting at a desk with his back to her turned slowly around and regarded her with such a friendly expression that she gathered courage to say, "Sir, I am looking for members of the Mormon church who rent the upper floor of this hall for their services."

The man was middle-aged; he had a long, homely face, but the eyes of a dreamer. He continued to smile as he answered, "Then you have found what you seek. I am Brother Forsyth. How may I help you, my dear?"

In a torrent Millie told him, finding it easy to unburden her soul to this stranger. "God answered my prayers. He sent me to you. Do you believe that is possible?"

"And why shouldn't it be?"

"I do not really believe in him." She faced the man squarely; she would not lie to him.

An expression flickered over his features that robbed them of their plainness. He placed his hand on her arm, and all the tenderness and faith of his spirit flowed into her.

"Ah, but God believes in you, Millicent Fenn. He loves you as much as he loves any of his children, and for the moment, that is all you need to concern yourself with."

Albert Forsyth located another elder of the Church, and they accompanied Millie back to Gloucester on the afternoon train. When they entered the house Almira was nodding by the bedside and Amos was at the back of the house, playing with the little white dog. Almira was frightened when she saw the two strange men with Millie, but something in the girl's face silenced her. She stood in the corner of the room and watched them anoint the child's head with oil, then cover the tangled flaxen hair with their hands and say the strangest of words. She felt the hush of the moment, but Millie felt more. Millie felt light—light all around and within her. She could almost hear the light singing, and she opened her eyes, startled.

Brother Forsyth had stopped speaking and stood back from the bed a bit. Millie saw Adria stir. She saw the blue eyes slowly open, flicker, and then dart wildly, looking for her. In a moment she was on her knees beside her daughter. "Welcome back, dear heart," she cried.

"Mother, I had the loveliest dream," Adria murmured sleepily. "But I cannot remember it, and now I am glad to be home."

Millie fed her broth and chamomile tea, and she seemed nearly herself again by the time the men left. Millie walked with them down the stone path to where the sea could be seen like a silver rope edging the shore.

"I have nothing to say," Millie began. "I could never thank you if I tried for the rest of my life."

"You could thank Him, and more easily than you know." Albert Forsyth patted Millie's hand, and again she felt the warm strength of him. "May we return to check on the child's progress?"

"Come for supper Saturday," Millie urged, and they agreed. She did not wait to watch them walk away, two dark figures against the chalk-white surface of the path. She raced back inside and was surprised to hear Adria's voice raised in distress. "What is it, Amos? What is Adria saying?"

Amos stood by the door, his head hanging, shuffling his feet in obvious discomfort. "She says it was a wee stranded dog she was after. She fell from the ledge trying to reach him."

"Where is he, Mother? Did he die in the storm? I so wanted to rescue him." Adria's blue eyes filled with tears.

Amos tugged at Millie's sleeve, and she walked a short distance off with him, where he stood on tiptoe and whispered into her ear.

Millie nodded her head, and he disappeared out the door and round the corner of the house. In a moment he appeared at the back door, pulling something gently along with him. Adria let out a low cry and opened her arms, and, with the perception born in some animals, the small dog trotted right to her and laid his head in her lap.

Thus Millie's main task for the remainder of the evening was to keep the house still enough to quell the excitement that burned in Adria's eyes. At last Millie was able to assure Almira that she could manage by herself and that the best thing for Adria was total quiet, and so Almira took her son and left. No word of what they had both witnessed passed between them, and Millie was grateful for that. As night fell like a soothing curtain, the small dog slept by the fire, and Adria grew drowsy herself. Almira sent the doctor back, and when he examined the child he shook his head again. But this time his eyes glowed.

"Nothing short of a miracle, Millie," he marveled softly. "We don't understand these things. It's God Himself who takes over in cases like this."

"I can let her sleep, then?"

"Let her sleep, let her eat—don't let her run and play yet. But she's going to be fine."

Still, it was difficult for Millie when she saw the child sink into a peaceful slumber. She didn't feel sleepy herself. Something within her still surged with the light she had felt.

I'll sit in the rocker beside Adria's bed and read until I get tired, she thought. Going in search of a book, she found her fingers rummaging the high shelf and bringing down the small, dusty volume that she had not looked at for years. She settled in the rocker with the Book of Mormon in her lap, opened to the spot Nicholas had marked for her, and started to read.

When her visitors came on Saturday she had so many questions for them that their food got cold while they answered her. She asked sharp, discerning questions and wanted thorough answers. By the time they were through they had sat at table over an hour after the meal had ended. Finally, pushing his chair back, Albert Forsyth said, "Why don't you come to meeting tomorrow and see some of these things for yourself?"

"No, I couldn't. I don't think I could yet."

The man saw more than timidity in her eyes. "You are drawn by the doctrine but you do not want the way of life. Why is that, lass?" He knew there was a reason, he could see it in her eyes and in the fact that she would not meet his gaze. "You needn't tell me until you are ready," he said gently. "Anyway, come if you'd like. You will be welcome, you know that."

He clasped both her hands in his own. And Millie wished she could just keep standing there, drawing his strength and tenderness into her own parched soul.

She did not go that week nor the next, but she kept reading, and her questions compounded. Christmas was approaching. Perhaps she would take Adria and show her the bright city in its holiday dress. Little harm in paying a friendly visit this one time.

They arrived a bit late. The opening song was in progress when they took a back seat. It was a song Millie had never heard before, but the words smote her heart; there was a power in the song that pierced to the soul of her being.

"The Spirit of God like a fire is burning . . ." She could feel it; she did not want to feel it, but she knew what it was. And it was different from anything else she had ever felt in her life—except for those moments when Albert Forsyth had placed his hands on Adria's head and brought her back into life.

> The Lord is extending the Saints' understanding,
> Restoring their judges and all as at first.
> The knowledge and power of God are expanding;
> The veil o'er the earth is beginning to burst.

How many times must Verity and Judith and Leah have sung these same words, and what comfort the exultation of this song must have brought to their hearts! Millie listened to the sermons; she listened as she never had back in Judith's house. She understood, but she shunned the understanding, because it still brought her pain and even the old sense of confusion.

When the meeting ended Elder Forsyth found her quickly. He placed his hand on her arm and smiled at her gently. "You need to talk to someone, Millicent Fenn. Is it yet time?"

She shook her head. Then, deciding suddenly, she asked, "Do you have any word of the people who left Nauvoo—where they might be now?"

His expression did not alter. "They have crossed Iowa and are making a temporary camp—Winter Quarters, they call it—in the territory of Nebraska. They hope to be able to move on by the spring."

Millie nodded, afraid or unwilling to ask more.

"Will you return next week for the special Christmas service?"

"Yes, yes, I suppose that I might."

Others spoke to her before she left the building, and some of them seemed genuinely interested in her and why she was there. She did not know if their attentions pleased or angered her; she could not decide.

Though the weather was cold, she walked around the Common with Adria, pointing out to her places of interest that brought back floods of memory too painful to hold. She had not the courage to approach the house on Walnut Street; perhaps in time. Altogether, the day was too much for her. She arrived home exhausted and shaken in body and mind.

As it happened, she did not return to Boston for the Christmas services. A huge storm blew up that made the prospect of travel impossible. Millie was secretly glad. She felt as if she had escaped something unpleasant and strangely imperative.

On Christmas Day Almira came with the boys, as she had last year. But the ordeal with Adria had bound the two women in a way neither had expected, and much of the old reserve between them was gone. Thus a feeling of true gladness and festivity, like a fine sifting of snow, brightened the day for them.

Late that night, long after her guests had departed and Adria had fallen asleep, Millie reluctantly drew out the Book of Mormon and opened to the place that told of the Savior's visit to the Nephites. He seemed more real to her in that setting than anywhere else.

"For you I read this, Verity," she whispered, because the reluctance that sat upon her was real. But something, deeply hidden yet uneasily stirring, disclosed a more profound intent to her heart. Surely, in some way yet mysterious to her, God had healed her loved child. How ungrateful she would be to not thank him, to not spare him one thought on this, the most sacred day of the centuries. She did not understand, and she knew not what she was afraid of in attempting to try. But the reading brought some of that warm, strong feeling back to her. And the last words that went through her mind that Christmas Day before she, too, slept were the words Albert Forsyth had spoken to her in her fear and anguish: "God believes in you, Millicent Fenn. He loves you as much as he loves any of his children." For the first time in her life she desperately wanted to believe that those words could be true.

Chapter Twenty-five

1 March 1847, Winter Quarters, Nebraska Territory

Dearest Millie,

I write this in hopes that it will indeed reach you, intending to send it back with a rider to one of the Iowa cities that is on the mail line.

We have experienced a most interesting and trying winter in this place. The Omaha and Potawatomi Indians, whose land this is, have been generous and kind to us. Not so the whites, who have tried to cause trouble, even with the friendly Indians. Yet we have survived and have even built a gristmill at this place to grind our wheat into flour. Those who are here left Nauvoo in various stages of preparation, and now it is essential that we all build up our supplies in order to preserve our lives as we begin the longer trek westward. So there is much work to be done here, despite the cold and thick, sticky mud and the general dreariness, accentuated by bellies that are hungry more often than full. It has been difficult for the children, and many have suffered from scurvy and malaria and other troublesome diseases. Indeed, I fear there have been hundreds of deaths in the camp. Leah's Jenny grew ill enough to frighten us, but Edgar and Giles laid their hands on her head and healed her of the sickness that threatened her life and her mother's sanity, and God was merciful to us, though many others have not been spared this deep trial.

This letter, written so many weeks before, did not reach Millie's hands until late in the spring. She held it lovingly, understanding for the very first time what Verity was talking about. *He spared me, too,* she thought, a wild joy surging through her. *He spared me and my child.* And gently the seed of belief sprang up in her; Albert Forsyth's words could indeed have been true. Eagerly she read on, longing to bridge the dark gap between Verity and her and to speak face to face with this beloved woman who still called her her friend.

There are always new births, at least among the Saints, to soften the sting of death and parting and to reawaken the promise of life. Patty Sessions and the other midwives in the camp are kept busy day and night. Mother cheerfully assists in the births and then in caring for the mothers and their little ones. She has even recruited Maggie to go with her sometimes. Indeed, I find myself looking upon Maggie as another sister, and so, I think, does she regard Leah and me. I do my share, as you can guess, by sewing, though there is little new cloth in the camp and sometimes even a scarcity of thread. When Mother finds a sister who is too ill to care for her little ones she brings them back to Leah, and Leah reads them all stories and organizes little games and activities. Quiet as she is, they behave for her and appear to relish her company. And so we get on, day after day, moving closer to the time of departure toward our unknown destination.

I might, in truth, be quite wretched here if it were not for the sisters and the love they bear one another. We hold many meetings where we sing and pray and encourage each other. And when the spirit is strong, we remember who we are and what we are doing here and whose work this is.

Words, only words. But this time they had a faint meaning for Millie as she read them, and she knew what it was the women were feeling. Had not the same Spirit whispered to her own heart?

Next month President Young will head out with the first group, and the remainder of us, organized into companies of hundreds, fifties, and tens, will follow as we are ready. I want to leave early. I would rather get on with this than sit here and wonder and fret. Giles promises we will be ready in good time, and he is a man of his word.

I shall try to write more before we leave, and as we travel, though who knows how many months may pass before my letters reach you. We are in the wilderness, but we have no enemies to harry us. We are homeless, but we have God to guide us, and the promise of peace and prosperity in a land of our own. Thus we feel blessed indeed. May God bless and keep you also, my dearest Millie.

Love,
Verity

With the coming of spring and good weather there was no excuse for Millie not to travel up to Boston. She found herself going to the Mormon meetings, not regularly, but often enough that she became accepted as a known, recognizable face, and before she knew it she was being included in sewing projects and quilting bees. She brought produce from her gardens to distribute among the poor, and crocks of flowers to adorn the meeting rooms.

One Sunday in June Sister Turner gathered several of the ladies together to ask their assistance with a matter that had just come to her attention.

"A little family of orphans lives not far from here," she explained. "As I understand it, the father was lost at sea a year ago and the mother has been ill ever since. She died last Monday, and no one knows what to do with the little ones. They will go to the poorhouse, I fear."

"Are they members of . . . your church?" Millie asked in a small voice.

"Heavens no, my dear. But we must not let them suffer if we can find any means to prevent it. Poor innocent things."

"How many are there?" asked another.

"Two boys and a girl, I believe."

"I could take one of the boys, perhaps," a sister offered tentatively. "What ages be they?"

"You know, I'm not sure. I only peeked in at them once myself. Huddled miserably in a heap on the bed, they were. Probably not a one over ten."

"I'll take them all." Millie was surprised at the strength of her voice. But she trembled as the other women all turned to her, amazement plain in their faces.

"Oh, are you certain, my dear?" Sister Turner asked after a long pause.

"They can share Adria's bed, and she can sleep with me." Millie was thinking out loud. "That way we'll have room. And I've work in plenty for them to do: helping in the garden, picking berries, catching fish for their supper." The others were listening intently now. "I've the sea and woods, all the great outdoors for them to run and play in. And, at least for the time being, with fresh vegetables and fish from the nearby cove, I'll be able to feed them, too."

"But that's a handful for a little thing like yourself," one of the ladies ventured.

Sister Turner placed her hand over Millie's. "She can handle it, this girl can. I've no doubts of that."

It was Sister Turner's husband, Jed, who had come with Albert Forsyth that first night and laid his hands upon Adria. Millie met the woman's eyes and smiled deeply. "Let me try it, at least for awhile. It would give them a respite, a chance to build their strength up."

"All right, but if it's too much for you . . ."

"And let us come, once a week at least, and help with the washing and mending . . ."

Somehow it all was arranged. Millie knew, listening to the women and watching their faces, that they held her in great respect now. She liked the feeling that gave her. She could justify their respect, she knew she could; and she was anxious to try.

Nicholas felt the July sun burn hot through the dark felt of his hat, but he didn't mind. It seemed he never got warm the whole ten months he was in Winter Quarters. He liked being out on the trail. Every turn of the wagon's wheels brought them closer to freedom and the home Brigham and the first company of pioneers had found for them. Even Helena seemed to bloom under the touch of fresh air and sunshine. She had been very ill most of the winter, and at times he had feared for her life. Perhaps the demands of the trail would harden both of them. He had been tickled to find that stout Gerry Hines and his new wife had been assigned to their same company. Nights by the campfire had certainly proved amusing with Gerry there.

The creak of leather, the drone of flies round the oxen's fore-locks, the distant sound of someone singing in one of the wagons up ahead, made Nicholas sigh in contentment. He caught Helena's eye and tried to convey, in the brief exchange of expression, his deep love for her.

"We're approaching the Sweetwater a couple miles ahead." It was Gerry himself calling to him, riding up on a fat little mule whose gray sides bulged beneath the short Englishman's legs. "Brother Hall wondered if you'd ride up and have a word with him."

Brother Hall was their captain of fifty. He probably wanted help taking across some of the widows and their wagons. Gerry fell into place where Nicholas had been riding, seeing as his wagon traveled right behind theirs, and Lizbeth and Frederick's right ahead.

"I'll take care o' the ladies." The little man winked at Helena and doffed his limp cap. Nicholas rode off with a warm feeling of peace and well-being—not knowing how long it would be before he felt that way again.

He wasn't even there to see it happen. The slope leading down to the river bottoms was rock-strewn and steep. One of their oxen caught its foot on a stone or in a rabbit hole and began to slide out of control, dragging the other ox and the wagon help-lessly with it. It had been raining the day before, and the soil was tightly packed and scored with deep ruts and gashes. If Nicholas had been at the reins, not Helena with the baby in her arms, and weakened by her long illness . . .

It all happened too quickly, Lizbeth explained to him after. The white bulk of the wagon rocked, then toppled over like a tent with the stakes pulled, throwing Helena and the baby hard against the unyielding earth. The back wheel of the wagon passed over them, crushing the baby's light skull and pressing against her rib cage. There was nothing at all that could be done. Gerry Hines had jumped for the ox's head when he first saw what was hap-pening, taking a nasty fall himself as he tried to grab hold of the beast, and breaking his leg in the process. Abel had been riding in Lizbeth's wagon, and thus he was spared. Gerry, his face red and spattered with dirt, insisted on carrying Helena's body to safety himself, huffing like a little red engine and dragging his useless leg behind him.

By the time Nicholas arrived they had laid her body out, with her child tucked beside her, on a clean rock slab, with a soft blanket to cushion her head. She looked peaceful, as though she were sleeping sweetly, and so she was. Nicholas threw himself over her body with a grief that overcame him, choking his breath and making his head rock with pain. No one could coax him away until long after dark when they let Gerry Hines try—Gerry, whose face was gray with his own suffering, blaming himself for letting the accident happen.

"Come away, lad. We'll cover her gently and put her in the wagon; then you can come and pick a nice spot with me—"

"I won't bury her here."

Gerry's eyes blinked in his round, swollen face. "You must take care of her properly."

"Here on these low, ugly flats that claimed her life—I won't do it."

Nicholas turned, yanked his horse's reins, and mounted, all in one movement, and disappeared while Gerry stood blinking. He rode all through the night and did not appear again until three hours past sunup, when the company had crossed the river and was moving along level ground. He had located a site on a high knoll with an old elm tree bent above it. Here he had dug through the moist soil with a stick, with his hands, with the hunting knife that rode at his side, until he had an enclosure deep enough to hold and protect her.

The company stopped and buried mother and daughter there. But when they pulled out Nicholas stayed, sitting stiff and silent beside the raw grave. It was two days before he caught up with the others and took his accustomed place. But he did not smile, and he spoke to no one, and his deep blue eyes were gray with a suffering that was almost too heavy to bear.

"Follow me closely, now. Hold hands tightly, and I'll show you the way."

Millie watched the three children march up the hillside, single file, in the wake of Adria, while the little white dog followed obediently behind. Both Adria and the puppy had been ecstatic when the children arrived, and things had worked as smoothly as clock-work ever since.

All Adria needed was this chance to bring out the kindness and compassion of her nature, Millie reflected, thinking over the past weeks since the quiet, wide-eyed children had arrived. The little girl fussed over them, saving the tastiest morsels to fill their thin bellies, letting them be the first to take turns, making sure they had enough blankets to keep warm when the spring nights were chill. Millie had never seen her like this, and it thrilled her to dis-cover the depth of perception and sympathy in the child. The amazed little family responded openly to Adria's enthusiasm and kindness; she was another child like themselves. Her love threw the door wide open, and it was no task at all for Millie to walk straight through.

The boys learned quickly, anxious to earn their keep and con-tribute their share. Under Amos's tutelage they learned how to re-pair broken boards and hinges, how to fish in the shallows for haddock and summer flounder with shrimp and minnows for bait, and how to clean and gut the catch for eating when the fishing was done. David was the oldest, and he was an excellent weeder, sparing Millie hours of work in the garden. Samuel, only six, would stand on a stool at the sink, with a long apron on, rinsing dirt from the vegetables his brother picked.

Eliza was three or thereabouts, and she was no trouble at all. Adria showed her how to pick flowers properly and which ones not to touch, and she would proudly present Millie with a fresh bouquet every day. They were an unlikely family, brought to-gether in storybook fashion, but they were happy, and Millie felt more at peace than she had in a long, long time.

Evenings when the work was done and they had eaten their fill of the day's catch and the garden's yield, the little ones stretched out on the cool boards of the floor and listened while Millie read story after story to them. Sometimes she would let Adria take a turn, and the boys were amazed at her skill.

"Would you like to read as Adria does?" Millie asked David one morning when no one else was indoors. She doubted whether either boy knew much beyond his alphabet.

"Nah, reading's girls' stuff," he said.

"I hardly think so," she replied evenly. "All of those books we have been reading from were written by men. If you want to grow up and work in the city, you must be able to read. If you wish to go to sea like your father before you, you must still learn to read, my lad." She put her hand on his shoulder, thin of both flesh and muscle. "It isn't a hard thing to do. I'll teach you myself, and then this autumn when school starts you'll already know how."

She could see that his pleasure was stronger than his fear, so the very next day they began, rising half an hour earlier than the others so no one would know.

These strange, precious souls, she thought, watching him bend over the book, his narrow face screwed up in concentration and his brown eyes lit with the beauty that learning always sparks there. *I know so little about them. Much like Adria, their past is a blank sheet to me. Yet God has entrusted me with helping to write their future.* It was a sobering thought, but one that brought her a great surge of pleasure. *God, whoever he is, has trusted me,* she decided. *So I will have faith in myself.* And each summer's day passed more beautifully and productively than the last.

As the autumn days pushed summer away with chilly fingers, the ladies from the church came more and more often to Gloucester. They were good workers. One day they would put up fruit, another vegetables against the winter hunger of four little mouths. A merchant donated cloth, and the ladies helped Millie sew good, sturdy clothes for the three orphans and, of course, for Adria, too. They tied quilts and sewed warm flannel sheets, and one day Albert Forsyth came with three other men and put up a second bed beside Adria's small one, then set in a good supply of wood for the winter. There seemed to be not one detail that the Saints overlooked. Millie knew they were grateful to her for shouldering what they considered the brunt of the burden, though she constantly reassured them of her willingness and of what a help the children were to her.

"We're all in this together," Sister Turner beamed at her one day when Millie had been protesting their kindnesses. "We're sisters. We help one another. That's why there's so much love between us."

Simply put. But Millie was beginning to understand. One

afternoon Albert Forsyth sought her where she worked in her garden. "Are you ready yet, Sister Fenn?" he asked.

"Ready for what?" Millie laughed.

"You ought to be baptized. You would be by now, but something's holding you back. Are you ready to tell me yet?"

They had the garden to themselves. The day was cool and languid; none of the other men were about and the women were all busy inside. *Maybe I can tell him just a little,* she thought. She had changed; she had grown stronger since the children came. And it was easier to talk to this man in her strength than it had been in her weakness.

Before she was through, though, she had poured out what to her seemed like every detail of what had passed in her life, from that first day in the house on Walnut Street to the coming of Nicholas Todd, the death of her father, her conversations with old Daniel, her marriage to Luther, her doubts and her loneliness, the storm that brought Adria to her, and then to Luther's death and the dreary prospect of life forever discontent and alone.

"You are a stubborn one," Elder Forsyth said when at last she sat silent. "You acknowledge God's hand in your life, but you still want to pick and choose."

"I may sense him sometimes, but I do not understand him the way you say you do."

"Understanding of God comes through love of God, and that from mainly two things: reading the scriptures and learning of him, then serving others and in that way practicing the principles he taught. You are doing both of those things, Millicent."

"It isn't that simple."

He reached over and placed his hand on her arm. "Oh, but it is. We complicate it; we block our own way by refusing to feel the Spirit or refusing to see the truth—or refusing to take life one step at a time."

Did he knew what strength and sustenance she felt when he touched her?

"What do you mean when you say 'the Spirit'?" she asked.

"Sometimes we mean the spirit of the Lord, which is also called the Spirit or the Light of Christ, which God is pouring out upon all his children in these last days, as he promised to do in the

Bible. This Spirit is withheld from the very wicked, but it strives with all other men, helping them seek and recognize truth and light in their lives. The other 'Spirit' is that of the Holy Ghost, who is one of the three personages of the Godhead."

Millie was shaking her head at him. "I need to read more— much more—to understand what you are telling me."

He continued as though she had not spoken. "The Holy Ghost bears witness of Heavenly Father and Jesus Christ to the spirits of men. And when you are confirmed a member of God's church, the right to the companionship of this comforter and rev-elator is given to you." He tightened the pressure of his hand on her arm. "Thus, one nevermore has to walk all alone through life."

There were tears in Millie's eyes.

"Are you ready, Millicent Fenn?"

"No, not yet." *Do not rush me,* her eyes said.

He nodded and smiled at her, and dropped his hand from her arm. "Come, let's go see if that good food I have been smelling this past while is ready to eat."

She walked with him into her kitchen, still warmed by the peace of his spirit and the things he had said.

Chapter Twenty-six

Great Salt Lake City, 31 August 1847

My dearest Millie,

We have reached the Valley, along with hundreds of others! Before the winter sets in we expect to have nearly two thousand people in this place.

To recount the tale of our travels to you would require reams of paper which I do not have. Nor could I accurately paint for you the scenes we have been through. But it would amaze and impress you to know how organized our companies were. When we made camp at night the wagons were drawn into a circle, with the livestock protected in the center. The fires were put out at nine o'clock, when all were expected to retire, for we arose between five and six in the morning and were on our way by seven—this for six days of the week. On the Sabbath we always rested and worshiped the Lord.

I wish you could see the great herds of buffalo that inhabit these plains; great, hairy, ragged, prehistoric beasts, whose thundering movements make the whole earth tremble and reel. And the bronze-skinned Indians—I saw them only at a distance, seated on horses with elaborate saddles. The horses' bodies were painted with designs and symbols in bright, rich colors and often the warriors were painted as well on their faces and their bare chests, with feathers festooning their hair. I wondered if we looked as strange to them, with our pale skin and our abundance of bulky clothing. Imagine how a sunbonnet with a wide brim that nearly hides the whole face must look to one of these spare, almost naked men?

Could I any better describe the mountains to you? Blue ridge after blue ridge of them stretching off into the distance, but those straight ahead all dirt and jagged rock and perpendicular cliffs—everything about them saying, "You do not belong here! We are greater and more ancient than you, and we will remain, unchanged, long after you have ceased to exist."

The Valley! Oh, Millie, it is a huge, empty basin, with the lake at its end. Save for a few scrawny cottonwoods, there is not a green thing in sight. Ground has been planted, though; nearly five thousand acres, much of it in winter wheat. The men are building three sawmills in the mountains and one gristmill, and they've raised a stockade or fort, made of logs and sun-dried bricks, called adobes. Within its walls we will be safe from Indian raids and attacks. There is organization here, as there always is with the Saints. While one group of men clears the land, another plows, another builds a road into the canyon, and yet another cuts timber. We are also building a great arbor or bowery where meetings can be held, and dances, and perhaps even dramas. And Brigham Young has already selected a site where a temple to the Lord will be built.

I have seen sunflowers, but mostly sagebrush—nothing but gray-green sagebrush on every hand. And mice, I fear, in the hundreds, disturbed by the plow. And crickets! Black, disgusting little creatures, which crawl on the valley floor and which the Indians, they tell us, gather to roast and eat. Oh, Millie, it is a wild and uncivilized place! And yet already it is home, because we are all here together, brothers and sisters, and we are familiar with each other's hopes and desires and pains. Brigham Young said, "I do not want people to understand that I had anything to do with our being moved here; that was the providence of the Almighty; it was the power of God that wrought out salvation for his people. I never could have devised such a plan."

Thus, with faith that God's hand does indeed guide us, the Saints can rejoice and be grateful for the blessings he grants us. I count you as one of my blessings, Millie; you know that. Mother says I must relate to you that she dreamed of you her first night in the valley, the very first night she spent here. She says you must be told of it, for, with her Irish blood, she sets great store by portents and dreams. In truth, though, I believe it was the Spirit that impressed this dream on her mind.

She said she saw you living here in the valley, and you dwelt in a large, lovely house surrounded by beautiful gardens. And although you were youthful as you now are, your home was filled with children! They were young, happy children— and you looked radiantly happy yourself. There, you have it. 'Tis a strange little dream; nothing more, I suppose. But it has made me miss you more sorely, dear heart. What deep, unearthly bond links some spirits to one another, Millie? I wish I knew. I wish I knew if Mother's dream meant anything.

Well, I fear I must close. I have no more paper, and my candle gutters in the dish. When you go to bed at night, remember that far out here, beyond the plains and the mountains, there are hearts that love you dearly and cherish fond memories of you.

Yours always,
Verity Winters

It took months for Verity's letter to reach Millie. When at last it arrived it was four months old and rather the worse for wear, but it was the one letter Millie would treasure above all the rest.

When she read of Judith's dream a warm feeling spread through her; not a shock or a thrill, but a deep, seeping warmth. Judith had seen her and these orphaned children. There was no possible way she could have known of them, and yet she had seen.

The following morning Millie took the train into Boston and made arrangements with Brother Forsyth to be baptized.

"You will be the first baptism of the new year," he told her. "Eighteen forty-eight. I wonder what else it will bring."

Millie wondered, too, though she kept her counsel. One step at a time. That was what God and Albert Forsyth himself had been trying to teach her. One step after another, and each step by faith.

Nicholas was cold and hungry, and the dreariness of the wide, empty valley depressed his spirits. The food the Saints had brought with them was nearly depleted, and where to find more?

He and Abel shared the last of their flour with Lizbeth and Frederick the week before Christmas. By spring they would be reduced to digging for roots in the ground, like the Indians. But would that be sufficient to sustain them until the crops matured and could be harvested? Nicholas wished that he cared. He wished he could break free of this prison of pain that had encased him since Helena's death.

It was unlike him to be laid so low, and it frightened him. Other men had lost wives, and there were widows as well in abundance, and motherly arms empty and yearning after little ones left behind in shallow, unmarked graves. A numbness prevented him from joining in, from contributing, from being part of this life. He had no heart for building a future in this place when all that was precious had been lost to him. Except for his son, all he had ever loved was left at places behind him, along the path of his life. And this parched, wind-swept valley held no future for him that he could see.

For weeks he was burdened with hopelessness; nothing could rouse him from his lethargy. Then Gerry Hines knocked on his door. It was a gray morning, much like any other. But the stout Englishman asked him to walk with him outside the fort for a spell.

They walked in silence for many minutes, and Nicholas sensed nothing.

"Look here, Brother Todd"—Gerry's sudden vehemence startled him—"it's time to come to your senses, lad."

Nicholas stared at him blankly.

"That's the truth of it, now," Gerry blurted, and when Nicholas did not stop him, he heaved up his chest and continued. "Don't you remember the days in Liverpool? Nothing to eat; people dying from sickness on every hand. And no hope—no hope for anything better tomorrow! Now, those were times to despair of! But what did you do? You shared the gospel, and you shared your own spirit. You starved for our sakes, you huddled in cold little rooms, you walked the stiff, wind-swept streets—all for our sakes. All for this! All for a future that only the gospel can give!"

He placed his plump, hairy hands on Nicholas's arms and gave him such a shake that he felt his jaw move in his head. "Enough of this, lad. Why, she'd be ashamed of you, Helena would. God helped you then, back in Liverpool, and he'll help you now. Just don't shut him out—don't shut us all out, Nicholas. Come now, there's a good lad."

Slowly, slowly he felt the darkness fall from him. He was weak and light-headed, but he could breathe again. He held out his arms and embraced his short, startled convert, pressing his face into the man's ample shoulder; then gave way to tears. And the sorrow that had gone rancid within him and tainted his soul loosened and lifted with the healing tears and a friend's love and faith.

Despite the pinched conditions of winter there was work in plenty to be done in the Valley, and Nicholas, feeling the freedom of his release, thrust in his sickle with all his might. The walls of the fort needed to be extended, and two additional blocks, one on the north and one on the south, were begun in preparation for arrivals to the valley who would come in the spring.

While he worked, Nicholas, who had been self-indulgent too long, questioned his motives and purposes and examined a faith that had been somewhat pompous and sure of the answers when he had been young. He took to walking along the line of the city creek in the evenings, alone, as he had walked beside the Mississippi back in Nauvoo. Here at last, the beauty of the country unfolded before him. At sunset, in the hour before twilight, the mountains glowed as though lit by some inner fire, and all the rough edges of the harsh land seemed gentled by the soft luminosity.

As he walked Nicholas prayed in his soul that the path his life should take would be opened up to him, that he would be shown what work the Lord wanted him to do. Day after day he prayed tirelessly, morning and night, until a peace of sorts settled upon him and he knew in his heart that his course would indeed be guided.

About the middle of March Bishop Grant called on him and informed him that the brethren were in need of elders to serve missions back east.

"We understand you served briefly in the Boston area once before, on your way to England."

"That's right. Yes. But that was several years ago."

"Well, would you go now? I know you've lost your dear wife and have only a small son to care for. Could your sister and her husband take him into their home for a season?" Under the ledge of his brow his intent brown eyes burned out at Nicholas. "The work in that area is progressing, and we feel we need to help it along. Your name came strongly into the minds of several of the brethren. I believe the Lord wants you there."

His words burned into Nicholas with a conviction he could not deny or ignore. "I will go whenever you want me," he replied.

"Good. We'll keep in touch, then. You'll go as soon as the roads are passable in the spring. We'll get back to you with further instructions."

He held out his arm and the two men shook hands, and Nicholas knew that Brother Grant had just brought him the answer he'd been praying for.

Albert Forsyth was waiting at the train station to meet the missionaries sent out from Salt Lake. "You've had a long journey, brethren," he readily sympathized, "but as soon as you're rested I want to hear all about the Valley and what Brother Brigham is up to out there."

They talked all the way back to the Forsyth home, where the two would be staying. But Nicholas had difficulty keeping his mind on the conversation. At least for a time he had been able to put Millicent completely out of his mind. The Lord had a work for him to do here, and he didn't expect him to get muddled up in old affairs of the heart. Besides, he didn't know if he wished to meet Millicent Cooper again, ten years older and married to some seaman. Perhaps she had changed. Perhaps it would be wiser to keep the almost flawless memory of her safe in his mind.

The following morning Brother Forsyth took them over to Boylston Hall where their meetings were held and filled them in on the facts and details of Church membership there.

"Have you proselyted anywhere outside Boston itself?" Nicholas asked.

"We haven't proselyted much at all, son, except on a haphazard basis. Course, it will be different having you here."

"Do you wish us to go further abroad, into some of the other coastal communities?"

"I don't think so, not yet." He turned a soft but penetrating gaze on the young man.

"Are all your members from right here in Boston, then?" asked Thad Newman, who had been sent out as a companion to Nicholas.

"No, no they are not. We have some from down Concord way, a family in Marblehead and another Cape Cod way, and Widow Fenn over in Gloucester."

Brother Forsyth did not fail to notice the new missionary's reaction when he said the word *Gloucester*. "Have you been in Gloucester before, Elder Todd?"

"Yes I have, sir, a few years back."

"Are you acquainted with anyone in Gloucester?"

"I was. Well, not really—it was so long ago."

The man was still watching Nicholas closely. Nicholas began to feel noticeably uncomfortable under that gaze.

"Well, then, why don't you run these things out to Sister Fenn for us? You might enjoy seeing the old town again. She's a widow with several small children to support, and the ladies have some shoes here for the boys, eggs from Sister Fenway's hen, and a few odds and ends, it looks like." He peered into a box sitting on a chair beside him, then closed the lid and handed it over to Nicholas. "You be careful with that, now," he said. "I'll head your companion in another direction, and we can meet up tonight. But you'd best stay in Gloucester for supper if you're invited. Sister Fenn is a mighty good cook."

He had no choice. Brother Forsyth took him to the station and showed him which train to catch, and even gave him change for the fare. It was a perfect day for late summer, with a cool breeze blowing in from the sea. He opened the window beside him, leaned back a little, and closed his eyes. It was as if the sea wind blew the years away from him and the time no longer existed between his first trip to Gloucester and now.

When Nicholas began to walk through town, the rich smell of Gloucester enveloped him. Every inch of the place was familiar, and he felt his heart begin to race in his breast. He detoured down by the waterfront, whistling "Truly, Truly Fair," and questioned the men on the pier to see if old Daniel was still around.

"He died several years back," one of them replied, a bit warily, as he scratched the stubble on his chin. "Did you know him, then?"

"Here and in Liverpool," Nicholas replied. "He was a grand old soul."

"He was that, indeed."

The men touched their hats to him as he walked off. He had not dared to ask about Millicent, too. He would go deliver his box to this Widow Fenn and then see if he had courage enough to ask her about Millicent Cooper.

Shuffling out of the main part of town, he realized that he didn't know where he was supposed to be going, but his feet were taking him by old habit down Hesperus Road. Seeing a boy scrambling up one of the sand hills, he shouted, "Can you tell me where Widow Fenn lives?"

The boy shaded his eyes and called back, "Straight ahead half a mile. Where the land rises sharp-like, veer off to the left. You'll see it, a little yellow house with gardens all around it."

Nicholas walked on for some distance before it began to dawn on him that he was heading for Millicent's house. But that couldn't be! He turned up the green slope and slowed his steps as he drew closer. His memories had grown too painful. He stooped and set the box on the ground, then started up the rock path to the cottage.

Only then did he see the bent figure in the garden. "I'm afraid I've lost my way," he said gently. "Is this Widow Fenn's place?"

She looked up. She straightened her back very slowly and rose to her feet. "I am Widow Fenn," she said, pushing her damp hair back from her forehead. Her eyes were wide and she looked very pale. "I believe, if I remember correctly, that it would be Millicent Cooper to you."

He said nothing. His eyes filled with tears as he looked at her.

"You've come back." Her voice was no more than a whisper.

"He sent me here."

"Who sent you?"

"Brother Forsyth, directly." A hint of the old sparkle began to creep into his eyes. "But before that, I believe the Lord sent me back here, Millie."

She stared at him for a moment. Her eyes were hard and appraising. "I believe he did, too."

It was a reply he had not expected.

"Will you come inside where it is cool, and have something to drink?" she asked him.

He followed her into the dim, quiet kitchen. "Brother Forsyth said you have children, several children." He sat down at the table, and she poured him a drink that tasted of lime and lemon and the last flowers of summer.

"I have," she replied. "But not a single one of them is really my own."

While he sipped his drink she told him how she was unable to have children after she married Luther and what sorrow that brought her, and then how Adria came to her. He listened carefully, his hand closed around the cool glass, his eyes never leaving her face. She told of Luther's death and old Daniel's death, then interrupted herself suddenly.

"I've mixed it all up. There is too much to tell; I can't tell it all."

He leaned across the table, still holding her with his gaze. "Begin way back, when I came, before I came. I won't leave until I know everything. Brother Forsyth even gave me permission to stay to supper if you asked me." A faint smile lifted the corners of his mouth, and the sight of it made Millie tremble inside.

"Then I shall begin with Judith and Verity and Leah on Walnut Street in Boston," she acquiesced, pulling out a chair and sitting across from him. "I wouldn't tell you about them before when you were here; my pride prevented me. But you need to know this to understand."

He listened, though amazement following amazement made his heart freeze in his breast.

"That illuminates many things!" he cried at one point. But then he began to grown solemn and quiet as her tale wove itself out. At last he could bear it no longer. "Why did you not answer my letters?" he asked, and his voice held a tense note of demand in it. "Although I was near dying I wrote to tell you what had happened. And when I was back in Nauvoo I continued to write, for over two years, Millicent!"

She swayed in her chair, and he put his hand out to steady her.

"I wrote to you, but you did not answer me." Her voice shook a little. "I received no letters! I thought you had died in Liverpool!" She buried her face in her hands.

"You poor thing! Oh, merciful heaven!" Nicholas cried. He leaned over and began very gently to tell Millie the story of his life. Every now and again she bit her lip as the tears welled up in her eyes. As shadows traced their patterns over the deserted garden, the children came tumbling in. Nicholas would have been happy to be introduced to them, despite the interruption, but Millie shook her head.

"There is plenty of time for the children in their turn," she said firmly, and sent them back outside with fruit and slices of bread. "Play on the beach until you hear me call," she instructed. That was a directive they could stand to obey, and they all scampered out in high spirits.

When Millie turned back to Nicholas, her face was more pale and drawn than before. "It was Almira," she said. "Despite her nastiness, her narrowness of soul, I never for one minute suspected her."

As she explained to Nicholas he rose in agitation and began pacing the floor. A sense of outraged injustice, of being the butt of a cruel game, rose in his throat like bile. But Millie was sitting quietly, her hands folded neatly in her lap over the gardening apron she wore. Experience in living had only deepened her beauty; even the shades of her hair had bronzed and darkened.

"Perhaps all happened as it was meant to happen."

Her words caught him up short. He threw a look of questioning appeal at her.

"I would never have married you if you had come back for me—" Millie added, cutting off his protest, "And if I had, it would have been a disaster. And Nicholas, think. You loved Helena, and she gave you two beautiful children before she was taken away. I learned how to love because God brought Adria to me. I needed so much time, so much growing to prepare myself. All the work you did in Nauvoo, your growth, your contributions there—I believe all that was essential. Five years ago, a year ago, even, I would not have been ready—"

"But it has been *ten years,* Millicent!"

A faint smile, like the ghost of a memory, passed over her face. "Yes, ten years almost to the month. Oh, Nicholas, if only I had known during all the dark, terrible times when I was groping, unable to hope or to see any future at all."

"It is so easy to forget that we are in God's hands," Nicholas said, and his face was dark with the memories of his own sufferings.

At length she walked out into the gathering darkness with him. A lone curlew circled above their heads, and all the loneliness of the deep, restless sea waves was in its cry.

The children, hearing Millie's voice, forgot their instructions and came running and stumbling to her over the sands. She gathered them into her arms one by one, and Nicholas, standing by watching, was embraced by her tenderness, too.

"I will return tomorrow," he promised. Then, catching up her hands, said, "Will you wait for me, Millicent? I am here on a mission. It may be a long time."

"A long time?" She turned her eyes and gazed seaward, over the dark world of water that constantly sang in her ears, sang with the fears and loves and longings of all mankind.

"I can wait, Nicholas," she said calmly. "I, too, will have much to do."

It was late when the train Nicholas rode pulled into the Boston station, and later still when he presented himself at Albert Forsyth's door. Only a dim lamp burned on the hall table; all the dark house was still.

"You stayed to dinner, I see," Brother Forsyth said as he opened the door to him. His eyes held an expression Nicholas was not able to read.

"We ate nothing at all, sir. We talked for hours—and hours."

"I was hoping you would." Brother Forsyth sighed, and then smiled when the lamp glow showed him the expression on the younger man's face.

"I felt pretty sure you were the man Millie had told me of, though I cannot for the life of me remember if she ever once actually mentioned your name. It was something about you, and about the way you looked when you asked about Gloucester." His eyes took on a gentle expression as he paused and considered for a moment. "No, it was more than that, son. It was one of those promptings of the Spirit that are so faint and still I might have overlooked it if I hadn't been careful."

They stood in silence for a moment. "Millie's a rare, special woman." Brother Forsyth placed his hand on Nicholas's shoulder. "But I suppose you know that."

"I want to marry her after this mission is over, Brother Forsyth—no matter how long that may take."

Brother Forsyth smiled, and his eyes were beautiful in the soft circle of light. "I believe you've found the mission you were sent here for, Elder." He gave Nicholas's shoulder a fatherly pat. "That's my own opinion, mind, but I'd be surprised if the brethren didn't agree."

The children slept at last after all the excitement of the stranger's visit. But Millie walked the old path by the sea, wishing she could draw some of its deep, ancient power into her soul. It soothed her to think that the ocean could contain all the secrets and horrors of man, generation following generation, and still be the same.

Then she remembered and looked up to the heavens that stretched over her head. Both the high, endless heavens and the fathomless sea were contained by God. Yes, and the small beating heart of a every man and woman alive.

Knowing that, she believed she would never again be afraid. Knowing that, she could walk away from the ocean and the cottage on the shore, and live in the house on the desert which Judith had seen in her dream, and find out what it was like to be the wife of a man she loved.

"Good night, Nicholas," she murmured, and her voice was only a breath beneath the voice of the tide. "Verity, I am coming." Her heart sang out the words, and her joy was full. She walked with a sure stride along the cool sand, and the coils of white foam curled under her feet. She walked with the sounds of the sea and the night wind in her ears, and she walked in peace—because she knew, past fear, past doubting, that she did not walk alone.